The Island of Bicycle Dancers

The Island of Bicycle Dancers

JIRO ADACHI

Picador

St. Martin's Press
New York

For information, address Picador, 175 Fifth Avenue, New York, N.Y. 10010.

www.picadorusa.com

Picador® is a U.S. registered trademark and is used by St. Martin's Press under license from Pan Books Limited.

For information on Picador Reading Group Guides, as well as ordering, please contact the Trade Marketing department at St. Martin's Press.
Phone: 1-800-221-7945 extension 763
Fax: 212-677-7456
E-mail: trademarketing@stmartins.com

Library of Congress Cataloging-in-Publication Data

Adachi, Jiro, 1965–
The island of bicycle dancers / Jiro Adachi.
p. cm.
ISBN 0-312-31246-6
EAN 978-0312-31246-6
1. Young women—Fiction. 2. Japanese—New York (State)—New York—Fiction. 3. English language—Acquisition—Fiction. 4. Bicycle messengers—Fiction. 5. Koreans—Japan—Fiction. 6. Korean Americans—Fiction. 7. New York (N.Y.)—Fiction. I. Title.

PS3601.D34I85 2004
813'.6—dc22

2003066681

First published in the United States by St. Martin's Press

First Picador Edition: February 2005

10 9 8 7 6 5 4 3 2 1

In memory of
Freddie, Lenke Manton,
Jim Pitt, and Hugo Garcia

ONE

Him

She looked for him—the bike messenger with the splendid caramel-colored skin. Other bikers went by, taxis, delivery trucks, buses, but no him. Slowly, she swept cigarette butts, bits of food, and store receipts toward the curb. She glanced down First Avenue again, then swept the trash into the street where it landed on top of a pigeon wing. Where was the rest of the bird? No bird, no blood, just dirty feathers and some broken bone curled against the concrete. Back home in Japan there were no dead animals or animal parts lying around. In her hometown of Kawasaki, there was only the occasional stray cat or dog. Once, she had seen a rat outside the Kirin bicycle race stadium, but that was it. New York had everything, she thought. *New York had him. Where was him?*

Where dat nigga at?

This voice in her inner ear came so quickly she had to go back over it and figure out what it meant, where she might have heard it. *Nigga, nigga, nigga.* She stared down First Avenue and tried to recall. The 7 train? The guy with the gold tooth at the bakery down the street? One of her older cousin Suzie's hip-hop tapes, maybe. There were so many bits and pieces of English passing by the Lucky Market window each day; it was like a fever dream—full and pressing. The words and phrases she heard crowded her mind sometimes, vied for attention—

like this one now. She could hear the voice so clearly but had no face to attach to it, no source. She tried to match it to the face of her messenger, but it didn't quite fit.

Suzie had told her it was good to be able to imagine different voices in English because it meant you had a good ear. In New York, there were too many different kinds of English. Sometimes her head was full of her aunt and uncle's Korean English, sometimes Suzie's American English going on about the Indian women who came into the nail salon dripping with yellow gold and the black women who spent all their money on nails that ended up looking like cheap jewelry. Her ear caught snippets of Chinese English from the high school kids on the 7 train, Spanish English everywhere, Russian English and Polish English near Lucky Market; black English all over, even from white people and some Asians—everyone trying to act black. Did her messenger act like that, too? she wondered.

More cars. A fire truck. What could she say to him? Would he think she was Korean? She imagined telling him that she was half Japanese and half Korean. He would want to know more, of course, and she would explain that she came for the summer. Work in the store. Learn English. The real problem, she would tell him, was that Japanese was spoken all around the neighborhood of the store—not even Japanese English but just plain Japanese—in restaurants and boutiques and hair salons. She couldn't tell if the speakers were tourists or people who lived here, but they were always speaking Japanese, never English. She had promised herself that they were to be avoided at all costs. Only English this summer.

An ambulance was trying to get through First Avenue traffic, its siren loud and steady. In the back, she imagined, lay a one-winged pigeon, a gray stain on a white sheet, eyes wide with fear.

Then she saw him: riding behind the ambulance—long, dark muscles like a wild animal. She drank him in with her eyes. He sat upright, in one hand a bagel and in the other an orange juice. Quick twitches of his hips steered the bike between lanes of traffic. An impossible, crazy dance. She caught her breath as he sped past. Then he was gone. No more him.

"Jae Hee!" It was the girl's Korean aunt, Hyun Jeong, standing in the doorway of the store. "Move from street!"

She never listens to me, thought Hyun Jeong as she waited for her niece to turn around. Hyun Jeong stared at the girl, who was gazing off into traffic as though she had just missed her bus. She mumbled to herself in Korean her growing list of complaints against this half-breed summer guest pawned off on her by her brother-in-law, this girl who didn't dress like a girl but wore a red-and-white baseball shirt and tight jeans on a hot June day. The crazy blond streaks in her short hair. She wasn't even here a full week before she changed her hair color the first time. How many color treatments had that scalp suffered in the last month since her arrival? Hyun Jeong had lost count. Just like Suzie, only worse. At least Suzie was pure Korean. This girl clearly didn't want to be Korean or Japanese. Yet she was skinny like most Japanese. Her head was big like a Korean.

"Jae Hee!" Hyun Jeong cried again as she stepped onto the sidewalk. "You sleeping?"

The girl didn't look at her aunt. She glanced over at Daniel, one of the store workers, who was outside unpacking a box of apples. He grinned at her and shook his head. He and José, the other worker, but especially him, seemed to know what was going on at all times. She spoke little to them, but when she did it was friendly. They shared new English words. They teased her about her hair colors. They helped her behind the register if the store got crowded. They called her by her Japanese name.

She had decided not to answer her aunt so long as the woman insisted on calling her Jae Hee. For a month now since her arrival, this was how it had been. This battle of names. Her father had told her this would happen and encouraged her to avoid any conflict by trying to use her Korean first name while she was in New York. There was no reason to keep it a secret in New York, he said. She refused, of course, because it seemed like bad advice from a Korean man who had spent so much of his life pretending to be Japanese to avoid being thought of as a *chon,* the Japanese equivalent of "nigger" for Koreans. Her father told her stories of when he first came to Japan, how there was a sudden lack of apartments at a real estate agency when he first looked under his Korean name. Then he changed his name but almost lost his first job as a newspaper ad salesman because the boss found out he was Korean. Her mother being the obedient *O.L.*, Office Lady, that she was, told her to listen to her father.

In any case, her aunt didn't seem to care about what name she liked to be called. As soon as she got off the plane, it was Jae Hee you look like a boy, Jae Hee you're much taller than when we saw you eighteen years ago. Jae Hee, Jae Hee, Jae Hee. Like she was trying to make up for twenty years of being called by her Japanese first name. On top of this, the woman was constantly nosy. How much was that bag and that shirt? Where are you going now? What did you eat for lunch? It was no wonder her own daughter, Suzie, came home only to sleep and have breakfast.

"Jae Hee!" her aunt called again, growing more shrill, but the girl still refused to look up.

The messenger was long out of sight already, but the girl felt suddenly disturbed that he hadn't bought his bagel and juice at Lucky Market. She was stuck with her aunt again. But, she decided, it was time for decisive action. With the toe of her sneaker, she slid the pigeon wing onto the flat straw of the broom, carrying it over to Hyun Jeong, who stepped out onto the sidewalk.

"What that?" Hyun Jeong asked. "No, don' bring here. No—"

The girl held the broom up toward her aunt. "My name is Yurika," she said as she dropped the pigeon wing at her aunt's feet.

"Shibal!" her aunt cursed as she moved past her into the store.

"You are also Korean," Hyun Jeong said a short while later when her niece was back behind the register. "You have Korean name. You don't have to make secret here." She had a concerned look on her face that Suzie had told her was never real—the way her eyes grew large and her lips formed *O*'s of worry. She slapped the back of her hand over and over. All the cutting was too much: cutting flowers, cutting meat, cutting vegetables, cutting open large boxes full of small boxes. She laid her hand palm up on the counter and watched the fingers curl closed as though still holding a knife or scissors. No good shape fingers, she thought in English as she reached for the extra-large jar of Tiger Balm under the counter.

"Everybody like Korean people here," she went on. "Not like Japan. Also, I know. Japanese woman always have trouble here." She massaged the balm into her hands. "Men so bad like that. This city not safe for Japanese women." She shook her head and laughed, making her permed ponytail shake like a used party streamer.

Yurika glared at her aunt, then scanned the counter, looking for the top of the Tiger Balm. The smell was nasty, like her. "You don't care the name I like—"

"In this store," Hyun Jeong said, "you are Jae Hee. It good name."

"Nobody call me Jae Hee," Yurika protested.

Her aunt tried to translate the meaning of the name but gave up. She was tired of always having to speak English to the girl. Why hadn't her father taught her Korean? Why hadn't he sent her to one of those Korean schools in Tokyo or Osaka? It was bad enough that she, Hyun Jeong, had to deal with the English her customers spoke, talking so fast, using all kinds of words she had no idea about; plus, she hated having to repeat herself because they couldn't understand what she said. She clicked her tongue against her teeth. "Okay," she said, returning the Tiger Balm underneath the counter. "I go down."

Yurika understood this statement meant her aunt was going down to the basement. She felt relieved and turned to the window. There was no messenger out there. Not hers, anyway. Sadness drew her face down. She had seen him from the store or the street almost every morning since she had begun working there. He looked so free. The times he had come into the store, she was stricken with speechlessness and could not say a thing. Was that why he had bought his juice and bagel somewhere else that morning?

Yurika didn't know what to do with herself, trapped in her uncle's store for a whole summer. The days passed with her pulling on rubber bands, shuffling matchbooks, selling cigarettes and coffee to commuters, aspirin and tampons to young women with their periods, bubble gum to schoolkids. There was Daniel to sometimes talk to, but he was often busy unloading truckloads of produce and packaged food while she rearranged the things under the counter: the first aid kit, telephone books, tape measures. Her two feet never left the ground.

Perhaps her messenger would stop in the store when he came back downtown. Maybe he had a delivery to make in the neighborhood and would need more juice or a candy bar. Maybe he smoked menthols like other messengers who came into the store. Was he a native English speaker? Did he speak Spanish? He looked like something Latin American. Daniel had taught her some words. *Bien,* she imagined telling the messenger if he ever asked how she was. He came and went frequently in her daydreams. *Gracias. Hola. Sí, bien.* She didn't remember how to say "good-bye."

With one eye on the front door and one eye on her work, she rang up bottles of water, juice, plums, peaches, and every other cold object American people liked to press against themselves to cool off in the heat of early June. But the image of the messenger stayed with her and would not leave. Distracted, her fingers began ringing up incorrect amounts at the register. After the lunch rush, she even left the register open.

"Wake up," her uncle, Sang Jun, scolded.

Sometimes, he looked to her just like her father—the square jaw and lean build. Except her father, who was the younger of the two, did not have as much gray in his hair and seemed a bit softer. With all the work at the store, Sang Jun stayed more fit compared to her father the *kai sha in,* the salary man who sat at a desk all day selling newspaper advertisement space and who enjoyed his wife's noodle soups at night.

Sang Jun and Yurika spoke little except when necessary. On her first day at the store, they had had their first person-to-person conversation. He had shown her around the store, how to use the register. In between customers, he asked her vague questions about his brother and sister-in-law. He seemed satisfied with her one- and two-word answers, and Yurika was surprised he didn't seem more interested. She wondered why but thought it might be rude if she asked, so she remained silent except to answer his questions. He didn't call her by any name, as though he didn't want to take a side between his wife and her. Sometimes, he gave her little English tips, which he seemed proud of. He told her that if an American asked how you were doing, always be positive—say, "Good" or "Not bad" or "Fine," something like that, then add, "And you?" Americans, he explained, liked to keep things moving when it came to conversation, and they weren't interested in any information that would slow things down.

Sang Jun noticed that the girl seemed to appreciate the advice, and sometimes he heard her use what he had taught her. She was a good worker, he thought now as he stepped outside the store to light a cigarette. But, like his brother, she was a bit of a dreamer. She needed to be watched.

Later that day, he told his wife about the girl leaving the register open. They were alone in the basement of the store, sorting through a dry goods delivery. "Her mind is somewhere else," he said.

"She misses Japan," said Hyun Jeong, making a face. "First time away from your brother and her *oka-san*."

Sang Jun frowned at her use of the Japanese word for "mother."

"Anyway, that's what happens to mixed children," Hyun Jeong went on. "A dog can't live in two houses."

Sang Jun touched a match to his cigarette and listened to the quickening of his wife's Korean. He was startled when she threw down an empty box of tea.

"Why give her a Korean name if she speaks Korean like a five-year-old—not even! A three-year-old! And she only uses that weak Japanese name!"

Her husband reminded her that since she was eighteen she had been using her Korean last name. "Besides," he continued, "she's here to learn English."

"Not from you! Not from me!"

"Speak for yourself," Sang Jun said in English. He prided himself on his language efforts. Although he had never had the time to take a class, he tried to read only English newspapers and listen to only English-speaking radio stations in the car or in the store. Occasionally, he even tried to listen to a Yankee game on the radio. He also had a thick, blue grammar reference book he consulted now and again and even knew the English names for the parts of speech. Hyun Jeong, on the other hand, never cared about English, never studied. It didn't matter to her that she was in an English-speaking country. She spoke Korean every chance she got, and as incredible to him as it was, for nearly twenty years she had spoken English only when it was absolutely necessary. Most of the English she knew came from television shows.

He watched her slice open another box. As she tightened her lips and narrowed her already small eyes, Sang Jun knew exactly what was coming next.

"Your brother should be paying us for her."

"Not this again." Sang Jun shook his head.

"He didn't send her here to learn English. They just wanted to get rid of her."

"You want to get rid of her—"

"Room or board or something! We have enough to worry about with Suzie."

Sang Jun dragged on his cigarette and shook his head.

"Instead we're paying her!"

"She works—"

"She's trouble. That's why she was sent here!" Hyun Jeong held up a box of Korean barley tea. "Your brother should have been drinking this every day. Then he never would have run off with that woman."

Sang Jun blew a ring of smoke to the ceiling. "You can't flush out love, *Yobo.*"

Over the next days, they watched the girl closely. They especially kept an eye on her when the sweaty bike messengers came into the store. These bike boys, as Sang Jun called them, were trouble. A few years earlier, he had caught two of them shoplifting beer into their messenger bags. They were no good. They shamelessly flirted with the girl in their crazy, impossible-to-understand English. They called her Baby, Angel.

One even called her "girlfriend." He was tall, with very white, pimpled skin. On his T-shirt was a picture of a German shepherd with the slogan THE LORD IS MY SHEPHERD, the sour smell of sweat filling the air around him. Sang Jun was pleased to see his niece defend herself against him.

"I'm not your girlfriend," Yurika said, ringing up his apple juice.

He smiled broadly, his mouth full of crooked teeth. "Not yet."

"No"—she shook her head—"never." But she felt her face flush because she heard her *v* like a *b* and knew she left off the final *r* so the word sounded like "neba."

The messenger grinned as he moved toward the exit, pointing his juice at her. "I'll be back."

He returned to the store almost every day, sometimes twice, sometimes more. Always talking too fast. Always making jokes. Sometimes, he came into the store with other messengers. Then he acted differently. He seemed more like them in the way he flung words from his mouth and said, "yo," every other word. Alone, he seemed more talkative, his words crisper, and there were fewer "yo's." He never came into the store with her handsome messenger, though, and she wondered if they knew each other.

Where is he? she wondered. Or, should the sentence be, Where is him? She became preoccupied with the countless English pronouns and their endless positioning in a sentence. Even as she made a mental note to consult her textbook later, her grammar logic began to collide with memories of spoken English she was not sure she should trust. Pronouns turned into multicolored demolition derby cars smacking against one another, engines roaring. These turned into terrible images of her messenger getting into accidents that came to her with such force that once she dropped a customer's change onto the counter and into the gummy bears and gummy worms and gummy fish that lined the display beneath the register.

"Don't worry about it," said a deep voice that seemed to come from somewhere far above her.

Yurika looked up. It was the tall, white messenger with the pimples again. This time he was wearing a T-shirt with a silhouette of a bicycle on it that read TECHNOLOGY ≠ EVOLUTION. He was buying his usual apple juice and grinned down at Yurika with his teeth of a broken fence. "Wanna see a trick?"

"Tu-lick?" Yurika repeated. She recognized the word but couldn't remember the meaning.

"Yeah, watch this," he said. He seemed to open his throat as he poured the juice down in a second.

Yurika gasped. "What did you do?"

He laughed and clapped his hands, which were covered with black leather from his torn bike gloves. "I can chug with the best," he said with a grin as he clapped his hands again. "Chug-a-lug-lug, three bikers in a Bug." His English dissolved into a fast, random assortment of sounds to her, some kind of story about him and two friends in a Volkswagen and beer, but the rest was a confusing set of sounds and jumbled signals.

"You Korean?" he suddenly asked, interrupting himself.

"Huh?" His question took her by surprise, and it took a moment for her to understand. She shook her head. "Japanese."

"But you work here—"

"I'm Japanese."

More flying words. He seemed to be talking about himself. Something something Scottish, something something English. His face stretched unnaturally long. "Huuuuguenot," he concluded.

Yurika tried to smile. Was he asking questions? Joking?

"Whitey." He stuck out a hand and spoke extra slowly. "My . . . name . . . is . . . Whitey."

"Whitey," Yurika repeated as she shook his moist, leathered hand. "I'm Yurika."

He asked her to spell it in English and after she did, he said, "Your name kind of means 'lucky.' "

She nodded. Suzie had explained this to her.

"Actually," he went on, "people used to shout, 'Eureka!' when they found gold." He nodded. "And it goes way back to the Greeks, I do believe." He moved toward the door, smiling in an almost shy way. "Later, Lucky."

Yurika didn't feel lucky at all, however, as she rode the 7 train home that day. On the contrary, she felt plagued by days' worth of incorrect

English over and over like a bad tune lodged in her ears. Neba. Tulick. She knew what some of her problems were. In Japan, she had done a brief language exchange with an American student. They had met in the *pachinko* parlor she was working in and had agreed to trade English lessons for Japanese ones. But when it became clear that Yurika wasn't interested in him romantically and that his Japanese was almost as good as hers, the lessons ended. She had, however, learned enough to be able to hear her mistakes constantly. They haunted her.

Looking around the subway car at all the Asians—the Chinese and Korean and Filipinos and Taiwanese—were they worried about their pronunciation while they took their subway naps or read non-English newspapers? How did each of them get through eight hours of everyday English? At the store, Daniel and José didn't seem to worry about it so much.

It would be a fine world if she could write to her parents and tell them that working in Uncle's store was not good enough for learning English in this short time and could they please send money for English lessons. Only two months left, she would remind them. She needed a class with a real teacher. Fast-talking bicycle messengers were pleasant for small talk, but they were not English teachers. She knew her parents had no money for this, though.

No, her parents had money enough only to send their daughter to the other side of the earth so that they wouldn't have to lie awake anxiously in their beds until the early morning hours when their daughter came stumbling home—if she came home at all. It was worth the money so they wouldn't have to receive embarrassing phone calls and visits from the Kawasaki police asking to speak to their daughter about one of her friends, so they wouldn't have to watch their daughter take a job in one *pachinko* parlor after another because she kept getting fired, so they wouldn't have to see their daughter drop out of yet another junior college.

There was probably more, too, Yurika realized. In Japan, she had been so excited finally to be going to New York. She hadn't noticed that her parents embraced the plan with a bit too much excitement—even going so far as to talk about her one day becoming a translator. In truth, she was realizing, they just wanted to be rid of her and were able to do so by simply giving her what she wanted—a trip to New York to learn English—but no money to take classes.

Yet here she was, surrounded by more kinds of Asians than she had ever imagined in one place. Not many Japanese, it seemed, but every other kind. She probably spoke the best English of anyone on the subway car, which she knew wasn't saying much. But if she could just learn the language, maybe she could do something on her own, something worthwhile out there in the vast land of English where no one cared at all if she were half sushi and half kimchee, as the kids in Japan used to tease her. English could be a way to start over, a way out of that life. But in the store, the sentences she used over and over were full of horrid, ear-twisting sounds and mistakes that made people not want to speak with her. Yes, she thought as the train pulled into the Main Street, Flushing, station, it is time to really learn English.

She felt a bit better as she got off the train and made her way toward the exit. As she rose from the station, though, her heart sank again. Everywhere she looked along Main Street, she saw Chinese and Korean characters on signs outside stores, on advertisements, on signs for sales, on public notices taped to walls, newspapers. She recognized many of the Chinese ones but had no idea what words they were making in Chinese. She felt bothered that she even had to wonder about that. Where was the English hiding? She found it only on bus stops and the parking regulation signs.

Face after Asian face passed her speaking in Chinese, Korean, or some dialects of India or Pakistan or Bangladesh that she couldn't even name. No one spoke English. She grew more agitated as she walked on. She stared at the drivers passing in cars and trucks. All Asian.

Turning off Main Street, her eyes fell to the ground because the sidewalk was a relief, neutral in language-free, dirty gray. Then she passed shreds of a Chinese newspaper and the wrapping of some snack with Chinese characters covering it. There was no escape.

By the time she arrived home, she was worn out from the overstimulation and frustrations of the day. Her head felt thick, her legs heavy. She could hear Suzie moving around upstairs in the kitchen, probably making tea, having just gotten home herself. Yurika trudged upstairs to the living room and flopped down on the couch, covering her face with her hands. She sighed. "My English is socks."

Suzie covered her mouth, trying not to laugh as she swallowed a mouthful of tea. "Cousin." She giggled, pointing to the pair of pink pom-pom socks on her own feet. "These are socks. You mean 'sucks.' "

Yurika groaned and put a brown corduroy pillow from the couch over her head.

Suzie's shift at Hannah Nails had ended at five, but she manicured on, working her emory board magic on her own nails. It was therapeutic for her and gave her time to think. She had watched this scene with Yurika play out to various degrees over and over the past month since her cousin's arrival. At first, there were just some shy questions about English Yurika heard in the store or somewhere else in the city. She had wanted to know what "tastayatago" meant in fast-food restaurants, and it took a while for Suzie to translate it into "To stay or to go?" Then came the stories of customers turned rude because Yurika had not understood questions or because they couldn't understand her—like one woman who left her vegetables on the counter and stormed from the store because Yurika had no idea what "arugula" meant. Suzie had to explain to Yurika that communication got "off sync" sometimes, especially with English. It happened all the time with her and her parents if she didn't speak Korean to them.

People were miserable, thought Suzie. They took their shit out on you and then blamed you for it. Then they wanted to be treated like gods or babies. That was the way at the salon, and that was the situation at the store, made worse by Hyun Jeong, no doubt.

Suzie liked being the English specialist with her cousin, though. At the salon, most customers just assumed she spoke only Korean. They were surprised when she didn't just ask them, "Square or round?" like all the manicurists asked before they started on a set of nails. Then, of course, they assumed she was really a college or a graduate student and was just working part-time to get a bit of extra money. As if there were something wrong with working in a nail salon. It always made her feel a bit embarrassed for the other manicurists who spoke Korean all day long while they worked. What did the customers think of them?

Suzie pushed one of the kitchen chairs out with her foot and smiled at Yurika. "You need tea," she said. "Come sit."

Sighing again, Yurika dragged herself to the table.

Suzie poured her jasmine tea. "You're in an English funk."

Watching her cousin's precise, high-speed filing mesmerized Yurika, so that a few moments passed before she responded. "What is 'whunk'?"

"Ffffunk," repeated Suzie, pointing the emory board to her bottom lip beneath her top front teeth. "It means 'a really bad way.' Like, I'm in a funk that I always break this pinkie nail. Or, I get into a funk when my nails look like shit."

"I'm real funk." Yurika sighed. "I need class for English."

Suzie stopped filing for a moment and looked up. "I could teach you." She checked her nails again. "I train all the new manicurists. I'm a really good teacher."

Yurika watched her cousin speak English. Koreans and Japanese—including herself—never opened their mouths when they spoke. It was an upsetting realization she had since arriving in New York. Americans, on the other hand, really opened wide when they spoke. You could see tongue, gums, and many teeth. At first, Yurika thought this looked vulgar, but after getting used to it, she began to like it. It was so strong and open. It made English that sounded clear and beautiful.

Suzie was telling her about how she was always helping the other manicurists at work with their English—phone bills, credit card business, things they heard in movies or on TV. The endings of Suzie's sentences flew away like wild birds. Her intonation rose up from her mouth and made leaps from her painted lips. There were flashes of teeth. Her tongue appeared for a split second, then disappeared. It even remained on the bottom right corner of her lip for a moment as though it needed a rest from the great effort of speaking accent-free English. Yurika knew that Suzie had learned English when she was a child, but the fact that she was so accentless and fluent at the age of twenty-five filled her with hope.

"I want speaking like you," Yurika said.

Suzie laughed and grabbed a pink flier for the nail salon off the counter and, on the back, drew a time schedule for one week.

"Okeydokey," Suzie said, pointing to the box for 8 A.M. "We'll start off each day with a one-hour lesson at breakfast."

Yurika nodded and smiled. "Okeydokey."

Suzie narrowed her eyes at her cousin and tapped the nails of her right hand on the table.

Yurika's first assignment was to ask someone a question each time she got on the train. So on the 7 train to and from the city, she tried to sit or stand next to women who looked close to her age or a bit older. Much to her surprise, many of the women she spoke to were not Americans either. Her most reliable question started with, "Does this train go to . . ." She surprised herself with the results. With a Russian woman who cleaned teeth for a dentist near the Empire State Building, she talked about how impossible it was to understand any subway announcements. A middle-aged woman from Puerto Rico and Yurika discussed the disgusting American habit of eating on the subways.

There was more homework, too. Because Yurika was having problems pronouncing the letters *l* and *r,* Suzie told her to ask customers who bought broccoli how they prepared it. Mrs. Manton added it to a salad for her husband, a cab driver, who liked "something fresh" after "breathing car fumes" for twelve hours. A tall young man with too much gel in his hair who always came into the store carrying a trembling Chihuahua "sautéed" his broccoli and "tossed it" in pasta. A pretty Thai woman with long, shiny black hair used hers in *pad see yu,* a stir-fry with flat rice noodles.

With the bicycle messengers, though, Yurika had the best conversations. They never bought broccoli. They were friendly to her, and it was easy to talk to them. Plus, she liked to see them together, especially when they were with Whitey. They never let him pay for anything. She was not sure why, but they were so generous to him; it was sweet.

Many of them spoke only a bit more English than her. Sometimes, the messengers heard different questions than the ones Yurika had asked, but regardless, they almost always answered something about their bicycles.

"You have always bicycle mind," Yurika said to Whitey one afternoon when he came in to restock his messenger bag with plums.

"That's how it is," he told her. "No bike, no money, and then . . ." He swung around to let her read the back of his T-shirt: NO MONEY NO HONEY.

She laughed and nodded, glad that she could finally understand one of his T-shirts. Whitey's way of speaking slowly grew on her. She felt a little sorry for the way he looked but was attracted to his English. It was very different from the other messengers. There were sudden bursts of words that seemed like a lot of warmup for what he really wanted to say. What she could pick up from these introductory stories was that Whitey was not always a messenger. She found out that messengers could make up to six hundred dollars in a good week, so he would work lots of months and then travel somewhere like the western

United States, Spain, Thailand, and some places that she had never heard of, like Dubrovnik.

From all the bicycle messengers, Yurika picked up lots of new vocabulary when she asked them about their bikes. She learned a short Dominican named Lefty had "squeaky" brakes. One biker named Wolf had "popped" his chain. A messenger named Jesus, who wore six leather-bound crucifixes around his neck, was saving up money to buy new "components." These words had cool sounds and intrigued Yurika. When she used them, she felt smarter. She made it a point to learn the names of bike parts: bracket, handlebars, saddle, pedal, and her favorite, spoke.

The messengers had *senmonyogo.* She translated this literally to mean "specialty-term words." To her, they were more than that. Their vocabulary became entry points into bicycle world, bicycle mind, bicycle mouth. Half language, half mechanics. You could take a tool to the sounds. Attach words to a frame. Grease up vowels and consonants. Ride away on a verb.

She learned the cool adjectives that went with the nouns, too, like "fine," "hot," "awesome," "wild," "the shit," and her favorite, "kickin'," as in, "I'm getting a kickin' new wheel pretty soon," which Whitey told her one day. A messenger named Bone, who ran a small bike shop out of his apartment, would be building it for him.

"Bone?" asked Yurika, tapping her forearm.

"His street name. He's broken a lot of bones." He shook his head. "Man, he's a badass."

"Almost bike messengers have such nicknames?"

Whitey paused, trying to make sense of her question. "Oh," he began when he realized her mistake, "yeah, most messengers have street names. But just for work," Whitey went on. "Nicknames are for all the time. Like, my family and friends call me Junior. Whitey's just for the street."

Yurika's eyes widened. "Junior?"

Whitey grinned and shook Yurika's hand up and down once. "James Harding Pitt the Second."

He explained that he got the name Mighty Whitey because he was the fastest white messenger at Quick Service, their company. There were also two Umbertos, U and U2. There were two brothers, one Lefty and one Righty, and others with names like Voodoo, Tank, Chain, Driver, Wolf, and Bone, the badass building Whitey's kickin' new wheel.

"Bone," Yurika repeated. A pirate came to mind, with a skull-and-crossbones tattoo.

Whitey held a fist in the air. "Street names make you strong."

Yurika paused for a moment to translate something from Japanese. "I have also other name."

"You do?"

She nodded. "Jae Hee."

"That Japanese?"

"Korean."

Whitey pointed a finger at her. "I thought you might be a mix." He asked which of her parents were which, and she told him. She explained that in Japan, she and her parents used a Japanese family name, Uda, from her mother's family. He asked if she spoke Korean, but she made a face. She paused to remember a phrase she had picked up recently to use for emphasis. "In fact," she said slowly, "I want learning English."

Whitey nodded slowly. His face was serious as if he understood about that situation. He had kind eyes, she thought. Kind brown, and they were softer than the rest of him.

"Yurika Uda," he said, trying to imitate her pronunciation but sounding a bit too sharp.

She shook her head and tried to explain that after high school she chose the two names of hers that she liked the best.

"So," she concluded, "Yurika Uda was become . . . is become?" She cocked her head, unsure which was correct.

Whitey smiled. "Became."

"Ah, so, so." She took a breath. "Yurika Uda *became* Yurika Song." She grinned. "Half sushi, half kimchee."

They both laughed, and Whitey held out his hand again for her to shake. "Nice to meet both of you."

She smiled. "Eh . . . I can call you Junior or Whitey?"

Whitey grabbed a pen and a matchbook from the counter and scribbled his phone number down for her. "Just call me."

Suzie liked her cousin's progress. Yurika couldn't always speak in complete sentences. She mostly didn't speak correctly, either. But her half sentences, phrases, and words were starting to come out with a rhythm that at times sounded like a native speaker. She already spoke better English than most of the manicurists at the store. Suzie was constantly trying to get them to speak English. She would say something in English, but they would answer in Korean, then blush when she scolded them and say—in Korean—that she was right, she was right, they needed to practice English. She loved seeing Yurika's improvement, and when her cousin said, "Riiiight?" stretching her *i,* Suzie knew that her cousin had been talking with some of the neighborhood locals around the store.

"Bicycle messengers," Yurika said.

"Are you flirting with these boys, Cousin? Do you know 'flirting?' Check your dictionary."

She spelled the word for Yurika, who consulted her pocket-sized computer dictionary, then blushed.

"You are." Suzie grinned. She threw her arms in the air in victory. "Told you I'm a good teacher."

"Whu-rut," Yurika attempted.

Suzie pointed to her own bottom lip again and said slowly, "Flirt." She pointed to her own tongue and opened her mouth wider and encouraged her cousin to try it.

Yurika tried to visualize her bottom lip beneath her top teeth, her tongue darting up behind her upper front teeth for the *l* sound, then rolling back on the roof of her mouth for the impossible *r*.

"Flirt."

Suzie held her coffee mug midair. "Good. Ten more times."

Yurika looked away, blushing at the idea of flirting in English. She wondered, though, if she would ever have the chance to practice this kind of English with *him*.

The opportunity came one late Friday afternoon. Yurika's messenger was riding up First Avenue, a few blocks south of the store. His face felt tired, covered with a mask of the day's traffic, his body stiff all over from particularly hectic deliveries that raced him back and forth from one end of the island to the other. On Eighth Avenue and Fiftieth Street, an ambulance almost ran him down getting through traffic. In Midtown, a woman driver from New Jersey in a white Buick sped through a yellow light, almost clipping his front wheel. And the list went on with lesser annoyances—long traffic lights, obnoxious cab drivers opening car doors that nearly took him out as he passed, traffic so thick that half of his runs took place up and down sidewalks dodging terrified pedestrians, cops at every other corner waiting for him to run a light.

He felt drowsy, eyelids heavy. He licked his lips, which tasted salty. At a stoplight on Ninth Street and First Avenue, he pulled up beside a red eighteen-wheel truck with tires as tall as his waist. To his right, a bus rolled to a stop. Crossing his arms on top of the handlebars, he rested his head on them, feeling sticky with sweat and dirt.

At times like this, the voice of his Mexican great-uncle, El Gato, came to him.

"Straighten up," he was telling him, as if Bone was a seven-year old learning to ride a two-wheeler.

"Drink up," he was saying, pushing a first shot glass of tequila toward him.

They were getting drunk, and the boy, now thirteen, was asking about his parents again.

"Your mother was a bitch and your father was a son of a bitch," El Gato mumbled. "No more 'bout that."

There were a couple of women the boy called aunts who lived in the same building, and there were supposed to be relatives in Puerto Rico, but no one ever talked about the boy's parents. Occasionally, while he was growing up, he would hear rumors from other kids' parents about his father as a violent man, about prison time for rape or murder, but no more. The image of his father in a windowless cell kept him awake at night. The boy had fantasies of opening the cell and freeing the man. These alternated with visions of his father being put to death in an electric chair, the families of his victims watching through a window.

Some messengers from his neighborhood brought the rumor with them into Manhattan, where it grew. At the messenger companies that knew him, it was believed he was the son of a rapist who murdered his victims, and he had been rotting in Sing Sing for decades. El Gato never said if it was true or not. Even on his deathbed, his liver the size of a car muffler, the old man wouldn't speak about the past. He had such an aversion to the past that while the boy was growing up, he wouldn't even utter a word of Spanish except to teach him how to swear, which he believed was necessary for survival along with learning English so the boy didn't sound like the son of a bitch he was.

"Pinchi cabrón," El Gato was saying as the light turned yellow for the cross traffic.

The truck began moving forward, picking up speed. The messenger jerked up as he felt the burning hot rubber of the truck's tires against his left leg as the truck continued to move. He was sandwiched between the driver's side of the bus and the truck. Each time a wheel passed by, it rubbed against the flesh of his left calf and thigh, throwing him against the side of the bus. Time slowed. The passengers on the bus, hearing the metallic banging of the bike and the thud of his body against the bus's side, moved to the window to see what was happening.

"There's a guy out there!" a man with glasses screamed to the bus driver.

A woman at one of the window seats began to cross herself, lips mumbling a silent prayer. The bus driver watched the scene, teeth clenched, in his rearview mirror.

As soon as the last wheel had rubbed past him, the messenger glanced around, breathing hard. He swung off the bike and picked it up so the frame rested on one shoulder, then limped out of traffic as drivers watched him pass. The bus moved on.

On the sidewalk, he first checked on his rear wheel. It was so warped it wouldn't even spin. The rest of the bike seemed fine. It was only when he lifted the bike again and began to walk up First Avenue that he noticed the burning sensation up and down the outside of his left leg and that he was walking with a limp. His outer calf and thigh were bright pink, shiny where the truck's wheels had burned off his flesh. He cursed and rested his bike against a parking meter, then sat down on the sidewalk and took out a cigarette. His hands were trembling. It could've been a lot worse, he told himself. He was still in one piece. He shook his head and inhaled deeply on the cigarette. Stupid motherfucker. Traffic continued up the avenue as usual.

He thought of Freddie, the first friend he had made as a messenger at a company called Early Bird. He was a big Jamaican rider who played bass and dreamed of being a full-time musician. One rainy day in early November, he got too close to a delivery truck. He was riding along right next to it on his fixed gear when he went over a wet manhole cover, slipped, and was crushed beneath the wheels of the truck.

"That's how it goes," he could hear El Gato say. "Can't fuck around in traffic."

And there were others. Angel. Hugo. For their kind it was practically a natural death. He took a long, final drag of the cigarette and flicked the rest into traffic. Slowly, he rose to his feet. A half a block away, he saw Lucky Market, with its bright assortment of flowers arranged outside.

Yurika's heart jumped when she saw him, but in the next breath she knew that something bad had happened.

"Your leg!" she exclaimed.

Before he could even say a word, Yurika had already moved to the other side of the counter with the briefcase-sized first aid kit from beneath the register. There were no other customers in the store. She opened the case and pointed to the antiseptic and gauze. "Please. You can use," Yurika said, noticing his strong smell of things burnt, which made her feel disoriented and warm.

He cleaned the wound, grimacing and gasping as he patted the raw flesh with antiseptic.

Yurika leaned in a bit closer. "This just happen?"

He nodded as he finished and stood up. He was more than a full head taller than her. The smell of his sweat filled her senses.

"You can walk?" she managed to ask. "You should have juice."

He glanced at his bike locked to a parking meter. "My rear wheel. Shit, man."

Yurika grew alarmed. He spoke bicycle English. No Spanish or black accent. Yurika's head filled with bicycle words, and she scrambled to make a sentence from them. "Broken spokes?" she asked as casually as possible.

He seemed to notice her for the first time then. His eyes were large and dark and moved quickly over her face and body. A kind of smile crept to the corners of his mouth. "You know bikes?"

She felt herself grow warmer, and she nodded. "Little."

He waved the used gauze in the air, unsure what to do with them.

"Ah, it's okay," said Yurika, taking them from him, then adding, "I'm Yurika."

He placed a hand on his chest. "Hector," he said. He turned at the sound of Hyun Jeong entering the store from the back room

She had been cutting flowers with Daniel, and her hands had begun to feel a bit stiff from the humidity and the heat of the back. Seeing her niece and a bike boy standing in the middle of the store, a dark wave of disapproval passed over her face.

"He burned leg," said Yurika.

"Nah," said the messenger, "it ain't so bad."

"Go to hospital," Hyun Jeong said, staring at the leg, then to Yurika, "You cut flowers now. I take register," and added in Korean that her hands hurt.

Yurika smiled faintly at the messenger. "You can—" she began, but stopped because she had no idea what she was saying. Her face flushed. She slapped her hands together. "It okay?" she asked, pointing to his leg. He nodded, and she gestured toward the back of the store. "Flowers," she said, unable to put together the rest of the sentence.

Reluctantly, she joined Daniel in the back room where he was busy cutting the stems off purple and yellow wildflowers. They sat beside each other on a long blue wooden bench. Two white plastic cutting boards lay across stacked milk crates before them. Daniel felt that Yurika's mind was still in the other room. She fingered the flower petals and rolled the stems between her fingers instead of cutting. Having watched the girl closely since her arrival, he knew she and Hyun Jeong didn't like each other. Hyun Jeong was always criticizing the way the girl looked, the way she did things. Sometimes she watched the girl with a scowl on her face.

"Wha's his name?" he asked now, not looking up. Yurika stopped fidgeting. She glanced at Daniel. His face was broad and dark, his eyes watchful. She felt exposed and again had that feeling that he and José knew everything that was going on at all times. It occurred to her just then that she barely knew anything about him except that his real name was Anarvaez, that he was from Veracruz, Mexico, and he was the kindest person in the store.

She quickly grabbed a new bunch of wildflowers and, in one swift motion, hacked off the stems with a cleaver. "Hector," she replied, trying to hide her grin, as the blood rushed into her face.

"Good name," he said with a nod. He stopped cutting for a moment and reached behind himself for his brown leather knapsack. Taking out a pen and a small pad of paper he used for new English words, he tore out one of the blank pages and wrote "Hector" on it.

"My mother make like this," he said as he crumpled the paper into a tight little ball. He reached into his bag again and pulled out a plain white handkerchief. Into the handkerchief, he put the ball of paper with the name on it. Then he carefully picked up wildflower petals that had fallen off onto the cutting board, making a thick circle of purple and yellow petals around the paper ball. Tying the corners of the handkerchief together, he formed a pouch and handed it to Yurika. "Is good luck," he said. "Keep somewhere."

Yurika stared at the little sack of good luck in her right hand. In another instant, she felt a surge of warmth move up her right arm, pool in her shoulders, then pour down into her heart before filling her completely. It was not the kind of warmth she felt when she had a fever or when it was hot out. It was the warmth she felt when she saw *him*. Hector. She smiled and turned to Daniel with a nod. "Good."

"Of course," he said, returning to his cutting. "My mother very smart."

TWO

Bicycle Love

Emory boards of every size. White, black, red, and blue pairs of dice. Lighters, half-filled boxes of Marlboro Lights. Bottles of Visine and extra-strength aspirin. And the collection of condoms. Suzie kept them in a small tin that once held jasmine tea. There were several brands, some in square packaging the size of saltine crackers, some smaller and rectangular that reminded Hyun Jeong of the salt and pepper packages used in fast-food restaurants. Hyun Jeong had discovered them years earlier but never said a word.

It was her Tuesday morning vice, this exploratory activity through her daughter's and husband's drawers and closets, as a reward for having to clean the house with no one's help. Sang Jun's personal things held no interest for her. The worst of his vices was a stray matchbook in one of his dress shoes. Suzie was an altogether different sort. She had gone from a regular, sweet little girl to a bored high school student with borderline grades to a cigarette-smoking sex fiend obsessed with nails.

Also, since Yurika's arrival, Hyun Jeong had noticed a proliferation of English grammar books and speaking texts among Suzie's things. There was even a book called *The Practice of English Teaching*. Pages and pages of it were highlighted in yellow and pink, and Suzie had scribbled notes to herself in the margins. This was a surprise because

Suzie barely made it out of high school. All the teachers had said she was a smart girl but lazy. After she graduated, she immediately enrolled in the Flushing School of Nails, became a certified manicurist, then quickly rose in the ranks at Hannah Nails. She was going to open her own nail shop one day, she said. Seven years later, and Hyun Jeong was sure all her money had been spent on going out to clubs, drinking, cigarettes, and the skimpy clothes she liked to buy—miniskirts, mesh tops, dresses with low fronts and low backs, fishnets, garters.

The newness of Yurika's things was a welcome change. Hyun Jeong dusted a few minutes, then went through her niece's clothing. Hyun Jeong had tried to prolong this moment to increase the pleasure and felt proud that she had held out for the first month of her niece's stay. She felt the time might have also given the girl a chance to acquire a secret or two she might want to hide in a pair of socks or the hidden pouch of one of her suitcases. The girl had a few fashion magazines out in the open along with some stickers of the Japanese superhero Ultra Man. Standing on the bureau she shared with Suzie were also two action figures of him—foot-tall hard plastic—one in blue and one in red. Big alien eyes and diamond-shaped head. Hyun Jeong stared at each, wondering what a twenty-year-old was still doing playing with action figures and stickers. Japanese, she thought, they're just like children with all their toys and gadgets.

She found a small, square photo album covered with Hello Kitty and other unbearably cute stickers. A cursory leafing through it showed there was nothing other than pictures in the book. Jae Hee at a restaurant with friends. Jae Hee with some bad boy- and girlfriends with snarls for smiles surrounded by Chinese characters in neon. Japanese had no qualms about using Chinese characters. They would steal from any culture. There was only one picture of her and her parents, but it must have been ten years old. Jae Hee and her parents at the Tokyo Tower. Sang Jun's brother looked more and more Japanese every year, thought Hyun Jeong. He had the same shaped head as Sang Jun, but rounder and softer all over—in the cheeks and eyes. He used to be the more handsome one. Japan and that Japanese wife of his had made him soft like those *udon* noodles he loved so much back when she knew him in Korea. She wondered if he liked introducing himself as Mr. Uda instead of Mr. Song. If he got any pleasure out of speaking Japanese instead of Korean. If he knew any Koreans anymore besides his older brother twelve thousand miles away. She had spoken to him for only a minute at a time over the years. Even Sang Jun talked to him only a few times a year.

In fact, thought Hyun Jeong, since her niece's arrival, the man had not called at all. The woman called once and the girl wasn't even home; Sang Jun made up some ridiculous progress report about how good her English was becoming—he was a good liar when he wanted to be. But no one was as good a liar as someone who pretended to be Japanese when he was really Korean. Hyun Jeong shook her head. Anything would be better than being a Korean in Japan.

She went through the rest of the girl's things but found no cigarettes hidden anywhere, no drugs of any kind, and all the clothes folded more or less neatly in the two drawers. It was only a matter of time before Suzie's bad influence changed all that. If the girl was bad when she left Japan, she would be worse after spending a summer with Suzie. Hyun Jeong checked the girl's empty luggage in the closet as well. Nothing. She must at least be keeping her money, some traveler's checks, somewhere, Hyun Jeong considered, but there were no papers among the girl's things except for some English—probably some dirty slang—scribbled on small scraps of paper.

Whitey was thrilled with Yurika's interest in slang. He looked forward to each visit to the store when he would present her with a small gift of English, usually something rude. He had noticed her when she first came to the store, but she seemed busy with too many things to notice him. As he rode down avenues and across streets, he imagined helping her pronounce her *l* for words like "love," "lips," "lap." He fixed his eyes on her curvy lips when she tried new phrases. The sight warmed his insides. Her eyes got shinier when she laughed, her dimples like punctuation marks of joy.

After a recent incident with a cab driver, Whitey came into the store and taught Yurika one of his most valued slang expressions. Placing both bike-gloved hands on the counter, he leaned forward and said slowly, "Up yours."

Pleased by the sound, Yurika repeated happily, "Up yours," then, "It's meaning 'angry'?"

"Yeah." Whitey laughed. "People will definitely know you're mad."

Yurika puzzled with "up yours," as she did with other English idioms. She saw the anger from one speaker rising up then spilling down to the floor and filling up into another person's body. She liked how direct English was. It seemed to her like all of Japanese was the opposite. To say one thing in Japanese, your words had to go around another person's age, position, feelings. English was more like a happy dog that came right up to you and smelled your crotch, then jumped up to lick your face. Short and to the point.

She practiced the phrase in mumbles when her aunt's shrill voice called her by the wrong name in the store. She repeated it like a silent mantra when she recalled how, during her first week in the city, she found Hyun Jeong in her and Suzie's bathroom at home, going through Suzie's makeup. Did her own mother go through her things? It was hard to imagine her mother doing something as sneaky as that. Her mother was like a shallow, pretty pond where waves disappeared as quickly as they were made. Hyun Jeong, on the other hand, was like a hole filled with mud where you could lose your shoe if you stepped in it.

For brief moments, Yurika found herself telling Whitey about Japan or about life with the Songs in Queens. He was a good listener who asked lots of questions as he rocked back and forth on the other side of the counter, chewing on a candy bar or sucking on a plum pit.

Whitey would always have another question for Yurika. Anything to keep her lips moving. It had been years since he felt this way about someone. When he had first started messengering five years earlier, there was a legal secretary he looked forward to seeing. He was twenty; she was twenty-one, fresh out of City College. Ginger Squizelli. Her name seemed an impossible mix of a porn star's and the Bensonhurst Italian she was. He dreamed of kissing the round of forehead flesh framed by an irresistible cowlick she had just to the right of the part in her hair. She said she admired the fact that he kept a journal, which he sometimes produced to jot down her observations about life in a legal office—the drawer full of spare shoes at each assistant's desk or the direct relationship between boredom and the size of one's ball made of rubber bands. She had a great smile and didn't seem to mind his teeth or skin at all. In fact, she seemed to see past these problems to the world traveler, as she liked to say, the chronicler of American life. He filled pages and pages with details of their five- and ten-minute conversations. To avoid the dirty looks of her office manager or, worse, one of the lawyers she worked for, Whitey crammed as much as he could into each visit.

After a summer of seeing her at work two, sometimes three times each week, he was about to ask her out, but she disappeared—law school, her coworkers said—University of Michigan. She hadn't said a word to him. As he was riding up Sixth Avenue that same week, it had dawned on him: she just hadn't cared enough to mention something that important. It just didn't matter. *He* just didn't matter. He was the invisible messenger who became visible only when he appeared with a delivery in hand. It was a feeling he had experienced again and again in office buildings all around the city but was only just realizing. Often, no one looked at him in elevators or as he walked down hallways. Once inside an office, assistants usually wouldn't even look up until you were standing right in front of them. Then they would rarely make eye contact. The only reason he started talking to Ginger was because she always made eye contact. She used to say, "Thank you." She used to smile.

Right in the middle of Midtown, Whitey welled up with loathing for his customers and self-pity for himself. He comforted himself in crosstown traffic as he raced past buses and in between cars. He took consolation in the power he felt knowing that the only faster way from one end of the island to the other was by helicopter. His bike, he realized, was his ticket to freedom. As long as he could ride, the world could never be such a bad place. As he pumped his legs and felt the sweat pour down his face, his heart felt glad to be alive. He was thrilled to make his living *on the outside*.

This was a distinction Whitey liked to dwell on in those early days of messengering: those who made their livings *on the inside* and those who worked *on the outside*. Those on the inside usually made more money, but those on the outside lived closer to the ground—they were in the air and in the elements. Those on the inside used their brains more. Those on the outside used their bodies and still a bit of their brains. Those on the inside moved from room to room and desk to water cooler. Those on the outside often ranged far and wide. Those on the inside often followed dress codes. Those on the outside wore what they wanted. Those on the inside were clock watchers. For them, it sure was the decade of the clock on the wall. Those on the outside knew the end of their day by the waning light. The exception to all of this seemed to be the cops, who had *inside* jobs on the *outside,* which is why they wore uniforms and were usually also overweight and out of shape but visible on the streets.

To Whitey, Yurika seemed like someone on the inside ready to move to the outside. She was right in between. You could see the spark in her eye. *A Korean Japanese with dimples,* he wrote on the day he taught her "up yours," *the future of America.*

With his slightly tattered spiral-bound notebook in his lap, he settled onto the mattress in the corner of his Avenue D studio apartment. Surrounding him stood piles of used paperbacks that doubled as furniture—American and world history supported an iced coffee and leftover pork lo mein; travel and true crime held a couple of half-filled ashtrays; rock-and-roll nonfiction and memoirs of various rebellions and revolutions acted as a semipermanent stand of bike tools. Whitey enfolded Yurika into his ongoing list of predictions about America's future. He saw the fastest-growing ethnic groups in the country forming an Asian-Latin empire where Yurika's dimples, her lips, her sloping back, her two-tone hair, became a beauty ideal from coast to coast, from Nuevo Saigon to San Singapore. He wrote about a future where the streets were filled with tasty ethnic cocktails like Yurika, people not fully part of one culture or another but smack in the middle of two or three. Their growing numbers were shrinking the world at an exponential rate, so that this middle, this in between, mushroomed into regions populated by people like Yurika of yellowish brown flesh and lovely eyes the shape of mango pits, the lands of the In Betweenese.

He wrote and he smoked. Still in his bike shorts, still sweating from a day of messengering and the heat, he pulled up his knees and propped his journal against them. His back stuck to the frayed poster that came with the original Beatles White Album, a collage he never tired of looking at. He had stared up at the poster for so many years that he had taken on the Fab Four's faces as his own. In weird, self-conscious moods, he was John in that greenish picture where he looks slightly Chinese. When his skin was having clearer days, he was George in three-quarter profile, smiling. When he was happy, he was Ringo, grinning at Liz Taylor as they danced. As he wrote, he was Paul in profile, unshaven, contemplative.

His words moved from Yurika and the rise of the Betweenese to the shrinking of the Anglo race, which he welcomed. He prided himself on being a living embodiment of his own race's cosmic downward mobility. In fact, Whitey had come to believe that his acne, which had really kicked in only when he was eighteen, was a gross allergic reaction to the Anglo trappings that surrounded him in the form of the short-lived Ivy League education his father had arranged for him in New York. A huge boil developed on his back during a reading of Plato's *Republic* in his Western Civilization class. St. Augustine made his chest break out. Witnessing huge, white, neckless frat boys trying to dance at a keg party gave him hives on his neck and cheeks. He hated looking at his own white face at that time, so he spray-painted BUSH LEAGUE across his mirror in red, white, and blue. Then he dropped out.

Whitey was much happier now that he was surrounded by Latinos, blacks, and other downwardly mobile whites—mostly artists and junkies of the East Village and the Lower East Side. His skin had improved considerably, though scars remained. Still, though, on days when he had too many deliveries to corporate banks in the Wall Street area or law offices around Rockefeller Center, small whiteheads appeared around his chin and on his earlobes. In this way, he wrote, he considered himself Betweenese—a Virginian-Anglo-white boy who never fit in with his own people—not at the private prep school he attended, not in any of the summer jobs at country clubs or banks his father had arranged for him. As a child, he had always rooted for Indians when he watched old John Ford Westerns with his family. He was drawn to food-oriented cultures and loathed his mother's holiday cornish hens; he liked rice with meals instead of potatoes. The white girls he had fallen in love with could not get past friendship with him because he was "too weird." When he dropped out of school, his father, after periodically ranting at him for a few days, finally got to what he felt was the real problem, asking with equal parts exasperation and contempt, "Why can't you be like one of us?"

They were sitting at the kitchen table, his father with a cup of black coffee, Whitey with a pot of green tea.

Whitey shrugged. " 'Cause I'm not."

He decided to return to New York the following week, find a job, find an apartment. Before he did, he sat for the last time in the living room of his parents' two-story colonial house. He wrote now about how his mother sat tight-lipped on the sofa while his father clinked the ice in his scotch glass and, as he liked to say, "cleared the deck." That meant that he stated, in five or six different ways, that Whitey—who was still very much James or Junior—would not be entitled to another cent of their money for as long as he chose this . . . what was the word his father had used, Whitey wondered as he lit another cigarette and turned a page in his journal . . . as long as he chose this *lifestyle*. The mattress on the floor, the sitar music, practicing *tai chi* on their front lawn for all their neighbors to see while they went to work—it was all too much for James Senior.

Whitey laughed. He knew there was more than that. Dropping out was just the main blow to his father's Great White Hope. Too bad they never had another son. He always imagined that there should have been an older brother. Perhaps that was the first crack in his father's plan. There was a daughter, Whitey's sister, but they never seemed to expect much from her. Right out of college, she married a bald military man almost three times her age and became the mother of two daughters before the age of twenty-four. At times, Whitey could understand his father's disappointment. Whitey was, after all, the first generation of the downwardly mobile of their race. There were no framed terminal degrees hanging on their walls. There were no pictures of Whitey on Capitol Hill shaking the hands of senators and congressmen. He and his father spoke only on birthdays and the big holidays, and they hadn't seen each other since he left home three years earlier. His mother had visited once that first year and was horrified that her son was living in a former storefront, surrounded by Puerto Ricans and derelicts. She left the city in tears.

Whitey stopped writing and stretched onto his back, an ashtray on his chest. Outside, the street was settling in for the evening. His landlord's son, Samson, was holding court with his neighborhood cronies. A *meringue* played in the bodega next door. It was such a different place of business than Lucky Market. Whitey wondered what kind of music Yurika listened to. The day he met her, he was having a good skin day and was feeling very George as he hummed "Here Comes the Sun." It wasn't until he left the store that he got self-conscious about the acne scars on his face and neck and turned into John, his mental radio turned to "Happiness Is a Warm Gun." He worried that he might disgust her, that she would not want to talk to him. Or worse, that she would talk to him but not really care. Would Yurika Song be another Ginger Squizelli?

In fact, Yurika looked forward to Whitey's visits even though she would have rather spent time with Hector. She liked the English Whitey taught her and was starting to feel more comfortable asking him questions about expressions she had heard or thought she had heard. He spent fifteen minutes explaining the various uses of the word "wasted" after Yurika had heard another messenger say it. She admired his quick mind. He didn't even have to think before launching into an explanation of the differences among "feeling wasted," "wasting breath," "wasting time," feeling like a "waste case," and the expression "waste not, want not."

It was in her lessons with Suzie, though, that she improved her vocabulary in English about Hector. Images of his legs and long, chiseled arms, the sweat on his thick neck, came to her with disturbing frequency and wiped her mind quite clean of English. At other times, she imagined having conversations with him. Sometimes he was a native

English speaker and sometimes he spoke no more English than Daniel. She wasn't sure how much English he spoke because they hadn't talked enough on the day he had the accident. His poor leg. Resorting back to Japanese, she quietly marveled at his thighs and calves, his broad chest, his muscular bottom. Finally, Yurika had no choice but to ask Suzie to review the names of body parts with her just so she could think about him in English.

"Why do you want to know?" Suzie asked, narrowing her eyes. Yurika blushed. Suzie turned mock serious and drew an outline of a male body in the lesson book. She had seen this kind of lesson in one of her textbooks and now took the liberty of adapting it to Yurika's potentially lusty needs. She had hoped they would get around to this. Her cousin was a strange mix of the street, with her attraction to these bike boys, and real naïveté. How much did she know about sex? She pointed her pencil to the privates.

"Here?" she asked.

"Maybe later." Yurika laughed, covering her mouth.

Suzie pointed to the leg. "Here?"

Yurika nodded. " 'Leg' I know."

"A leg woman." Suzie sighed. "Mmm." There was hope for her cousin yet.

They began with the toes and worked their way up through the ankles, shins, calves, knees, thighs, hips, even the privates. Suzie lingered there for a moment, this region being her other area of expertise in addition to nails. Their lesson turned into secret, urgent whispers. Suzie found out that Yurika was not a virgin, that she had been with a couple of guys in Japan, one a boyfriend, but the sex sounded positively uninspired.

Suzie went over the name and nickname of each part of the male privates with loving detail, revealing to her cousin the sizes and shapes of her most memorable lovers—the man from Bombay who liked to do it sideways, the beautiful Rastafarian who liked to enter from behind, and one mystery man at a club who liked to do it standing with her legs wrapped around him.

Yurika was amazed at how much good information Suzie could share on the subject. Much more could go on down there than she had ever imagined. The five years that separated their ages made quite a difference. Yurika wondered what kind of experiences she would have by the time she was twenty-five. She used to have a boyfriend at one of her junior colleges, and they had gone to *robu-ho,* love hotels. But he was a *Yankee,* a bad boy, and all he wanted to do was find some Iranian selling phone cards and pot, go to a *robu-ho,* smoke, fool around, and make phone calls. His name was Ryo, and he always liked Yurika on top, moving fast. She would look down at his stoned face and know he was somewhere far away. Then there was Masa, an older guy she met at a *pachinko* parlor. He preferred if she used her hands with some moisturizer, and he didn't like kissing. None of it was very much fun. Maybe it was just Japanese men, Yurika thought. She wanted to ask Suzie if she had ever been with one of them, but she was too embarrassed.

Suzie taught Yurika body part idioms ranging from "having balls" to "pulling someone's leg" and "kissing someone's ass." She explained the differences between having a big dick and being a big dick, between being a dickhead and dicking someone around, a blow job and a blow off. She told her cousin about a drunken evening with two men in Brooklyn, what she called a "double whammy," an expression good for impressive things that came in pairs.

She grabbed Yurika's arm. "Who is he?" she demanded.

Yurika told her cousin everything, about the sight of her messenger flying up First Avenue, his legs, the arms, the skin like, like *"nan-take,"* she mumbled, making fists. "What can I say for 'good skin'—not good skin . . . can I say delicious color skin?"

Suzie grinned. "Only if you've tasted it."

• • •

A few days passed, and Yurika did not see her messenger at all. Maybe his leg had gotten worse. When a second week nearly finished and there was still no sight of him, she grew sad. She dyed neon red streaks into her already blond-streaked hair. After experimenting with a variety of hairstyles and disliking them all, she went with two pigtails sticking out behind her head like flames. It was how she felt—burning, heated—but for what?

Maybe to Hector she was just another cashier who couldn't speak enough English. Maybe, too, men with delicious colored skin didn't care for women with yellow skin. Yurika could plainly see she did not look at all like the Puerto Rican and Dominican girls in the neighborhood around the grocery store. Their breasts were ripe. Their wide, full lips glowed with ruby red lipstick. Their eyes gleamed like hungry tigers. Gold hung around their long necks, on their ears, and, in some, even capped their teeth.

Yurika felt plain even with flames coming out of the back of her head. She was a bit too flat-faced, her head too big. Maybe her eyes were pretty, but they were not pretty in a round-eyed way; hers were the shape of plum pits and probably too small for her head. When she smiled, the dimples in her cheeks made her look three or four years younger. Her body was tiny compared to these other women—her breasts too small and high, her shoulders too bony, and maybe worst of all, the terrible curse from her mother: her hips were wider than her chest.

She glanced around the store. Daniel and José were outside stocking the fruit and vegetable bins, talking in Spanish. Hyun Jeong was in the basement kitchen preparing a late lunch. Sang Jun was making the rounds visiting with other Korean grocers in the neighborhood. She snatched the yellow tape measure beneath the cash register. Making sure no one was coming into the store, she wrapped it around her hips:

thirty-five inches. Slipping the tape measure to her waist and pulling it tight, it measured twenty-four inches. She held her breath for the last, most important measurement. Crouching behind the counter, she quickly wrapped the tape measure around her chest. Immediately, she knew it was hopeless. The loosest tape measure in the world could not increase her meager thirty-two inches into something like ripe fruit. There was just enough for a handful on each side.

The rest of the day, she was hopelessly preoccupied with her bowling pin figure, and that night she grew feverish in her sleep. She dreamed that she had become a hunchback, and no one in the store noticed her enormous hump or that she breathed like an overworked horse with every step. She was preparing the store for a special sale that remained a mystery to her until the last minute. Finally, colored cardboard cutouts of racing bicycles hung everywhere with the words GIRL SALE written on them. In the window stood a large bowling pin covered in a bike jersey that read BIKE MESSENGER GIRL SPECIAL—10% OFF WITH I.D. All her messenger friends rode their bikes into the store, covering her freshly mopped floor with tire tracks. They performed circus riding tricks up and down the aisles. Whitey stood on the top bar of his bike, arms out to the sides, coasting down the frozen food section. In the drink section of the store, she found Hector sipping a half-gallon carton of orange juice with a straw. When he finished, he folded up the carton like an accordion and began to play a mad carnival tune that smelled of decaying orange blossoms. Then everything stopped. Hector opened his mouth to speak, and his breath smelled of bicycle grease as he said, "I'll buy you."

Although Yurika was thrilled that she was beginning to dream in English, she didn't tell Suzie or anyone else about that particular dream. It stuck to her insides, sometimes rising to her tongue, where it left the faint taste of orange rinds. Bike messenger girl special. Were there any bike messenger girls? she wondered. Staring out the window of Lucky Market, she watched for one. Messengers rode past occasionally, but none of them were female. If there were women, would they dress like men? She imagined a messenger makeover for herself—a skintight jumpsuit in blue or red like Ultra Man, her hair a brightly contrasting color, a bandanna tied around her neck.

As her mind filled with bike-messenger merchandise, Yurika came to a satisfying interpretation of her dream. It was telling her to have a sale at the store especially for bicycle messengers.

On her way to the subway that evening, she noticed that several stores offered discounts to local hospital workers from Beth Israel Medical Center, MTA employees, even commuters. A drugstore on the corner of Fourteenth Street offered 10 percent off for senior citizens.

Over scallion omelets and miso soup the next morning, while she and Suzie worked on "may," "might," "could," and "should," Yurika shared her idea. "Uncle might to try—"

Suzie narrowed her eyes. One of her books had said that flat-out correction during speaking practice wasn't helpful. Instead, a teacher should echo a student's mistakes so that the student could better focus on the problem and possibly self-correct. "To try?" Suzie asked. "Uncle might *to try?"*

Sure enough, Yurika shook her head. "Uncle might *try* special sale at the store."

Suzie nodded. "Good." Then she laughed. "Do you know the word 'cheap'?"

Yurika checked her dictionary for the word and frowned. "Not expensive?"

Suzie laughed. "Next meaning maybe."

"Oh." Yurika sighed. "Not generous."

Maybe she would have to do some research. How many messengers came to the store? How much money did they spend? Over the course of the day, she wrote down a list of questions for messengers in a small black-and-white, pocket-sized notebook with "English" written on the front. *Ask to them,* she wrote, *please could you say what juice you like more? What foods is your most favorite of Lucky Market, please? Are you smoker?*

She noted that on the average, fifty-eight messengers came into the store between 7 A.M. and 7 P.M., about five every hour. She kept lists of every product purchased and the amount of each with tax. Almost every purchase made by them, she noted, contained some form of sugar or caffeine, mostly both. Each day she totaled Cokes, Mountain Dews, Pepsis, juices, chocolate milks, coffees, and later in the day when the messengers came in walking slowly or with limps and their eyes glassy with fatigue, forty-ounce beers like Olde English and Colt 45. She kept running lists of food ranging from brownies, pink and yellow cupcakes, KitKats, bubble gum, licorice, ice cream, nuts of every kind, bananas, and peaches—anything, it seemed, to fuel them through a day.

"What you write?" Hyun Jeong asked one afternoon.

Yurika looked up, startled. "English homework," she said. "Business English."

"Ah, bijnish English," Hyun Jeong nodded, silently noting that the girl was picking up Suzie's secretive ways.

During her evening commute home, Yurika added up the totals of messenger purchases on a calculator. On the average, messengers spent $261.50 cents every day. Even if they received a 10 percent discount they would still spend more than a thousand dollars each week. Plus, the sale would surely attract more messengers. But maybe it wouldn't work. She scanned her memory for recent English slang acquisitions. *I hope,* she wrote, *Uncle Sang Jun has balls to make good sale.*

Just before she left work on the Friday evening of her first research week, Whitey entered the store, dressed in cut-off jeans and a T-shirt that read INFIDELS ARE PEOPLE TOO.

"Cool hair," he said, reaching over the counter to flick one of her flaming pigtails.

Yurika blushed. "It's different little."

"Yeah, I dig it."

"Ah! You don't work?"

"Nah, I took the day off," Whitey told her. "I had some stuff to do."

They spoke at the same time, she asking what he had to do, he wanting to show her something. Yurika agreed to meet him on the corner of Eleventh Street and First Avenue in half an hour, just after she got off work.

She didn't tell Sang Jun where she was going. "Bye-bye," she waved as he spoke to the pretty Thai woman who liked to stir-fry her broccoli.

"Okay," he replied absently, and she was gone.

Yurika's eyes opened wide. Whitey stood beside the largest bicycle she had ever seen. It was as long as the cars in Japan. Two seats, two handlebars, four pedals, red like the lips of Puerto Rican girls, almost like her hair, and trimmed in gold. Yurika stood staring with her mouth open, one hand on top of her head.

"Wanna ride?" Whitey asked.

"It's . . . it's," Yurika gasped, "it's big double whammy!"

Whitey laughed. "We call her Big Red." He was pleased with himself and felt thoroughly Paul—optimistic, in charge, making things happen.

Passers-by slowed and watched as Whitey helped Yurika onto the backseat. He explained that it was called a tandem bike, and he was borrowing it from his boss.

"Can we fly?" Yurika asked, still amazed at the length.

Soon their legs were moving in sync. She giggled at their speed, which was nearly the same as the cars beside them. Wild breath filled her lungs, and now she was glad she had flames coming out of the back of her head.

The wheels of the bike hummed beneath them. It was after rush hour. Traffic was thinning. They rode in their own lane up First Avenue, past the tall red-brick apartment buildings and all the stores that were closing up for the day. The sky was still blue, and the heat from the day seemed to vanish as the cool air swept past her cheeks and over her head. For the first time, she noticed the long muscles on Whitey's legs as he maneuvered the bike up the avenue. When he rose up out of his saddle to sprint through traffic lights about to change, the folds and curves in his shoulders became more pronounced; his thighs and calves seemed to ripple with long, precise ridges. She grinned with the rush of speed, the feel of the road beneath her.

They passed the United Nations as it gleamed in the light of the setting sun. As they passed through Sutton Place, Yurika threw her head back in glee, seeing the blue sky above her and the tops of buildings passing them. A bird flew across her line of vision and disappeared down a side street. Entering Central Park from Fifty-ninth Street, they picked up speed. Other cyclists and some tourists pointed at the two of them.

Yurika's stomach knotted. "It's safety?"

Whitey turned around and yelled, "Let go of the handlebars! Put your hands in the air! Go ahead!"

Yurika shook her head with a laugh.

"Let go!" he shouted again. After a bit more encouragement, she did. At first she let go of the handlebars but kept her hands hovering over them.

"Sit up straight." Whitey straightened his back to demonstrate.

Slowly, surely, she did. The park was beautiful, not what she expected. As they rode up the hill leading past the Metropolitan Museum of Art, she raised her hands off the bars, then her arms. She sat back, still lifting her arms higher until she was stretching to the sky and the tops of trees. She rested her hands on the top of her head, sat back, and closed her eyes. Her feet pedaled to Whitey's steady rhythm. A summer evening breeze cooled her face, her arms, penetrating the light cotton of her sweater, sweeping over her torso and down around the small of her back.

They slowed as they reached a straightaway on the road. Whitey pointed out the reservoir to the left. People were running and some stood with their hands on the wire fence as they looked over the water at the sun setting over the West Side. Whitey showed her the best kite-flying fields just past the reservoir on the left side of the road and where a garden lay to the right.

The park was much bigger and more gorgeous than Yurika had ever imagined. She was embarrassed that she had never been there before. In Japan, Central Park had the reputation of being as dangerous as the subways, especially at night. It was the place where joggers were raped and homeless people begged for money and gay men spread AIDS by having sex behind trees. Where she expected to see crumbling walls covered in graffiti, there were huge trees. Where she expected to find swamps filled with car parts and garbage, she rode past small lakes with ducks on them. She was expecting gangs of black kids jumping out of the bushes but instead found statues hidden between greenery and on top of rocks.

Whitey glanced back occasionally and grinned. Yurika looked happy. She was full of wonder, staring up at the canopy of trees, the playing fields, the roller skaters dancing to their disco, dogs chasing each other and rolling in the grass. He wanted to ride with her through the night and right out to Far Rockaway to watch the sunrise on the beach. He felt joy spark in his chest, and this feeling fueled the pumping of his legs as he rode her past the joggers and walkers and speed skaters. They circled the park until dusk settled. Whitey suggested they go to Sheep Meadow and watch the city's lights come on, but Yurika said she needed to get home. Slowly, they pedaled down Fifth Avenue to the 7 train subway station at Forty-second Street.

Yurika got off the bike first. Her legs felt like rubber, and at first it felt strange to stand on hard ground. She stood to the side as Whitey dismounted and leaned the bike against a street lamp lit for the night. He was so comfortable on bicycles, Yurika thought, a cowboy and his double-whammy horse. She could still feel the power of the bike in her body. What were the words for that? Her brain felt too tingly and aerated for any English. English brain had turned off. Bicycle mind had turned on. All she could do was smile.

"So beautiful," she ended up saying.

Whitey clapped his bike-gloved hands together as he rocked to and fro. "I can show you the whole city—bridges, parkways, parks. Have you seen Coney Island?"

Yurika laughed nervously, understanding only the beginning of his sentence. "My subway entrance," she said. Her hands pressed against each leg, and she fought hard not to bow at him. "Oh." She stepped forward again. "Maybe we have sale for bike messenger at store. Tell messengers."

"That's great. I can chug a whole lot of juice then." He wanted to ride her away to Belvedere Castle or some high, grand place. "Do you need to ride back downtown?" he asked. "The city's great on bike at night. We can ride to Flushing."

She backed away again. "I'm so tired." She began down the steps as she thanked him again.

"Yurika," Whitey called out, taking a step forward then glancing back at the unlocked bike. He wanted to grab her, kiss her. She seemed far away, and he felt a little foolish as she descended the stairs, still waving at him. Then she was gone.

THREE

Bike Boys

"You want a Thai massage?"

Sang Jun shook his head. "Not now." He lit a cigarette and stared up at the ceiling.

"You're supposed to smoke *after.*" Riya's long hair tumbled from the top of her head. She paced back and forth. "You can smoke anytime," she went on. Her dressing gown of midnight-blue silk swirled around her as she made a face. *"I'm* not anytime."

"Of course, of course." Sang Jun motioned for her to come sit next to him. He handed her his cigarette. It dangled from her mouth as she squinted at him through the smoke, sizing him up, wondering what was on his mind. Her nails lightly scratched the ridges of his forearm as she took a long drag from the cigarette and gave it back.

"You know, sometimes, I have so stress." He tapped the ash into an empty beer can at the side of the bed. "Business, family—"

"So?" She swept her hand around the walls of her East Village studio. "Is this Lucky Market?" From the exposed brick and white walls hung Thai weavings and photos of elephants from the hill tribes surrounding her home in Chiang Mai.

Sang Jun loved her place because it was just like her—a little beautiful, a little wild. He had been seeing her for almost three years now, and each time he approached the door of her building, he still felt a tingling in his stomach. After they had met at the store, she invited him over to draw him, which she did and continued to do. But every visit was different. Sometimes she was a confidante, sometimes a lover, sometimes a strict artist who would not let him move even if his bladder was ready to burst while she was sketching him.

Framing her face with her long fingers, she blinked at him. "Do I look like your family?"

Sang Jun let out a laugh then fell serious. "It's my niece."

Riya nodded. Sang Jun had told her about the girl long ago and Riya had looked forward to meeting her. She saw her in the store sometimes now, and they were friendly. They talked about how to prepare *pad see yu* and the difference between Thai noodles and Japanese ones. She was cute, Riya thought, with just enough spark in her eyes to make her interesting and probably troublesome in the ways Sang Jun had told her about. The girl had mixed with a bad crowd in Japan. One of her friends stole a motorcycle. Another was caught with drugs. None of them finished college. They went from one job to another just like Yurika. The girl, in fact, reminded Riya of some of her art students.

Sang Jun talked and smoked. Riya admired the clean line of his square jaw, his lips. She moved her body closer to his, and he put his arm around her. As she played with the flecks of gray hair around his ear, he explained that anything could happen to a girl who got in with the wrong people in this city. Riya wondered if he wasn't more concerned about what his brother would say if something happened to her.

"Bike boys," he said with disgust.

"Motorcycles?"

He shook his head. "Messengers on bicycles. Crazy ones."

"Is she doing drugs?" Riya asked. "My students do a lot. Are there black guys?"

"Black, white, brown, all kind." He shook his head. "I show you something."

He leapt out of bed, looking to Riya like a big boy in his white boxer shorts and dark socks. From his leather briefcase he produced some papers that had been stapled together. "She give to me," he said, handing them to her. It was a proposal that read SALE FOR BICYCLE MESSENGERS.

"She waste her time like this," Sang Jun said, slapping the paper and lying back down.

It was neatly prepared in English. Colored bar and line graphs projected costs and sales for all products. What a careful hand, Riya smiled to herself—just like her uncle's girlfriend. She slid her hand slowly down Sang Jun's belly, scratching lightly as she went, pretending to read, waiting for a sigh to come from her lover's mouth.

Sang Jung sank into the bed. He tried to relax, but his mind kept returning to his niece's proposal. This was not good. When he was at the store or at home watching TV with Hyun Jeong, he could not stop thinking of Riya, of her long fingers and her sweet smell of frangipani. He ached for her. As soon as he felt her nails on his flesh, he grew aroused, so she was not always aware that his attention had wandered. In fact, Sang Jun was a restless man by nature, and at that moment he couldn't get his niece's proposal out of his mind. It was a textbook perfect sale on paper. When he had seen it two days earlier at breakfast, it reminded him of his university years, sitting beside the love of his life, Jong Eun, wondering what their children would look like after they were married. Her eyes sparkled when she spoke of standard deviations, profit margins, wanting to be a mother. But his heart shrank away from the memory again, especially with a hand inside his boxers.

Closing his eyes, he reached inside of Riya's robe, even as his thoughts filled with his family gathered around the Sunday breakfast table.

. . .

There he sat, sipping his cup of hot *oksusu cha*. Hyun Jeong served him more rice and *miyukkuk*. The smell of the seaweed soup filled the room, and he watched as his side dishes were refilled with kimchee and spinach.

"Your English improve," he told his niece, flipping pages of the proposal.

"What'd you expect?" Suzie said, shaking her head. She knew the answer was, "Nothing," but she might surprise them yet. She had a knack for teaching English. Even though she loved nails, at work she caught herself daydreaming more and more about being in front of a class of hot Latin men, writing vocabulary on the board, doing pronunciation drills. The image gave her butterflies. She wondered how one went from training manicurists to teaching English. If she could get a certificate to do nails, surely she could get a certificate to teach English.

Sang Jun glanced at his daughter. She was rubbing the tips of her fingers with vitamin E oil, her long black hair in a messy pile on top of her head. Shadows surrounded her bloodshot eyes. Sometimes she so reminded him of Jong Eun. He recalled her sitting on the edge of the hospital bed after one radiation treatment. Pale, tired. Suzie was still called Su Jung then—a healthy six-month-old with a mother who had six months to live. It was a terrible joke. His voice lowered. "What time did you get home?"

"The sale, Dad, the sale." She squinted at him and adjusted her frayed robe.

He grunted and looked down. His niece kept looking at him, but he didn't make eye contact with her. Her proposal seemed perfect yet completely ridiculous, given whom it was for. If he could keep every messenger out of his store, he would do it, with their sweaty smell, bad language, and loose hands slipping drink and food into their endlessly deep messenger bags. Still though, he pretended to consider the plan because he didn't want to discourage her outright. After all, what would his brother say? Probably, he would blame everything on Hyun Jeong and say how one should never marry the sister of the love of one's life. He was an idealist that way, Sang Jun thought. Look at him—he ran away to Japan for a Japanese woman. Who was he to say what was right or wrong? Suzie needed a mother. Hyun Jeong was there. They looked enough alike with their small chins and sharp eyes. No one in America, including Suzie, would ever know the truth. Plus, in America, mothers and their children were famous for hating each other. They were always on talk shows accusing each other of horrible things. But, of course, Suzie did find out. The nosy twelve-year-old going through her father's things. There was Jong Eun's old passport, pictures. She demanded to know everything, then locked herself in her room crying and raging for what seemed like days. When she emerged, she was a changed girl. She no longer called Hyun Jeong Mom, and she spoke to them only if it was necessary. She became wild and began to play nasty tricks on them.

Sang Jun stared at the pages of the proposal and wondered if Suzie would have become so out of control if Jong Eun had raised her. Jong Eun had joy where Hyun Jeong carried around a suitcase full of spite. Jong Eun had patience where Hyun Jeong had selfishness. Jong Eun smelled naturally sweet where Hyun Jeong smelled naturally of aspirin. When he had his first business exporting Korean food, Jong Eun would sit at the breakfast table in a robe, a mug of steaming tea beside her as she used a pencil to punch in numbers on an old adding machine. She was single-minded and focused. In this way, the two sisters were similar, but Sang Jun didn't trust Hyun Jeong to do the books. He turned to her now and asked for a calculator, pencil, and paper, then added his niece's neat columns of numbers, putting small check marks next to each sum.

He was stalling. In his ear, he could hear Jong Eun whispering,

Don't be silly, Dangsin. This girl will be strong. His mind drifted to the memory of her lying in her sickbed, Suzie in her arms. Blue light of early morning filled the room—the color against the pale hospital walls thin like paper, like the handwritten good-night notes she stuck in his kimchi when he arrived home late. Almost twenty-five years later, the bitterness of his loss still gave him an ache in his chest. He still could not believe she was gone and that their time together had been so short, not even three years.

He cleared his throat.

"Here it comes," Suzie said.

Sang Jun barked at his daughter in Korean.

"Whatever," she said, picking up her vitamin E and turning to her cousin. "I told you he was cheap." She shuffled out of the room, the bottoms of her slippers chafing across the linoleum floor.

Sang Jun cleared his throat again and looked at his niece. She was staring at him, unblinking, her head cocked slightly to one side, a slight snarl beginning to form on her mouth. "You work hard." He put the proposal down. "But bike boys"—he shook his head—"no good."

"They steal from us before," Hyun Jeong chimed in. "I tell you." She gave a laugh. "You waste time."

Yurika stared down at the table, the corners of her lips twitching.

"You listen, Jae Hee."

Blood rushed into Yurika's face. Stabbing random bits of okra with her chopsticks and grinding her teeth, she realized something: she wasn't Korean enough for them. Her aunt refusing to call her by her name and constantly criticizing. Her uncle never called her any name. They didn't want a sale that wasn't a Korean one. It wasn't about the bike boys. She glared up at them.

Sang Jun remained silent, but Hyun Jeong caught the look in her niece's eyes and slapped the table. "Now you listen, Jae Hee—"

Hyun Jeong began to lecture her about how she shouldn't start staying out late with bad bike boys, but Yurika didn't hear her. Angry

English welled up from deep inside her. She didn't have to think what to say because she had been practicing it in many quiet moments: when Hyun Jeong called her Jae Hee, when she remembered Hyun Jeong going through Suzie's cosmetics, every time her shrill voice squealed out an order at the store or in this house where no one laughed except her at stupid things on the TV. For every time this woman said something bad about one of the messengers, about Whitey's skin, for her arrogance and snobbery, for her bitchiness and disregard for other people's feelings, an angry, volcanic, acid splash of English flew from her. "I'm up yours!"

After she stormed from the room, Sang Jun and Hyun Jeong sat in a stunned, confused silence. After a few moments, Hyun Jeong spoke—in Korean—as she rose to clear dishes. "She's not learning good English."

"Bitch," shouted Whitey.

His brakes were either too tight, too loose, or the brake pads got so crooked that they squealed against the rims. He stood back and stared at his bike, a midrange Japanese racer he'd upgraded with Italian and French components. The chrome-alloy frame was totally wrapped in black electrical tape to protect it from the street and to hide the make. Light enough to ride all day but heavy enough to absorb the shock of all those miles. It was a good bike, and it looked handsome on this new mechanic stand.

"Fucking brakes are killing me," he whispered. He was already sweaty from the heat, but the stubborn brakes made him drip with perspiration and frustration. At least he had the mechanic stand. It was so amateurish to turn the bike upside down to do repairs, and he was relieved that those days were now over. He was also glad Bone agreed to exchange the stand for a couple of pairs of Campagnolo pedals

Whitey had "found" for him on a pair of touring bikes locked to a parking meter in Tribeca.

A little side business—in exchange for parts, service, and tools, Whitey stripped bikes for Bone. He felt bad for the people he stole from, but he stripped only bikes that looked like they belonged to people who could afford to replace the parts. Plus, with the mountain bike craze, the field had opened up. It was an exciting time for this sort of thing. Just the day before, he had lifted a quick-release front wheel with big, knobby tires, an anodized rat trap, a pair of toe clip straps, and two rear brake pads. Bone took the parts and built Frankenstein bikes he called "conversions." These he sold cut-rate to messengers and people in his neighborhood. Nobody asked questions. Everyone paid cash. In the grand scheme of things, Whitey figured, this little ecosystem of bike part redisbursement helped more people than it harmed.

He wondered about Bone. Was it a coincidence that the son of a convict was building bikes from stolen parts? At least he wasn't committing violent crimes. Which is not to say the guy didn't have a violent temper. He had broken one messenger's nose with a **U**-shaped bike lock. That had cost him his job. He got this job at Quick Service because in this business, no one asked for references or résumés. If you could ride, you could work. If you didn't work out, you didn't work. Bone mostly kept to himself. Even though Whitey and he were friendly, Bone never spoke about his past, and Whitey never asked.

In terms of Whitey's participation in this fencing operation, the real problem was the cosmic one—his own brakes were always acting up, and he knew what this meant. It was the price he was paying for stealing. He would be cruising down Second Avenue and then brake for a light or a drop, only to have this ear-piercing screech rise up from his wheels. It was shabby, and he hated shabbiness. In one way, there was no sense to it. He knew how to repair brakes. The problem was that he just didn't want to stop this business yet. Bone was building him a front racing wheel with Mavic G40 rims and a Kevlar beaded tire, and Whitey didn't want to pay eighty bucks for it. But maybe, just maybe, though, this would be his last parts-for-service trade.

Meanwhile, he couldn't get these damn brakes fixed. Whatever angle he approached from, even using his third-hand tool, there was a problem. He took a few steps back and lit a cigarette, then turned on the radio that sat on a small pile of travel guides. At the top of the news, a highjacking was in its third day. Some guy was still on trial for killing his wife by slowly poisoning her. Eighty-five people were dead from tornadoes in the U.S. and Canada. And, in the orbiting shuttle, a Saudi prince became the first person to read the entire Koran in outer space. Whitey had just begun to sink into a reverie about what he would do if Yurika was being held hostage by Japanese-hating terrorists when she called.

He dropped his socket wrench to the floor. "I was just thinking of you. This hostage thing is going on, you know, and—"

Yurika had no idea what he was saying, but it was good to hear his voice. It was always full of hope.

"I'm not good," she said.

Whitey closed his eyes. She was calling from a pay phone on the street, and the noise from traffic made her voice small, far away.

"What happened?" he said louder into the phone.

"So, I got big fighting to my aunt."

"You got big fighting, huh? What'd she say?"

"She so nasty."

"Where are you? It's pretty noisy."

"Flushing."

"Come over," Whitey shouted into the phone. "You can help fix my bike."

• • •

She had never been so far east and downtown from Lucky Market before because everyone had warned her about Alphabet City. Flushing had Koreatown. Canal Street had Chinatown. And Alphabet City had heroin, homeless people, and crime. But the day was bright, and people were everywhere. Like Central Park, Alphabet City was not what she had thought. Where she expected burned-out buildings, she saw sometimes run-down but mostly respectable brownstones with brown, white, and black locals sitting on stoops, trying to cool off in the heat. Small, half-naked kids ran in and out of the water spraying from an open fire hydrant. A small man wearing a fedora stood on a corner beside a huge block of ice that he was shaving into paper cones and flavoring for overheated children. Few people noticed her except for an older Asian woman walking toward her. Their eyes lingered on each other. The woman, who began to smile as she got closer, had a jet-black ponytail that hung to her waist, and she was carrying a large drawing pad.

"Hello," said the woman. "Lucky Market girl, right?"

Yurika grinned. *"Pad see yu!"*

"Yes." The woman laughed. "Good memory. You working today?"

Yurika shook her head, suddenly self-conscious about this spontaneous English conversation. She hesitated with her words. "I'm . . . go see friend."

"Oh, good."

"He gonna teach me about bike."

The woman's big eyes lit up. "Boyfriend?"

Yurika made a face and shook her head. "Just friend." She pointed to the drawing pad. "Ah, you make something art?"

"I teach drawing. Wanna see?"

Yurika nodded, and when the woman opened her drawing pad, Yurika's mouth fell open. There, on page after page in pencil, bright yellow, and blue crayon, red pastel, charcoals, lay her uncle. Faces, nudes, studies of him in profile, his jaw, his ear, him smiling, looking angry, looking sad, looking happy, looking ecstatic with mouth open and eyes tightly shut. The woman closed the pad.

Yurika was speechless. She lifted her eyes to the woman's face, which had a slight smile. She was older than Yurika had thought, perhaps in her early forties. But very beautiful, smooth skin, sharp eyes that seemed to smile as well.

"I'm Riya," she said, producing a little blue card with her name, her contact information on Tenth Street, and the words LIFE DRAWING. "This can be our secret," she said, leaning in toward Yurika. "You know 'secret,' don't you?"

Yurika nodded. The woman's eyes were so clear. Yurika wanted to keep staring into them.

"Come and see me. I'll draw you. We can talk more."

Yurika managed a faint nod.

Riya walked on, turning around once. Yurika was still standing there, card in hand, mouth open. She waved to her, and Yurika held up a hand.

Slowly, Yurika turned around and began walking again, the images of her uncle's body—red face and blue feet and yellow privates crowding her mind.

What the fuck?

She knew that voice in her head. It was one of Whitey's expressions, and it kept repeating over and over in her inner ear until she arrived at his street-level apartment on Sixth Street and Avenue D. She held up Riya's card when Whitey opened the door.

"Uncle secret life," she mumbled.

Whitey stepped onto the sidewalk and glanced back and forth along the avenue. He wiped his hands on his cutoff jeans and wiped his forehead with the edge of his black T-shirt that read simply MEAT. He nodded to the super of his building and some of his handymen leaning against a parked car. "Those guys bothering you?"

Yurika shook her head as Whitey ushered her into his apartment.

She sat directly on the slightly tilting wooden floor and seemed in a daze as she told him what had just happened.

"Your uncle's got a floozy."

"Froojy?"

"Floo-zy," Whitey repeated slowly. "A girlfriend." He laughed. "Who can blame him?" he asked, thinking of Hyun Jeong. "Wanna beer?"

He produced two cold bottles of a Czech beer with a name Yurika couldn't pronounce. It was cold and delicious. As he explained how his apartment used to be a store a little smaller than Lucky Market, Yurika thought about the last time she had any alcohol—in Japan with her friends. They had gotten drunk at a sake bar the night before she left for New York. Thankfully, her flight was the following evening because she didn't wake up until the afternoon. Her mother had hovered around her futon, cleaning the room until she woke up. Today, though, she would not get drunk. This was a friendly drink on a hot summer day. She watched Whitey as he talked, noticing how he made eye contact only every few sentences, like he was suddenly shy. Somehow, he had gotten back on the subject of her uncle. He was explaining how men and women cheating on each other was a kind of American tradition. "It's why people say this is the land of the devil," he told her, "like those fuckin' hijackers."

Yurika nodded absently as she began to notice the things of his apartment. There were piles of books surrounding the mattress on the floor.

"So much books," she said.

"Furniture." Whitey laughed, and then in another moment when Yurika understood the joke, they laughed together.

Yurika was reminded of apartments in Japan, the way everything was compact—the small sink in one corner, and next to that a small oven that sat on top of a half refrigerator. The walls seemed very New York, though, with slightly tattered posters, one of the Beatles, one of

Lou Reed, another of a musician Whitey told her was Nigerian—Fela Kuti—and others of bands she had never heard of like Spike Driver and The Turds. In between these were cutouts of professional bike racers from Europe and America that seemed to race around the entire room and even onto the ceiling. There were maps of the countries he'd traveled to and a vertical map of Manhattan that listed every avenue and street and also divided the island into sections from one tip to another. Whitey stood behind Yurika as she gazed at the minutiae of the island. The map had been given to him, he explained, by the first messenger company he had worked for. The island was divided up because each section was a rate zone so a dispatcher would know how much to charge for delivery runs.

Whitey wiped the side of his face on his shoulder. Yurika was sweating, too. Small beads of sweat covered her lower neck. The collar of her pink T-shirt had been torn out, so he could also see moisture on parts of her shoulders. Shoulders worth biting, he thought as he lowered his head toward the back of hers. He closed his eyes and inhaled deeply. She smelled salty with a slight hint of some kind of hair product.

Yurika turned with a laugh and checked her pigtails, which she had just touched up with a bit of orange dye.

"No, no," Whitey said, "everything's fine. You smell good." He so wanted to kiss her, but he didn't because she laughed again and slapped his arm as she moved toward the bike in the center of the room. Instead, he began telling her about the well-lubricated parts of the bike.

"This," he said, pointing to the bottom center of the frame, "is the bottom bracket." Yurika looked closer as Whitey continued. "Do you know ball bearings?" She did not, of course, but as she leaned more forward to look, the top of her T-shirt fell open. Whitey prided himself on the fact that he was not the kind of guy who stared at women's breasts when he talked to them. However, his peripheral vision had developed considerably for just such moments. As he explained how the super-stiff crank arms extended from the bottom bracket, looking at her face, he could also see the gentle slope of flesh down her neck and chest bone and the soft rounding of both of her breasts. She wore a blue bra with a touch of lace. He spoke slowly, lovingly about axle grease and parts that rubbed against each other, about the rising seat post and handlebar stem, about the tension in the spokes that pressed against the soft rubber inner tube. He was mortified by his own words but could not stop himself.

"You have good bike mind," Yurika told him, catching only the names of the parts and some of their functions. She had always loved the design of bikes but thought it was more of a boy's thing. Sitting there now, she felt herself drawn to Whitey's words and the bike before them; it was like learning a new secret handshake.

He held up an oddly shaped tool that could have been a cross between a miniature hammer and a tiny monkey wrench. "This is a chain remover," he announced. Picking up the chain from the ground, he went on. "As you can see, the chain has already been removed." He showed her how the design of the chain had one inner link and one outer link. "The outer link is called the male, and the inside one is the female."

"Why?"

"I'll show you." He held the two ends of the chain together on the chain tool and began to turn a small arm that slowly pushed a tiny peg from the male link into the female link, reuniting the chain.

"So," said Yurika, "male to female."

Whitey nodded. "Sexy, right?" He handed her the chain on the tool. "Try to open the chain again. Turn the arm about six full times."

He liked looking at her hands. They were small but elegant, with articulate fingers and nice nails that weren't long or painted, just plain, attractive.

Yurika forgot herself as she got absorbed in the business of bicycle mechanics. She had no pestering aunt, no store to report to, no window to look longingly out from, no Japanese to translate from, no Korean to be ashamed of. In Japan, her interests, if they could be called that, had been shopping and going out with friends, with the occasional dabble into learning more English. There had been nothing as stimulating as the language of bicycle repair and now the hands-on experience of it. After dragging herself through high school and attempting junior college a couple of times, Yurika had unwittingly resigned herself to a life of rote jobs and restless ambles up and down the streets of Shinjuku and Roppongi. Here, in Whitey's apartment, though, with her fingers and nails slowly becoming covered in dirty bike grease, she felt satisfied in a way she had not felt in a long time. There existed only the frame with its strange black electrical tape, its parts, the names for the parts doing slow laps around the bicycle stadium in her brain, and the warm baritone of Whitey's voice telling her to tighten that cable or add a bit more grease to the chain. She was even able to fix Whitey's brakes.

"You rock!" Whitey said, putting a warm hand on her neck and giving it a small shake. "I can't believe it—I've been trying forever to fix those!"

Yurika laughed, and the sight of her dimples made Whitey smile. His teeth reminded her of the rotting smile of a security guard she sometimes saw back home in Kawasaki. He worked at the Kawasaki stadium where the Kirin bicycle races were held. Sometimes she and her friends would go, and the guys would place bets. The bike racers were like beautiful machines, all with thighs like tree trunks and barrel chests. Each stayed in his lane for the entire race with the only burst of energy coming the last lap, when all the racers would bounce from their saddles and pump their legs for the finish line. Then there would be a surge in the crowd, people almost rising to their feet but not completely.

Yurika began to tell Whitey about these races and was surprised that he knew all about them. From a stack of magazines in the corner of the studio, he produced a *Bicycle Racing Illustrated* that had an article about racing in Japan.

"Strong sprinters," Whitey said, nodding.

Yurika told him that the thing she liked best about going to the races besides the bikers was watching the people in the crowd. "Yakuza guy with girlfriends," she said. "Just like movie." She described cool guys with hair tonic in dark suits and sport shirts, tattoos up and down their arms, mute women with big hair and tight dresses.

"I wanna go," said Whitey. "Bring a camera."

"You can't take photos. Not allowed."

"Why not?"

"Hmmm. Maybe so bad impression from Japan."

Whitey sat back onto the floor. "So what's your impression of this country?"

Yurika picked some bike grease from beneath a nail. "Just I know New York little."

He lit a cigarette. "Yeah," he said, "New York is definitely not America."

"But, here there's not *mindu conturoru.* Do you know?" She scribbled it down on a piece of paper.

"Mind control?"

"Mine control," Yurika tried to imitate. "In Japanese we say, *mindu conturoru.*"

Whitey repeated her words. "What the fuck?"

Yurika explained that it was a kind of Japanese English as she looked around the room. "So, because you smoking, then I wanna smoke. If I don't smoke then maybe you don't like me. In Japan like this for everything—clothes, music, speaking, school, family. So many mind control."

Whitey shook his head. "Man, that sucks."

"So." Yurika nodded. "That's Japan. I like here more."

"You should stay here, then."

Yurika looked at Whitey, then abruptly glanced at her watch. It was almost eight o'clock. She had meant to stay only a couple of hours. "Ah—" She jumped to her feet. "I'm so late again."

Whitey felt his heart sink, but he tried not to show it. "I'll walk you to the train."

"It's okay," Yurika began, but Whitey wouldn't hear of it.

"It's a shitty neighborhood and even shittier after dark."

"But not dark yet—"

"Close enough."

He dug through a drawer in his kitchenette and produced a key on a tiny wrench. "For you," he said. "Come by any time, even if I'm not here. My house is your house." He leaned his face in close to hers. "Escape from Lucky Market."

For the second time today, Yurika was speechless. First with Riya. Now with Whitey. She liked him as a friend and didn't want him to get any wrong idea. She turned over the key in her hand and shook her head. "You're very kind."

"All right?" Whitey asked. "Any time you want. I don't get back here till like nine or ten anyhow, so if you wanna hang out after work by yourself, this is the place."

Yurika got the gist of that sentence, and she felt a wave of relief—to have a place to go, to be alone. She slipped the key in her pocket and looked up. Whitey's eyes were big and brown, and she asked him why he looked unhappy.

He fumbled around with some words, scratched his forehead to hide his face a little. Then he patted the side of her arm. "Did I tell you how I found this place?"

The story lasted until they got to the subway entrance. Whitey elaborated on it a bit so he could explain the meanings of key words such as "psycho," "nut job," and "bounty hunter" to describe his former roommate. He also explained the meanings of words like "sanctuary" and "lifesaver" to describe the apartment.

"Like candy Lifesaver?" asked Yurika.

Whitey nodded. "Just like."

As they walked, they stopped to admire a passing posse of four older men on bicycles that were decorated with Puerto Rican flags and fixed with stereos, streamers, lambskin seat pads, oversized bike horns, and more. One even had a pair of bullhorns mounted on the handlebars. Whitey explained that they were the members of the Puerto Rican Schwinn Bicycle Club. They were fixtures in the neighborhood whom everyone loved to see. Tourists had their pictures taken with them. They rode together in parades. Yurika was amazed and couldn't stop shaking her head. She asked Whitey if there was a good word for a sight like that.

Whitey thought for a moment, then turned to her. "Funky," he said, nodding.

Yurika was confused because she knew that "funk" meant some kind of bad way. As they walked, Whitey told her the multiple meanings of the word and related phrases like "funked out," "funky ass," "give up the funk." When they reached the subway entrance, Yurika placed her hands flat on the top of her thighs and bowed deeply. *"Hi, domo arigato,* Whitey-san, *domo.* Very good *sensei*—ah, teacher."

The Japanese Whitey had picked up in his travels was little more than those words. He wanted to kiss her on her way back up to standing, but again he didn't. Instead, he held out a hand and taught her a kind of handshake some of the messengers liked to do: you slap your hands together and pull them away slowly, snapping the very edges of each other's fingers for good luck. Yurika liked it and wanted to practice it a few more times until she could do it smoothly.

In fact, they were having a hard time saying good-bye to each other. Yurika was dreading the sight of her aunt and uncle. Whitey was dreading the sight of his bike tools without Yurika's hands on them.

In the end, they said good-bye in as many languages as possible. Yurika said it in Japanese, Korean, English, Hawaiian, and Italian, and Whitey said it in French, German, Portuguese, Russian, Thai, Spanish, Pig Latin, and Ubi-Dubi. Then they exchanged several *adios*es as Yurika descended into the subway. Whitey had walked several blocks before he realized he was singing a version of the Beatles' "Hello, Good-bye" to himself: "You say *sayonara* and I say *hola, hola, hola.* I don't know why you say *sayonara,* I say *hola."* He was feeling positively Ringo.

Whitey began showing up at the store three, four times a day. He would talk to Yurika when she was ringing up customers. Once, Sang Jun even had to remind him that she was working. Worse to Sang Jun was that Yurika didn't seem to mind him. In fact, if he weren't so unattractive, Sang Jun might have thought that he was her boyfriend. The bike boy often showed up at five, and the two of them went off somewhere. They spent July Fourth together running around the city and seeing the fireworks. He felt relief that with this tall bike boy with the bad skin, she was at least spending time with someone closer to her own color. Several times, he had to tell her with some firmness that staying out late with the bike boys was a bad idea, but like Suzie, she didn't listen. In fact, she was getting more and more involved with the bike boys. Apparently, she had told them that there would be a sale because many of them kept asking him if this size Coke was on sale or if these cigarettes were discounted because of the sale. One afternoon, a messenger the girl called Lefty, who smelled particularly bad, cornered him and wanted to know if he could order some bicycle merchandise and discount it as part of the sale.

"This is grocery," Sang Jun exclaimed as he escaped to the back room. "No sale." He took over the flattening of cardboard boxes from José. Picking up a razor, he sliced the corners of one box as he mumbled to himself, "Dirt. Bad smell. Same like they English: Yo, man. Yo, guy."

His niece was beginning to speak like them, too; he'd heard a "yo" slip from her mouth while she was talking to one of them. There was a crazy handshake as well. She had also started to dress like them, wearing a red bike cap backward on her head, used army shorts, and T-shirts with incomprehensible slogans and foreign bike brands on them. He didn't want to give his brother any bad reports, but he was now sure that the girl was sent away for the summer to give his brother and sister-in-law a much-needed break.

Over the last few years especially, whenever Sang Jun had talked to his brother, Tae Hyun, and asked about Yurika, there was a noticeable strain in his brother's voice. He would hesitate and give a low hum into the phone while he searched for the words that might make the situation sound not quite as bad as it was. "She's having some trouble," he would say, or "her friends are a bad influence." When Sang Jun asked if she was getting into trouble, the answer came as something like, "No, but her friends are." *Her friends* were keeping her up late and out all night. *Her friends* kept her from studying. So when Sang Jun's brother asked if Yurika could go there for a summer and practice her English while she did some work around the store, it was understood that she needed to get away from these *friends.* Sang Jun felt there was no need to harp on the point and embarrass Tae Hyun. Clearly, he and his wife couldn't handle the girl, and her friends were a convenient excuse for poor parenting skills.

Hyun Jeong reminded her husband at every possible opportunity that she had been right about the girl from the start: she was trouble and her parents wanted to get rid of her. Tae Hyun should have given them room and board money for her, and the two of them should not be paying her to do a job a monkey could do. Wherever Hyun Jeong was, Sang Jun could hear the buzz of her perpetual complaining. All that was wrong in her immediate world could be traced back to the girl's arrival: the extra cleaning around the house, the lack of sleep because the girl was staying out later and later with that terrible-skinned bike boy and who knows what other street vermin—as if it wasn't bad enough to have one girl in the house who stayed out all hours of the night—the extra cooking, the long-distance lies that everything was fine. In fact, how could anything be fine with a half-Japanese, half-Korean delinquent who didn't speak enough Korean to order *bi-bim-bop?* Wasn't it strange that the girl's parents never called when the girl was around and only once a month and the girl never called them back? There was probably even a dip in sales because she was charging all her bike boys pennies as they walked away with the store, item by item, in their huge bags. Hyun Jeong mourned the loss of money that they were paying the girl to disrupt their lives not just for a week, which would have been the polite duration of a family member's visit, but for an entire summer. As if things hadn't already grown difficult because of Suzie's long-term wild behavior, were they expected to whip this girl into some kind of shape? And of course the girl would arrive during the terrible heat of summer along with the terrible news of a hijacking, a trial of a dreadful man who killed his wife—imagine such a thing—and her own husband disappearing whenever he wished. How did she know that Sang Jun hadn't poisoned her sister in the first place and made it look like cancer?

As this question left her lips, Hyun Jeong was restocking the canned tomatoes. By the time she realized that Sang Jun was listening in the next aisle, he already had her by the scruff of her neck and was pushing her into the back of the store and down to the basement kitchen.

"Shut up and make kimchee," he growled in her ear before storming out of the basement and locking the door.

This humiliation fueled Hyun Jeong's search-and-find mission the following Tuesday morning. Yurika had new clothing and had acquired more things. The walls were starting to be covered with pictures of cyclists in skintight outfits and faces twisted in pain. There were piles of clothes on the floor and on the chair by the desk. Hyun Jeong wanted to just throw everything out, but she resisted and instead went through every pocket, every neon fanny pack scattered around the room. She examined every new bike tool that lay on the desk and on the floor. She tried to translate the slogans on the girl's T-shirts while she searched for hidden pockets on them. She sat on Suzie's bed, frustrated, glancing at the mess of Yurika's things. Of course, the girl's true disorderly state had finally come out. She was more and more like Suzie as time went on. They both left messes wherever they went, knowing whose job it was to clean up. They did this to spite her; she was quite sure of this.

But where was the girl's money? Just all this stuff and those stupid action figures. Hyun Jeong slowly turned her head. The Ultra Man action figures stood on the bureau, side by side. Rising from the bed, she walked over to them, picked up the red figure and turned it over. The arms moved. The legs moved. She gave it a shake. There was something inside. Squeezing the neck, she gave a pull to the head and off it came. There, stuffed into the body of the red Ultra Man, were tight rolls of money rubber-banded together. Emptying them onto the table, she could see that it was all Japanese yen, so she stuffed them back into red Ultra Man, put its head back on, and gave blue Ultra Man the same treatment. Decapitated blue Ultra Man kept the U.S. bills—tight rolls of twenties, tens, fives, and ones. Hyun Jeong smiled.

Of course the girl would keep her money in toys. So Japanese. So childish. Why hadn't she discovered it sooner? Picking up each roll and handling it, she tapped a roll of twenties on the bureau as she figured out what she thought would be an appropriate but inconspicuous amount of room and board to claim. She opened up the roll of twenties and counted: two forty. She took two twenties, then two bills from each of the other rolls except the one of singles. Seventy dollars for almost two months of room and board. The little half-breed was getting a bargain. Carefully placing a rubber band around each roll as it had been before, Hyun Jeong shoved Ultra Man's head back on and stood him next to his red friend. Certainly, she would see them again next Tuesday, she thought. As she left the room, she wondered what the exchange rate with the yen was these days.

Yurika did not discover the missing money for days. She was preoccupied with becoming, as Whitey kidded her, a "homegirl." They hung out at Whitey's place where Yurika worked on his bike and read bike magazines. They sought out some of the hidden nooks of the city Whitey had discovered over the years—an ancient tea parlor on Bayard Street and a no-man's-land full of car parts called Cocoa Hill. Whitey taught her as much slang as possible. Yurika learned homegirl gems such as "no way, José," "fuck that noise," and "chill out." He also gave her the occasional history lesson because he was appalled at how little she knew. She had heard of names like Hitler and Mao but had no idea who they were. About the Japanese occupation of Korea she knew next to nothing. She didn't know what had happened to the American Indians. She didn't know anything about July Fourth.

That day, especially, was a revelation to Yurika. They walked over the Williamsburg Bridge and wound through the streets until they arrived at an overgrown patch of land next to an oil plant that overlooked the East River. Passing through a fence that had huge chunks cut from it, they walked along a trail surrounded by weeds and tall grass that led to a moored and rusted barge that looked out on Manhattan. There was a handful of people already on the boat, some drinking beer from a cooler. Yurika and Whitey made their way to the helm and watched the fireworks against the backdrop of the Midtown skyline. They were so close they could even clearly see the firework boats anchored in the river. It seemed to Yurika to be such an insider's view of July Fourth in the city—away from crowds—no police, no vendors, no Japanese tourists.

A few local kids were setting off cherry bombs inside the hull of the boat, which scared her a bit, but Whitey only laughed and told her to try to listen to the language the kids were speaking. They were dressed in baggy T-shirts and even baggier trousers, not unlike all the hip-hop homeboys and homegirls she saw everywhere these days, even when she was in Japan. She could understand only a few of their swear words. What was the rest of it? Whitey made her guess, but she couldn't do it. As it turned out, they were speaking a perfect blend of homeboy English, which Whitey explained was more or less street slang, and Polish. Yurika was amazed because it was really another language altogether, maybe spoken by only a handful of wild kids from Brooklyn. Were they fluent in either language? What did they speak in school? Did they go to school? There were too many questions flying through Yurika's head for her to stop one and ask it of Whitey. Instead, she watched mushroom caps of red, white, and blue fire explode in the sky, reflect against the skyline, and rain down over the water.

It was then Yurika realized that, not unlike these street boys, she too was learning her own kind of English. She had her grammar and sex-related slang that Suzie taught her, the bike English from the messengers, the store English customers spoke, and the words and phrases that she was learning from Whitey.

A spray of yellow sparks lit up the night sky. They floated down and became tendrils of gold hanging over the water. Yurika felt warm inside. She was making her own English. She was growing a second tongue. There were words and phrases and attitudes for this New York life that she had no words for in Japanese.

"English life," she mumbled to herself as an explosion of red, white, and blue like a water fountain showered over everyone. In her English life, she could stand on an old boat watching fireworks while street boys set off cherry bombs of Polish English. In her English life, she could have a dream boy like Hector—maybe, she reminded herself, just maybe; at least it was possible. English life gave her a friend like Whitey who, unlike friends in her Japanese life, had curiosity about things and people. He asked more and more questions of her that created more English life in her. Like when they walked over the Williamsburg Bridge. It took her the entire time to describe to him how to make the perfect bowl of rice. He kept asking questions and fed her vocabulary and expressions. He made her repeat herself over and over, so that by the time they stepped foot in Brooklyn, he joked, she could have hosted her own cooking show with lines like, "The secret to perfect, steaming bowls of rice is to rinse the grains before they're cooked."

At the height of the fireworks, Yurika looked at Whitey. He was entranced like a boy, his face turned up to the sky, his mouth open, his skin changing color with every explosion in the sky.

He glanced at her for a moment. "Are you watching this?" he shouted. "This is what we call a 'mind fuck'—something amazing. Get it?"

Yurika nodded. A huge umbrella of orange lights opened up, showering blue sparkles everywhere. Everyone gasped as the blue rain glimmered as it fell slowly to the water below. Yurika grinned. She thought of her parents. They never would have imagined this kind of education for her: in English life, there was more mind fuck and less *mindu conturoru*.

"What the fuck?" Yurika mumbled to herself as she counted again. Still seventy short. A day and a half's money from the store. Had she been careless in counting her cash? It was the one thing she had gotten good at this summer besides bike repair. Where was that money?

She sat on the floor next to the headless blue Ultra Man. Suzie was out for the evening. Upstairs, she could hear the TV and Hyun Jeong's occasional shrill laughter. She recalled her aunt going through Suzie's cosmetics and wondered if the woman was crazy enough to also steal. The idea was too impossible. She tried to put it out of her mind and decided that she must have made a mistake about how much money she had to begin with.

She could hear her uncle telling her to pay more attention. He was out that night as well, and Yurika wondered if he was with Riya. Putting her money away, she pulled the blue card from her wallet and sat on the bed beside the phone. Riya's last name was an impossibly long one with sixteen letters that Yurika could not even begin to pronounce properly when she tried. She felt so curious about this woman who had pages and pages of her uncle's naked body on her drawing pad. Grabbing the phone, Yurika dialed. The phone rang and rang, and just before Yurika was about to give up, Riya picked up. There was a moment's pause as Yurika considered hanging up.

"Hello? Who is this?" Riya sounded annoyed.

"Ah, hi, I am Yurika. From Lucky Market." She listened carefully to hear if Sang Jun was in the background.

"Yes, I'm glad you're calling."

Yurika was surprised at how formal she sounded.

"Did you think about what I said?"

It was impossible to tell if the woman was being discreet and not saying Yurika's name or if she were speaking normally. Yurika closed her eyes and listened for any sounds in the background—coughing, talking, movement—but there was nothing. Would Riya have told Sang Jun about their chance meeting on the street?

"I can go there after five," Yurika said. "What day?"

Riya suggested a week from the following Monday. "Bring a robe in case you want to pose nude."

The words didn't make sense at first. Yurika repeated the sentence to herself, and could hear herself become flustered when she figured them out. "Ah, *nu-do.* No clothes!" A laugh escaped her.

"Yes," Riya said, and Yurika could hear her smile. "See you soon."

Yurika tried to sound calm but was imagining her parts in charcoal and pencil next to her uncle's privates. "Yeah," Yurika said, unable to stop grinning, "see you."

It was difficult not to tell Suzie about this woman. Whenever she talked to her cousin, though, she managed not to think about it because Suzie had far more interesting things to share. She was exhausted from a string of weekday nights "club hopping" in the city. Once again she had met the guy who liked to do it standing. Yurika and Suzie lay in their respective beds on a Wednesday morning as Suzie, her eyes still closed, told her cousin of a bathroom stall at one club where she and "the standing man" did it silently, wordlessly, vertically, completely.

"It's so nice to be lying down," she cooed with a sleepy grin.

"You don't know his name?" Yurika asked.

"Standing man," Suzie replied. "That's his superpower." She smirked. "He's got such a nice butt. Legs like steel."

Yurika thought of Hector. It was impossible that Standing Man and Hector were the same man. How could Hector ride all day and then dance and have sex standing up all night long and work the next day? Still, though, the image of Hector naked and aroused inflamed her insides and made her sweat when she thought of it in the store that day. She wanted to press against his skin. Not say a word. Just quietly wrap herself entirely around him to feel his hardness, heat, the smell of his flesh.

Suzie's words lingered in Yurika's mind for the rest of the day as well. She hadn't seen Hector go by for more than a week. "Steel" didn't seem like a good word for his legs. He was more like an animal. That was his superpower. Her animal man. She reached into her pocket for the pouch Daniel had made for her weeks earlier. It was still intact, but not so fresh anymore. All day her attention shifted to the window, scanning the street for her animal man.

"Looking for me?"

It was Whitey. "Yo, my homeboy," Yurika said with a laugh as she extended her hand over the counter for a messenger handshake.

"Homey, homey, don't you know me?" he shot back, which Yurika never fully understood except that it seemed like the response Whitey preferred. He talked in fast clips about something, which she picked up only at the end of his sentence. ". . . the wheel, the kickin' wheel, the hot-shit wheel."

Yurika nodded but wondered about "hot shit" because a few other messengers also used it. She guessed that because it had to do either with the bad smell of burning rubber or being on the street all day too close to dog shit, it meant something about a strong experience. "Why is wheel hot shit?"

Whitey slapped his hands together and started rocking back and forth. "Kick-ass French-made rims of superlight alloy, tires with the same stuff they make bulletproof vests from—Bang! Bang!" His hands had become guns as he shot at Yurika, then his fingers became bullets bouncing off his own chest. Yurika glanced to the back of the store to see if anyone was watching.

Whitey pointed at her with both hands. "You wanna come with me to get the wheel? You can check out this guy Bone's place. It's all bike, man. Totally hot shit. Tomorrow. But I got something good for today, too."

He had decided to show her the West Tenth Street pier. As they walked, he told her about how crazy Bone was. Once, he saw him flick a lit cigarette down the windshield and into the engine of a cab stopped at a light. Whitey laughed and shook his head. "Oil fire. Damn thing almost exploded." He turned to Yurika. "Some of the guys from Mexico call him Tres Huevos."

Yurika squinted at him. The name sounded serious.

"Three balls," Whitey said, grabbing his crotch. "Supertough guy. We say 'ballsy.' "

"Bo-ru-zi," Yurika repeated, imagining again a pirate, this time with a face covered with scars.

"More *l* more *z*."

"Bo-dzee, bo-dzee."

As she practiced this under her breath and Whitey talked, Yurika noticed that although he occasionally gestured with his right hand, letting go of the bicycle, the bike kept moving beside him like some kind of obedient pony. Yet Whitey didn't even seem to notice. He also sometimes lifted his bike by the handlebars and bounced it on the front wheel to emphasize a point he was making. Once this made a heavy woman walking in front of them spin around and snap, "Watch that thing!" It was a man in a wig and woman's clothes.

"Sorry, ma'am," said Whitey.

"Damn right," said the man, glancing at Whitey's messenger bag and bike. "Keep that thing in the street."

They walked right in the middle of the street, something Whitey often liked to do. Especially on streets where traffic went the opposite way from them. Naturally, he moved for cars, but still, it made Yurika nervous. Whitey told her just to keep her eyes open for cars and enjoy the freedom and thrill of walking down the middle of a New York City street. As they walked, he explained a bit of history of the West Village—Stonewall, the Halloween Parade, AIDS. A dispatcher he had worked with died from it.

Yurika asked if he knew any messengers who had died in accidents.

"A couple," Whitey replied. "But the city doesn't really care. It's an old story." He counted off the many haters of bike messengers on his fingers. His left thumb—the police; his pointer—the store owners like her uncle; then the pedestrians, the cab drivers, the mail-room clerk pinkie; back to the thumb with security guards, then secretaries, people in elevators, ring finger bus drivers, and the pinkie car drivers. Whitey taught her the phrase, "Don't kill the messenger," and sighed loudly as they crossed Hudson Street. He believed that there was a predisposition for people to hate messengers because of a genetic memory of the bad news they have had to deliver through the ages. Yurika missed the specifics of this idea but, because of the seriousness in Whitey's voice, understood that it was important. "So," Whitey went on, "there's a long history of messenger abuse. But also, I think people are jealous that we get to be outside riding around."

Yurika turned to him. "I'm jealous. Messengers looking like so free."

"But—" He stopped and pointed to the street where a messenger was holding on to the back of a truck speeding west—"they get crazy."

"So cool," Yurika said, the image of her animal man racing through her mind. "I wish I could be messenger."

Whitey felt the blood flare up his face. He had imagined her telling him this. Actually, over the years he had fantasized about many women telling him this. He would heroically talk them out of it or train them to ride the streets. But now, hearing those words leave the lips he had spent so much time staring at as they formed short *a*'s and puckered *r*'s—he stopped walking, put a hand on Yurika's shoulder, and kissed her. It was only a second, but he closed his eyes and didn't open them again until his face was moving away from hers.

Yurika's hand touched her lips as he moved away.

They stood in the middle of Tenth Street. A honk from a delivery truck made them jump to the side of the road. They walked on. Whitey let it all out. How he'd wanted to kiss her for weeks. How he looked forward to seeing her and hanging out with her. How he was so glad they were becoming friends. How he wanted more. How he hoped for more. The more he talked, the more he could feel himself revert from a fairly clear George face to a cloudy, green John one.

Yurika was confused. She was trying to listen to him but became distracted by her own thoughts. Was he supposed to be her special person who kissed her? She thought of the bikers that hung on her wall at home. *Bicycle Racing Illustrated* was the only thing she read in English these days, and it was Whitey who had bought her the issue as a gift. He was the one who pointed out François "The Badger" Mercier climbing a mountain road ahead of the pack. He was the one who showed her the great Irish racer, Kyle O'Foulain, sweating through his jersey. He was the one who would imitate the up-and-coming American, Paul Blaze, with his mouth open and head to one side. But Whitey didn't look like any of them. Could she ever even touch his face? She thought of the Puerto Rican girls around the store and was reminded of her own less-than-attractive shape and big head. Of course, she couldn't tell him about Hector, but she also wouldn't know what to say to her animal man if she were alone with him. She certainly wouldn't have the balls to kiss him.

Whitey had fallen silent. They walked on and sat on the edge of the pier, listening to the sound of the water lap against the buckled and cracked concrete beneath them. Yurika looked around. There were men with men, women with women, men with women, people with dogs. They were black, white, brown—but not Japanese. This was Whitey's world. She was far away from Kawasaki, but she wasn't alone.

"It's okay," she finally said.

"What's okay?"

"I understand why you kiss me." She shook his shoulder. "*Tres huevos.* Very balls."

Whitey gave a chuckle but didn't know what to say. He crossed his legs and stared down at his worn sneakers. He wanted to kiss her again but instead pressed his lips together for any remnant of her mouth left behind.

"You are my only friend here," Yurika said. "Maybe one day I have

American boyfriend, but first just friend. Just I need now."

Whitey nodded. He felt a pang of the familiar. There was Cassie Windsor in middle school, the beautiful field hockey player and *friend.* There was Mindy Simmons, the editor of his prep school's yearbook and *good friend.* In college there was Leshelle Divine, leader of the Coalition for a Free South Africa and *best buddy.* Now there was Yurika Song, cashier, blossoming bike mechanic, and *only friend.* Somehow, maybe, it was a step up.

"Maybe one day?" he asked.

Yurika nodded, thinking of Hector again, as the sun lowered over the Hudson River and New Jersey's pink, orange, and indigo sky. Whitey told her about how the sunset was so colorful only because of the pollution over New Jersey, but Yurika cut him off.

"You are so nice," she began. "Only I have kinds of bad boyfriends, bad guys."

Whitey was surprised to hear anything about her having boyfriends.

This time Yurika counted off on her fingers. "Don't go to school. Don't get a good job. Always drink. Do some trouble. Always say bad words."

Whitey had seen this before, too. Cassie Windsor had dated an All-American soccer player who ended up going to jail for credit card fraud. She ended up with a misogynistic white boy who graduated first in his law school class.

"Why do you date these guys?"

"I don't know." Yurika shrugged. "Just I like them." She could see her mother's lips narrowing in disapproval. Her parents couldn't stand her boyfriends. "They're criminals, not boyfriends," her father had said.

"Just you like them," Whitey repeated as he stared off at the sunset over New Jersey in all its polluted splendor. That's how it always was, he thought. There was something in everyone deeper than plain-and-simple sense that wanted to be fucked with, tormented, twisted, then laid to waste. Whitey took one of Yurika's hands in his and held it silently as they sat together. Neither said another word until the sun dropped behind the horizon, leaving behind lovely bands of pea green and neon yellow clouds.

"Do you know what a one-night stand is?" Suzie asked between mouthfuls of rice. Yurika had never seen her eat so much so quickly and asked her why she was so hungry. Suzie threw her head back and let out a laugh. She finished chewing, hand over her mouth. Her eyes gleamed. "Standing man."

Yurika imagined someone standing at a bus station an entire night. She shook her head. Suzie explained the meaning of "one-night stand" and how she had now experienced three of these with the standing man. Yurika's mouth hung open as she blinked at her cousin, who had resumed shoveling rice into her mouth with chopsticks like a Chinese construction worker she'd once seen in Chinatown. As she chewed, she served herself green tea in a shot glass and sipped the whole of it down at once.

"Still no name?" Yurika asked.

Suzie shrugged.

"He knows what's your name?"

"What your name—"

"Is," Yurika shot back.

"Good." Suzie sucked some food from her back teeth and shook her head. "That would suck. Then I wouldn't be the hot mystery woman."

After hearing this news, Yurika had second thoughts about asking Suzie her advice about Whitey. Suzie finished her meal, though, wiped her mouth, pushed her plates aside, and stretched her arms across the table to take her cousin's hands in hers.

"So tell me now about the man with the delicious skin."

"Nothing," Yurika said, glancing down. "Not even one day look."

She ended up talking about Whitey and how they liked to hang out after work.

Suzie had another shot of tea. "This guy likes you," she said, wiping her mouth.

"But it's okay." Yurika held a hand to her chest. "We have good feeling. We understand both—*ha-re?*—we understand—"

Suzie nodded at her. "We understand . . . eee . . ."

Yurika squinted. "Each other?"

"Yes," Suzie said. "Excellent. We say, 'It's platonic.' There's a vocabulary word for the two of you." She wrote it down in Yurika's notebook.

"Pu-ra-ton-ic."

"l, l, l," Suzie pointed to the tip of her tongue behind her top front teeth. "Lust, lick, lay."

Yurika nodded, though she didn't catch the words. After Suzie explained that "platonic" meant "just friends," Yurika thought she remembered some word in Japanese that was similar sounding. She checked her electronic dictionary, but it wasn't in there. She wished she had a better vocabulary. She wished she had paid more attention to her English classes in school. In Japan, though, English was by far the most boring class taught in junior and senior high school. Now she couldn't even remember what her teachers looked like, to say nothing of their names. They stood in front of the room speaking only in Japanese because they could barely speak English themselves. They made everyone do grammar exercises and write essays full of mistakes that no one ever caught and read lots of stories with words no one could pronounce. In fact, until she came to New York, English to Yurika had been a kind of dead language except for Hollywood movies and passing tourists. In New York, English was so alive. It was like a huge octopus—very clever and sometimes hard to catch but with so many wild and beautiful writhing limbs. In Japan, in fact, almost all her subjects in school seemed liked dead subjects at the time she was falling asleep in them. When was she going to use geometry? Why did she need to know the anatomy of a frog? She could not even muster the interest to study for any subject exams that might have gotten her into a university. While most students she knew in high school went to their *jyuku,* private schools where they crammed for these subject tests for five hours after regular school, she sneaked into the bicycle races with her friends or went shopping. What was the point anyway? It was well known in Japan that the only purpose of high school, the only reason why it was so difficult, was to get into a good university. Everyone knew that once you got into a university, life was easy. University was for status, not education. You only had to survive high school.

Bicycles was the subject that made Hector notice her. When she spoke about bikes, she felt closer to him; it didn't matter that he wasn't around. When Whitey instructed her on how to adjust gears, she sometimes imagined it was Hector talking. When she cleaned Whitey's chain, she imagined Hector's smell of bike grease like warm bananas. When she wrapped Whitey's handlebars in new tape, she tried to imagine what Hector looked like aroused, his size and shape. Bicycle repair, she liked to imagine, could be a secret passage to Hector.

Yurika told Suzie about Whitey's wheel and how he had invited her to go to the Bronx to pick it up at a messenger's apartment.

"His name is Bone," Yurika said, "because he broken so many bones."

"You know what else 'bone' means?"

Yurika shook her head.

"Have sex." Suzie nodded with a grin. The very mention of it caused a slight tingling somewhere behind her nose. When she was thoroughly sexed up, everything in the world became an extension of sex—smells, words, body language—and it was all good. It made her hungry. "Can I finish this rice?" She pointed to the pot of it between them.

"*Dozo*—ah, go ahead." Yurika watched her cousin. Her skin glowed from her experience with the standing man. She wondered if she could ever feel that way about having sex. Her ex-*Yankee* boyfriends were more interested in finding the right *robu-ho* before and smoking after. Something about going to the Bronx with Whitey, though, excited her. In her inner ear, there was a buzzing sound but not an annoying kind like when she used to be up all night working in a *pachinko* parlor. It was the sound of a spinning bicycle wheel, growing inside of her, and with it, the desire for Hector. She began repeating the names of bike parts to herself while she rode the subway and worked in the store. Sometimes she could hear Hector saying the names as well. *Spoke, wheel, frame, chain.* The words came naturally. Her fingers remembered the feeling of working on a bike. But something was still missing.

On that Thursday morning, she realized what it was and leapt from bed with great excitement. "I'm gonna get a bicycle! Today!"

Suzie had not slept well and at first didn't understand what her cousin was saying. She had tossed and turned all night, her nerves in a pinch. On her dresser sat an application for an English-language teaching certificate program that a private language school in the city ran. She was racked with self-doubt and haunted by the misery of her high school experience. This training program was supposed to be very practical; half the time you were actually teaching immigrants who were paying just a nominal fee to be taught by teachers-in-training. What if the students didn't like her or do what she said? What if they just didn't believe that she could really teach? The application deadline drew near.

Yurika, meanwhile, was telling Suzie about Bone's cheap conversions and how she would get one of those. For the occasion, she put on an orange Campagnolo T-shirt from which she had cut the collar and sleeves, along with a pair of baggy green army surplus shorts. It was as close as she could get to looking like a biker, and she was pleased. She emptied out her blue Ultra Man of its bills. The thought of her being able to ride around the city, the freedom, made it hard for her to concentrate at work. She couldn't wait to tell Whitey. In a fit of nervous energy, she dusted all the cigarettes, lined up all the candy before the counter perfectly, and prepared several filters full of new coffee. When she had to open the register to make change for customers, she made sure all the bills were facing in the same direction, faceup. She organized the tools, first aid kit, and all the miscellaneous items beneath the cash register.

"Hello, Mrs. Manton," she said in loud, clear English when the woman came in for some eggs. "How is your husband?"

"Listen to you," said Mrs. Manton, "you speak so good now."

When Lefty came into the store to buy cigarettes, he too noticed something different about Yurika.

"Nice smiling," he told her, making her blush.

Hyun Jeong grew suspicious. She had heard about drugs that give people more confidence. Once, she found a film canister half full of tiny colored pills buried in Suzie's drawer; maybe the girls were sharing them now.

"You so different today," she told Yurika. "Some trouble about that guy?"

"No trouble. Just happy."

This made her aunt even more suspicious. No one had a right to be happy at Lucky Market. "Something's wrong with the girl," she told her husband when he arrived at work.

Sang Jun grew alarmed. "What's wrong? She looks fine."

"I don't know," Hyun Jeong whispered in Korean. "I think she's taking drugs."

Sang Jun thought of what Riya had said about her art students. It was the first question she asked when he had told her about the girl and the bike boys.

"Some problem maybe with girl," Sang Jun told Daniel outside the store. "Keep eye on her. Try talk with her, find out."

Daniel told José the same, but the two of them could not understand what their boss was talking about. The girl was in the best mood they had ever seen her in. She wasn't spending all her time looking out the window longingly for the bike boy. She was talking to all the customers. The counter was cleaner and better ordered than they had ever seen it when the boss or his wife was taking the register.

It was a busy day, and the time went by so quickly that even Hyun Jeong did not have time to talk about her niece again. Shortly after five, Whitey appeared at the door. He motioned to Yurika that he would meet her on the corner. Her uncle was in Flushing to buy some kind of new machine for the store, so after saying good-bye to her aunt, who was in the back cutting thorns from rose stems, she left. She and Whitey walked across town to the D train as Yurika excitedly told him about her plans to buy a bike. As they rode the train all the way up to Bedford Park Boulevard in the Bronx, he answered her many questions about sizing for frames and if she could choose her parts and colors.

"Don't worry," Whitey added. "I'll be there."

Bone lived on the top floor of an old six-story brick building that had turned a dingy brown. The tiled hallway was dimly lit. The smell of years of roasted chicken seeped from the walls. Muted television voices—some in Spanish—floated through the empty halls.

Bone was expecting Whitey, who was late as usual. He paced back and forth, occasionally glancing out the window. Finally, there was a knock at the door.

"You're late," Bone said as he opened the door. A smile crept across his face when he saw Yurika. "Hey." His eyes glanced up and down. "Nice T-shirt."

Yurika froze. Hector. Bone. Hector was Bone. Tres Huevos. All the same. He seemed shorter than she remembered. He wore his bike shorts and a black tank top. The smell of sweat, sweet bicycle grease, and things burning overwhelmed her, and she blinked several times, swallowing hard. Whitey was already inside the small one-bedroom place, staring up at the bicycle wheels and frames hanging from the yellow ceiling.

"You know this homey?" Bone asked, motioning with his thumb and turning to Whitey.

Yurika remained outside the apartment. Her mind raced. He and Whitey were talking rapidly inside, then both stopped, turned, and stared at her. Whitey spoke first, introducing them. Yurika stepped into the apartment. The wooden floor creaked beneath her as the warm, pungent odor filled her senses.

"Yo, I know her," Bone said, watching her as she looked up at the ceiling. "She fixed up this motherfucker," he said, slapping his left leg with a laugh, "and probably saved my fuckin' life." He put a hand on her back and glanced up and down at her. "Didn't you, baby?"

His hand was warm, and Yurika felt electricity shoot through her body. That afternoon when he came into the store suddenly seemed so long ago. She had imagined so many meetings with him since then that it was hard to believe this was only the second time they were seeing each other.

"She wants a bike," Whitey said.

"Yeah?" Bone said, still eyeing her as she ran her fingers over the wheel-trueing stand on a table.

Yurika glanced at Hector, feeling the heat rise in her neck, her face. "You have so much things," she said, but her voice sounded small and thin.

Bone moved beside her, touched her shoulder, and led her to a portion of the wall that had small shelves full of different-size spokes and the screws that attach them to the rim. He picked up one of the screws and held it up. "Know what these are called?"

Yurika smiled and glanced back and forth between them. "Screw?" she offered up.

Whitey laughed nervously. Bone put it back in its box. "Nah, I tell you later." He turned to Whitey. "Lemme get your wheel, yo." From the corner next to the window, he grabbed a wooden pole with a hook at the tip and took down a wheel from the ceiling. The rim was the color of charcoal and thinner than any Yurika had ever seen.

Whitey took it carefully and stared at it for a moment, whistling. He held the hub with one hand and spun it with the other. "This kicks, yo."

Yurika laughed. "I know 'kick.'"

Bone laughed. "I bet you do."

Their eyes lingered on each other's for slightly longer than a moment, until Yurika could no longer stand it and looked away.

The two messengers exchanged some fast talk, but Yurika caught only a few curse words. She was distracted by all the bike stuff in the apartment and that it all smelled of him. She was afraid to look at Hector and unsure what to call him. Between her boiling hormones and her broken English, she was almost afraid to say anything at all. He and Whitey sounded like they were arguing, but she knew they were not. It was their messenger language. Strong, aggressive, full of words like "motherfucker" and "shit." Yet Whitey seemed nervous, talking more than usual, rocking back and forth.

Each wheel and frame hung down from above, each tagged with a name and a price. Some were new; some were repairs. Silver, red, blue, yellow, and gold illuminated the room with a metallic glow. Touring the place slowly, she spotted one frame she especially liked that was the color of honey. The workbench was covered with screws and cables and cable housing of all colors in strands and bits. On the yellow walls that were covered with posters, she recognized the Colombian "King of the Mountain" Hugo Garcia, the Italian legend Francesco Moser. She began looking at the parts that were piled in tall aluminum baskets and boxes that lined the floor against the walls. The small hairs on her neck stood on end. Yurika had heard that in ancient Japan, there was a special room where samurais kept their weapons and armor. Only a few could enter. This was the room she was standing in now.

"All right." Bone shook Whitey's hand. "Lemme take care my other customer here."

"I'm gonna help her," Whitey said.

Bone made a face. "We gon' be a while, yo."

Whitey started to take his messenger bag off. "No sweat, man."

Bone put a hand on the bag, his voice lowering. "I said we gonna be a while." He nodded slowly. "Is gonna be cool."

"I told her I'd help." Whitey's voice sounded tight.

Yurika glanced at Bone, who was shaking his head with a smirk. "It's okay," she said to Whitey, trying to sound as polite as possible; then, in a clear voice, said, "I'm fine."

"Is my business," Bone said, opening the door for Whitey, who backed into the hallway unevenly.

"I call you later," Yurika said, waving to him. She stood toward the back of the apartment, illuminated from behind by the light from outside.

"D train to the Seven at Forty-second Street," Whitey called out, his instructions echoing in the hallway.

Bone stood by the open door. As it began to close, his voice was a low hiss. "She gon' be jus' fine."

FOUR

Dropped

Whitey rode around the city all night. He sprinted through yellow traffic lights and pedaled down the middle of streets, sitting upright with his arms crossed. He clung to the back of late-night delivery trucks speeding crosstown. He hopped onto the sidewalk when traffic thickened. He switched directions according to the changing of the lights and the flow of traffic. The night became an endless run with all the speed and urgency of work but without a single drop. As the miles added up, his hands grew numb, as did his toes and his groin. His neck ached. His heart ached.

Everything he saw reminded him of Yurika: an Asian woman standing by a velvet rope outside a club; a couple sharing sushi in the window of a Japanese restaurant; the neon signs of Koreatown offering *bulgoki* and *bi-bim-bop* specials; the glow of a subway entrance; a Korean grocer on Third Avenue standing outside having a smoke.

Whitey pulled up to him and asked for a cigarette, and they stood beside one another smoking silently as the sweat poured down Whitey's face.

"Good bike," said the grocer.

Whitey nodded and took a deep drag, blowing smoke up to the sky. "Good smoke."

"How much?" the grocer asked, pointing to the bike.

"You wanna buy it?"

"No, no. Just I ask."

"Come on," Whitey said. "Good price."

The grocer waved a hand and gave a short hum before he spoke, searching for words in English. "My cousin got new one, mountain bike. Sometimes I use."

Whitey jabbed at the air with his cigarette. "Everyone's gettin' that fat tire stuff," he mumbled, "but I steal that shit for fun"—he slapped the head of a parking meter—"for that motherfucker and his fuckin' business." The grocer watched him with narrowed eyes. "You're lookin' at me like I'm some kind of freak, man." He held out a hand for the grocer to shake and spoke slowly. "I'm upset about a woman. She's half Korean."

"Half Korean?"

"And half Japanese."

"Oh." The grocer nodded slowly. "Problem."

Images of Yurika with Bone flashed through Whitey's mind. Him kissing her. Touching the flesh of her back. Whitey turned to the grocer and pointed to his bike again. "How about three hundred?"

"No, no," laughed the grocer.

"Two-fifty," Whitey added, pointing to the front wheel. "That's brand-new." He started explaining the difference between aluminum and composite rims, but the grocer, it turned out, was a materials engineer in Korea and knew all about them. His accent reminded Whitey of Yurika—the missing "the's" and *a*'s, the *l*'s for *r*'s, and *r*'s for *l*'s.

The grocer offered Whitey another smoke and said, "No wife? No kids?" He shook a finger at him. "Enjoy. Don't worry, be happy."

Whitey slapped the grocer on the shoulder and winked. "You still enjoying?"

The grocer grew serious and dragged on his cigarette. "Sometimes.

So much work." With his fingers, he outlined two boxes. "This my family. This my work."

Whitey felt a dull pain in his chest. His body felt thick in the head and feet, empty in between. Tossing his cigarette to the ground, he shook the grocer's hand again. "Gotta go."

The grocer watched Whitey disappear down the empty avenue. He turned back to his store and glanced at his watch: almost 3 A.M.

Whitey sprinted down to St. Mark's Place, drank a quart of orange juice, then sprinted up Third Avenue. He rode so fast that he dropped all the traffic he approached. He could feel the eyes of drivers on him as his body moved passed their windows. He thought of the restless population of people who claimed these hours for their own—for work, for play. The graveyard shift made the nine-to-five possible. Each building had its night dwellers, a slight checkerboard of lights in windows, the occasional silhouette of a person in profile or a face in a window smoking a cigarette. He imagined a messenger shift at that hour, deliveries moving in and out of shadows, the pleasure of empty lobbies, all the bike lockup space he could wish for. There was comfort in darkness. Boundaries blurred between buildings and street corners and passing trucks, between his body and the bike, the bike and the pavement. All the parts of the city got along better at night. He turned down a side street filled with shadows and stillness.

All he could hear was the spinning of his wheels and the white noise of the city. It was a hollow sound, an endless exhale of a sleeping monster. He felt small. His mind was aswarm with voices and images. His father was asking him over and over why he couldn't be more like one of them. They were through paying his way, he was saying as he ran his finger around the rim of his scotch glass. That drink would always remind him of that man. His coveted collection of twenty-five- and thirty-year-old bottles, each with its own velvet box. His drinking cronies talking about their grown children in their law offices and medical residencies and investment banking firms. Perhaps Yurika's father liked aged scotch. There were the two of them taking measured sips, speaking fragments of English to each other about how smooth it went down. The sheer impossibility of such a quaint image made Whitey smile.

He saw himself passing through the marble entryways of law offices that floated above the city at 60 Rockefeller Plaza. Passing men and women in pressed suits walked with a fast clip. Ginger Squizelli was smiling at him, but now she was creating the packages to hand to assistants for delivery instead of receiving them. Yurika sat at a desk, a paralegal in training, Ultra Man stickers surrounding her computer screen and a desk drawer full of neon markers and Allen keys smelling of bike grease.

The thought of her slowed him down. There was no future between her and Bone, he thought. *Just I like them,* he could hear her say. Her answer was as simple as it was pitiful. He pedaled once or twice, then the image of her kissing Bone made him coast. A fresh sheen of sweat covered him. There was enough humidity that particles of moisture floated beneath the yellow light of street lamps. Every midtown building rising into darkness seemed to hold a secret, as if Yurika and Bone were up there, watching him, silently judging. A plane flew overhead. A police car passed. Whitey entered Central Park from the southeast corner and disappeared in shadow. Making his way to Sheep Meadow, he found it closed so he heaved his bike over the fence, then hopped over, pausing to wipe his face on his sleeve. Lying down in the middle of the grass, he sighed at the night sky.

Nausea overtook him in waves. His eyes stung from sweat. For a long while, he lay still, his fingers lightly moving over the scars on his cheeks as he mumbled about Bone and Yurika, and him being such a stupid motherfucker and a shit-for-brains going up to the Bronx with her. Of course Bone would make a move on her. He always took advantage of whoever was around. That's how he managed to have half the messengers in New York stripping bikes for him. He was like a snake charmer, with all the right notes to play for each and every one of them. He got everyone doing the same petty larceny dance. "Start with the small stuff," he'd say, and he'd even give you your own set of Allen keys and show you what he meant; then he'd hand you a pair of small wire cutters and tell you, "Forget the cables 'cause they only get in the way—clip, clip, clip, a few turns of the size six Allen key, and you got yourself a pair of handlebars." He made it look cool, then made you feel like you could do anything. He knew that when it came to doing the deed, you'd have so much adrenaline pumping through you that you'd work like lightning so you wouldn't get caught. And, shit, if you did, it wasn't his problem—you were the one stripping the bike, not him.

Two policemen on scooters sitting on the east side of the meadow heard the cursing coming from somewhere in the middle of the meadow. It got louder and more agitated. Something about bones and girls and stripping. The two men mumbled to each other and one took out a megaphone from the trunk of his scooter, flashing a light.

"Meadow's closed."

Whitey froze for a moment then turned toward the voice, a flashlight to the east. "Fuck off," he shouted, standing and lifting his bike from the ground.

"You got one minute," came the answer.

Whitey stood up and reached into his bag, grabbing the first tool his hand came across, a round, steel spoke wrench. "Kiss my ass," he shouted back at them, throwing the wrench as hard as he could in their direction. It hit something metal, so he started running, his bike on his shoulder. The engines of the scooters started up. A police radio crackled. Reaching the fence on the western side, Whitey vaulted his bike and then himself over to the other side. In another moment, he was sprinting south through the park, behind him the police in their scooters.

Flying out onto Columbus Circle, he could see a police car a block away, heading toward him down Broadway, lights flashing against the empty storefronts, the siren going on and off intermittently. Whitey shifted into high gear, went into a crouch, and began wildly pumping his legs. Racing against the thin traffic coming up Eighth Avenue, cursing and grinding his teeth, sweat pouring down his face. He rode onto the sidewalk at Fifty-sixth Street and headed west, ducking into an alleyway and behind a Dumpster. The police stopped their car on the corner. The block looked empty, still, at a few minutes before 4 A.M.

Through the predawn darkness, Hyun Jeong made her way to the store. The girl must be there, she thought as she marched down First Avenue. Her mind raced between sudden pangs of worry and flashes of anger that they had ever agreed to take the girl. Who did she think she was? It was bad enough Suzie went out to God knows where. She slowed her step. Maybe the girl was with Suzie.

It would be just like Suzie not to call to tell them this. She had loved to torture them ever since she found out about her real mother. Hiding in the house so no one could find her. Pretending to choke on chicken bones. Smearing blood from her bloody nose all over her belly. Yurika had something of that blood, too. Torture blood. That was the Song family. Sang Jun's brother had run off and married that Japanese woman for just this reason. To make the whole family suffer for showing favoritism to Sang Jun, the elder brother, the responsible one. And their spawn, this little devil from Kawasaki—she was doing it now. Disappeared to spite Hyun Jeong, to make Hyun Jeong look bad and feel worse. This was what happened when you mixed good Korean blood with something else. Things just didn't turn out right.

Still, thought Hyun Jeong as her step slowed, what if something dreadful happened? The papers were full of rapes and murders and kidnappings. She scowled and picked up her pace. It would serve the girl's parents right. The girl too. This was not a city to play around in.

But, of course, they would not call her parents to report that their daughter was not home yet at, at—she glanced at her watch—at almost four-thirty in the morning. Sang Jun still had too much respect for his brother and wife. He wouldn't want to smear the proof of their failure as parents in their faces. She shook her head. What was the point of being nice at this hour? She entered the store and went straight for the phone. Daniel was surprised to see her there.

"Where's girl?" she asked.

Daniel shrugged.

The phone rang and rang. Get up, you lazy man, thought Hyun Jeong. Your niece is probably being dragged through the streets by crazy bike boys. Finally, a sleepy voice came on the line. *"Anyong—"*

"Did she call yet?"

Sang Jun grunted. "No."

"Call if you hear." She hung up and turned to Daniel, explaining that the girl had not come home that night. She asked again if he had seen her. Daniel shook his head and said he had seen her leave with the tall bike boy.

"Ah." Hyun Jeong made a face and waved a hand through the air. "No more bike boy."

Daniel went into the back to cut up carrots as she took over the register. She paced back and forth behind the counter, mumbling to herself in Korean, occasionally glancing out the window. The night drained from her, leaving her limbs stiff and her fingers cold. She reached for her Tiger Balm and applied some to her hands. She was up to her pinkies in squishy grease when Whitey walked through the door.

"You," she began.

"I'm working," Whitey snapped as he marched through the vegetable aisle and headed for the back. He found Daniel. In broken Spanish, he asked where Yurika was.

"Not here," Daniel said, nodding once and pointing a carrot. "She also look for her."

Whitey spun around to see Hyun Jeong right behind him, rubbing two greasy hands together. The menthol smell made him blink and step back.

"Where's Jae Hee?" Her eyes were bloodshot and glassy.

Whitey squinted at her, not understanding. "Yurika's not here?"

Her voice rose. "Where she?"

"How the fuck should I know?" he shot back, pushing past her and out of the store, straight for a phone.

It was the middle of winter in Yurika's dream. The sky over Kawasaki hung low and gray. The bike stadium had become a home for her and thousands of other people. Dirt clung to their faces and clothes. Everything smelled of burnt bike grease. People lay strewn around the track in makeshift beds and homes made of bike tires and sewn together bike seat cushions. Wet clothing hung from brake and derailleur cabling stretched between parts of bike frames that rose from the ground. She and her mother had made a fire from piles of spokes and were cooking miso soup. Her mother was instructing her to feed more spokes into the fire. Yurika watched each spoke get red, then white hot before it burst into flames, and each time it did, she gasped. They heard a siren and both turned their heads toward it. "They're bringing more people," her mother whispered. Yurika tried to concentrate on the fire. A man with broken glasses who looked like an older version of her father walked through the stadium ringing two sets of bike bells mounted on handlebars, waking everyone with cries of, *"O-hio! O-hio-gozai-masu!"*

Yurika's eyes opened. It was just getting light out. Bone's bed but no Bone. Phone ringing. She watched it. One more time. Two more times. Then nothing. She pulled the bedsheet around her and sat up as a slow fear crept up her insides, giving her a chill. She was starving and in a strange man's bed somewhere in the Bronx. Where was he? she wondered. What would Suzie do? Yurika hugged her knees in close and realized that Suzie probably had not had sex anywhere but a bathroom in a long time.

Yurika smelled Bone on her skin. Her evening and night with him returned to her in slow waves that lapped at the back of her mind. She fell back onto the bed. A slight smile crept over her lips. Her body still felt warm in the places he had enjoyed, remains of a smoldering fire—around her ribs, her thighs, between her legs. Where was he?

Covering her face with her hands, she saw an image of her aunt and uncle flash before her. She felt a twinge of panic. Should she call them? It was too early. Plus, she couldn't bear to hear what they would say. Sometimes, back home, she had stayed out all night in the Roppongi district drinking with her friends and American GIs. They were from places like Ohio and Iowa and had big white teeth. She used to call home to tell her parents where she was. Her mother was the phone answerer in the house. Never her father. The first thing her mother always said was, "Can you hear me?" in an unnaturally loud voice. Then she would complain about their phones and how new ones cost too much money. When Yurika first started going out, her mother used to tell her what kind of dinner was saved for her, but after a while that stopped, and over the television in the background the only thing her mother would say would be, "Okay, okay." There were long silences that Yurika took for her mother giving up. Then Yurika stopped calling altogether.

Where was he? When had the night ended? When had they left the workshop and collapsed in bed? When did she fall asleep? After all of her imagined conversations with him, she was disappointed that they barely spoke. "You like that?" he asked a few times. She nodded, moving where he put her, opening what he wanted. *I dig fucking you,* he said once, and she understood this was a good thing, though not how to respond.

Terrible English, her aunt said in one ear. *Terrible fucking English,* Suzie laughed in the other—*touching, sucking, feeling, nodding, squeezing, kissing, pulling, sweating, bending, lying, standing, smelling, folding, finding, losing.*

Yurika thought of his hands. They moved slowly over her, then grabbed her ribs or her shoulders, her behind. As the evening settled into night, with the noises of men playing dominoes on the sidewalk, salsa music rising up, she felt far from everything familiar and clung to the feeling of his hands. His hands, her home. His smell, her memory. Smell with no hands was not enough. She filled herself with him. Nothing like the Japanese guys back home. A knot formed in her chest. Where was he?

She glanced around the bedroom. Bike clothes lay everywhere—in piles on the bureau, hanging over the closet door, scattered across the floor. There were no photographs, no personal effects. It was as if the other room, the one filled with bike parts—those were his personal items. Finding her underwear on the floor in the bike room, she put on her panties and bra and stared at the rims hanging from the ceiling in the early morning light. They hadn't even spoken about the bicycle she wanted. One moment he was telling her that the name of the little screw for a spoke was called a nipple, and in the next moment her shirt was coming off. She went to the window. Looking up Bedford Park Boulevard, all she saw was a single car moving up the hill. To the right, more cars, a woman pushing a carriage full of laundry, holding the hand of a small boy.

She felt anger and indignation rise up. "What the fuck?"

"What a fuck," thought Bone as he rode around the reservoir near his apartment, his parts sore against his saddle. The air was still, the sky a clear blue. He imagined his father waking up in his windowless cell, not knowing if it were day or night. Sometimes, Bone imagined that he could feel his father alive, growing tired but still wondering about the people he once knew on the outside. At other times, he felt nothing and knew his father had died in prison, an old man. He preferred to think of him as a lean, tattooed, good-looking Puerto Rican man with a mustache. The women probably used to go crazy for him. All those Catholic girls he must have popped.

Bone thought of Yurika, though he couldn't quite remember her name. She was like those Catholic girls he grew up with, at first seemingly innocent but the most curious, the hungriest. He liked how she kept burying her face in his chest and in his neck, inhaling him.

"Maricón," he said as he dropped into a crouch and began pumping his legs to catch up to a rider ahead of him. He'd seen this guy before, a white boy from Riverdale who had a million questions about this kind of derailleur or that kind of frame, this kind of brake set, that kind of cyclometer. He wasn't much of a rider, and Bone loved to remind him of this every time he dropped him on a ride. Shifting into his largest gear, Bone gave a "yo" as he cruised by.

"Hey," said the Riverdale guy, and Bone could hear his gears shift and the turning of his crank as he tried to catch up, and then all sounds from him faded. Dropped again.

"Hasta luego," Bone mumbled as he watched his cyclometer slowly rise to twenty-three, twenty-four, twenty-five miles per hour, smooth like a shark through water. He imagined Yurika at his place, still asleep, and him walking through the door, sweaty. She would be lying on her stomach, her bare back uncovered, curving into that fine butt, her arms outstretched beneath a pillow. Sweat poured down the sides of his face as he left the reservoir at 205th Street, sprinting the last block past Harris Field, throwing his arms into the air as he coasted onto the overpass above the D train yards.

He liked the idea of an Oriental girlfriend. They were quiet, sexy.

The Puerto Rican girls he'd been with talked way too much—before, during, after—they wouldn't shut up. You had to exhaust them before they were out. Then they would still be mumbling some kind of afterword as they dozed, asking if he liked it, telling him about past boyfriends. He'd been with only one Asian woman before, Nancy Yee, in high school. She was Chinese but, having grown up in a Puerto Rican neighborhood, she acted like a homegirl—big hoop earrings, tight clothes, thick makeup. Pretty but loud. This girl was different, Bone thought, and reminded himself to check what her name was. He knew it started with a *Y* and ended with an *o* or an *a.* He rode slowly and mouthed different names aloud. "Yourio," "Yukoko," "Yumiko." Whatever. He wouldn't really have to say her name or speak much, anyway.

As soon as he stepped foot inside his apartment, he sensed she wasn't there. The apartment seemed too quiet, and then he noticed her clothes were gone. He went to the bedroom. Bringing a sheet to his nose, he could still smell something faintly sweet from her. He glanced around. There was no note, nothing. *"Puta,"* he could hear his uncle, El Gato, whisper. "Just like your mother."

Bone went to the window and leaned out, glancing up and down the boulevard: a few cars, a truck, no girl. For a brief moment, he understood why she left, but this passed and he felt anger swell up in him that she hadn't waited.

"What she gonna wait for?" El Gato was saying as Bone moved back to the workshop. "You're the *pendejo* who left first."

Yurika reached into her bag and pulled out the chain remover she had taken from Bone's place. It was covered with black dust and grime and looked like it hadn't been used in some time. He had other ones. This one was at the bottom of one of his tool kits. Next, she pulled out a racing saddle with a golden seat cover, then a set of tire tongs and a flat tire repair kit, a six-inch adjustable wrench, and a reflector that fit onto spokes. She had no idea what she would do with these things, and she was not sure she would see him again. The thought made her stomach sink. She turned each item over in her hand. A one-night stand was not enough. She shouldn't have left. Maybe he went to buy some breakfast for them. He was just like a *Yankee,* though, and *Yankees* never bought breakfast. In fact, they never even ate breakfast. She smiled to herself. They didn't smell like Bone. They didn't bone like Bone.

Sitting in a corner of an empty D train car heading downtown, she fell into a reverie of the night before, her mouth slightly open, her lap tingling with Bone's parts. She had made sounds all through the evening and into the night. She never made sounds in Japan. Last night, gasps escaped her lips. Moans. It didn't sound like her because she had never heard herself like that, sounds rising up from her deepest belly. In fact, she didn't realize she was doing it until a while had passed. It was Bone who made her aware of it when he growled in her ear, "I wanna hear you." Then she stopped, of course. But only briefly. She could not keep her mouth closed.

At 125th Street, people crowded into the train heading downtown. A tall woman with too many bags sat beside her, squishing her into the corner. Yurika noticed that people were looking at her—her lap full of bike stuff, her bright orange T-shirt that had become thoroughly wrinkled, her black and red hair flecked with blond sticking up and out, her flesh still smoldering. She put her bike parts back into her bag. The smell of Bone rose from her upper lip, so she curled it to smell better, which gave her a kind of snarl. This seemed to make people turn away. She closed her eyes and rested her head back against an advertisement in Russian for accident lawyers.

A sense of disbelief began dawning on her. She and him. Animal man. Her nose tingled. Her lap tingled. Uncovering his body, the whole of it, the parts of it, the creamy color of it in the folds of his hips, his arms, the insides of his thighs, the magnificent round butt and *tres huevos*—Yurika smiled—it was all too much for her senses to take in. If they hadn't fallen asleep from utter exhaustion, she would have liked to be that way with him for days and days, until they were so starving for real food that they would have no choice but to devour each other.

She wondered if Riya ever felt this tired after being with Sang Jun for a night—if he ever spent an entire night—if they were even really together. What if Sang Jun just posed for her?

Yurika began to doze. Bits of her night with Bone played out in her mind as the train rocked her into a deeper sleep. Once again he took her hands and placed them on his bare behind. She had to close her eyes because it was too exquisite, too firm and perfect a feeling. Then she moved her left hand around, following the lines of his torso to his privates, his bone, as Suzie would say. And, as she drifted off, it was Suzie who appeared in her half-dream state, giving her a lesson about how to sleep on a train: *Keep your mouth shut, don't drool, don't let your head fall on your neighbor's shoulder, and don't let go of your bag.* But it was no use. The movement of the train and the overwhelming memory of Bone's flesh put Yurika into a state of utter narcolepsy, and she slept deeply—mouth open, head bobbing from one side to another, lips brimming with saliva—until the train pulled into its last stop at Coney Island, and she was awakened by some early morning beachgoers playing salsa music from a boom box as they got off the train.

"Yo, Bone might not be in today."

The dispatcher, Ian, was busy doing his *Times* crossword puzzle in pen so he didn't look up. "Why's that?" he asked, pressing the pen against his pale cheek.

"He's busy with this Asian chick." Whitey spoke loud enough for the handful of messengers milling about to hear. "Actually, she's a sweet mix of Japanese and Korean."

Messengers were coming in for their pack of tickets for the day and going out. Some were waiting for their first runs of the day, and on hearing this news from Whitey, gathered around, their voices lowering in case Bone walked in.

"He get some nice ass, boy," said Wolf, peering over his black sunglasses.

Lefty, whose permanent five o'clock shadow seemed to brighten, gave him a high five. "Right? One time I saw him with this one chick, man, aiiiiiye!"

"Yeah," Whitey began, "she's a sweet one. It fuckin' kills me."

"Language," said Ian. "You know Jim's new rule."

Lefty's brother, Righty, came over from the coffee area and slapped Whitey on the shoulder, laughing so you could see his missing bottom tooth. "He takin' your pussy, bro? What kind of trade can you get for that?" Everyone cracked up, and Righty almost choked on his coffee.

Wolf grinned, looking more lupine than ever with his long jaw and unruly tufts of black hair. "Yo, Bone's wi' that fine *mami* from the store, right?"

Whitey swallowed hard and tried to laugh. He just wanted to get back to his bike locked up outside and hit the streets. "One and the fuckin' same. 'Scuse my fuckin' French, Jim, wherever the fuck you are." He told them about going up to Bone's place for his new wheel, how Yurika went with him because she was thinking of getting a bike.

"That was it," said Wolf, "right?"

Whitey nodded.

"Damn"—Righty shook his head—"that motherfucker moves in." He glanced at Whitey. "Nice new wheel?"

Whitey nodded with a half grin. He liked these guys. He didn't have to talk much for them to understand. They sometimes met up at the band shell in Central Park after work and got high. Once they started laughing so hard that Lefty peed in his bike shorts. But now, Whitey just wanted to get out of the stuffy second-story office, with its windows facing a brick wall, its thick smell of bike grease that always reminded him of bananas gone bad, the shabby fluorescent lighting and gray linoleum floors. He grabbed his tickets for the day and stuffed them into his bag.

"You keepin' Bone's social calendar now?" asked Ian. "Or just doing some light pimp work?"

"He's the fuckin' pimp," said Lefty, "not my nigga Whitey."

Righty agreed and took another sip of coffee. "Yeah, yo, we strip, he fucks."

"Word." Wolf shook his head and slapped Righty's hand. Lefty was nodding.

Whitey couldn't help but grin. "That is so true."

Righty slapped him on the back and let out a hoarse laugh. "We should get pussy for parts."

Ian glanced up. "Come on, fellas, Jim doesn't want that kind of talk here."

"Now, now," said Chain as he came from behind the counter. "Our great leader wants clean mouths."

"Show us how it's done, bro." Whitey slid a newspaper from the day before closer and flipped through pages. The other messengers drifted away, going off on Righty's last joke and comparing how much service they had coming from Bone.

"Is this the young lady you were courting?" asked Chain. He was a big man with hands like black baseball mitts, and he rested one now on Whitey's shoulder.

Whitey shook his head and fidgeted with the strap of his bag. "Didn't quite fly like that."

"Ah, our enterprising Mr. Hector Davila," Chain began, with a flash of the silver cap on his top front tooth. He was the most senior messenger, sometimes a dispatcher, and spoke the most proper English of them all, so he could get away with calling Bone by his real name. "Careful what you share with your colleagues about Mr. Davila."

Whitey glanced up. Chain's eyes were huge and yellowing at the edges. He knew the deal. He was the one who told Whitey about Bone breaking one messenger's nose with a U-shaped bike lock. Chain was the one, too, who told Whitey in confidence that Bone's father was in prison. Chain was here to set people straight. He oriented new messengers and let them know that it was only a matter of time before they got into an accident, the only question that mattered being how badly. He had read everything from *The Art of War* to *The Art of French Cooking* and knew things in a quiet, encyclopedic way. While the other messengers shared the bicycle booty they stripped for Bone, he and Whitey would have lightning-fast conversations ranging from the draft riots in nineteenth-century New York to the best way to kill cockroaches. He knew all the messengers and was paid extra by Jim to make sure there were no bad feelings among messengers and between messengers and dispatchers. Chain knew Bone and understood that he rode alone, worked alone, and didn't like people in his business.

Chain looked hard at Whitey and saw that the lines under his eyes were like the back roads of a tattered map. "You talked to her?"

"What am I gonna say?" Whitey shot back.

Chain squeezed Whitey's shoulder and inhaled deeply. "This, too, shall pass." He began to move away but turned around. "Keep your eyes open out there."

Whitey's insides churned with a queasy mixture of sleeplessness and disgust. He rushed to the bathroom on the other side of the room, just making it in time. "I'm melting," he whispered as his insides rushed out. There was a large, dead waterbug on its back by his feet, and he kicked it to the side. He touched his fingers to his face. This gesture was a kind of punishment he inflicted on himself when he was feeling full of self-loathing. He imagined pulling the whole mess of his face right off, scraping away every scar and pimple, then hanging it up to dry. Yurika might go for that, he thought. Not this face. He pulled at his hair, eyes shut tightly.

There was a commotion of voices from the office. Bone had arrived.

"How's the dragon lady?" It was Ian.

Whitey froze. It was almost impossible to hear what was going on with Bone's low voice and the din of the office. The other messengers chimed in: ". . . bitch . . . fine . . . up the butt . . . Whitey . . ."

There was laughter, then many voices at once, impossible to hear Bone's, but Whitey understood that this was a rare opportunity to tease Bone, and everyone got on board. He also knew that it was his fault. Maybe he should stay in the bathroom all day. Just flush himself down into another realm, the soggy flip side of the city where everyone looked and smelled bad, no one had sex, and life was the sound of an endless dripping faucet magnified a million times, dumbfounding everyone into slow motion and a wordless stupor. He knew, though, that he would have to go out and talk to Bone. He also knew that he would get no rest until he talked to both of them—Bone and Yurika—though he had no idea what he would say or should say, or what would come of it.

"Whitey be talkin' up my shit?" Bone asked Wolf, his large eyes getting larger.

"Sí, pero, she sound fine, yo."

Bone stopped smiling and moved his face in close to Wolf's. "You want those gears fixed?" Wolf nodded. "Then shut the fuck up."

Ian slapped the counter. "Watch the mouth, Bone."

"Fuckin' Whitey," Bone said with a shake of his head. "That his bike out there?"

Lefty tugged on his messenger bag. "Yo, Bone, man—"

Bone swung around. "You want that new fork, *maricón?"*

"I'm not sayin' nothin'."

"Damn right." Bone turned to Ian. "Yo, where's Whitey?" Ian shrugged. "Then gimme my tickets, so I can get the fuck away from these *cabrones."*

"Language, language," Chain piped in. "If Jim walks in—"

"All right, Bone." Ian handed him a stack of tickets. "I'm moving you out."

Bone took out a pen from his bag and began filling out his first ticket of the day.

"Pickup," Ian began. "Nine West Fifty-seven, third floor, see Hannah, reference Morgan, going to Sixty Water, eighth floor. That's an eight o'clock pickup, rush, got it?"

"I'm gone."

"The rest of you. Get out there and call in."

"Mr. Davila." Chain stood up, squaring his shoulders. Messengers began to shuffle from the office. "A word."

Bone swung his bag around to his back. "Chain, you heard my run—"

"Just a word." He put an arm around Bone and walked him to the door. From behind, they looked like a seasoned coach with one of his better players, talking strategy. Chain stood almost a full head taller than Bone, but he walked with a slight limp, whereas Bone moved across the floor with animal grace.

"Take it easy on Whitey," Chain began.

"He here?"

"Unimportant."

"His fuckin' mouth—"

"He likes that girl."

"Come on, Chain—" Bone slid out from the older man's arm. "Respec' to you, Chain, but tha's not your *pinche* business."

"No, it's not—"

"So?" Bone backed down the stairs, hands in the air. "Tha's all, Chain. Whitey get in my business, I'm a have a word with him."

"Take it easy, Hector." Chain's deep baritone resonated through the stairwell.

Bone mumbled under his breath as he made his way outside. New messengers were arriving for the day. The messengers who had been inside before were now hanging out on the metal stoop, drinking coffee, smoking. One whistled the theme from Iron Fists Theater. But Bone was busy scanning the triangular sitting area out front. The other messengers watched him and mumbled to each other. Bikes were locked around parking meters, bus and parking signs, the stairway railing leading into the office, the two park benches between the sidewalk and the office, even one sapling tree the city had just planted.

"Yo, Bone."

He swung around. It was Whitey.

Bone pointed at him and told him to keep his mouth shut. Then he turned around and walked. Whitey followed him.

"I gotta talk to you about that girl."

"None of your fuckin' business."

Whitey felt the adrenaline race through him. He reached for Bone's shoulder. "Come on, man, this is serious—"

"Watch that," warned Bone, slapping Whitey's hand away and walking away. "Crying to those guys like a fuckin' *culo."*

Whitey followed him and started talking. His legs felt weak from his night of riding and his mouth was dry. He was saying that he and Yurika had been spending a lot of time together and that she meant a lot to him. He was speaking faster and faster as his nerves got more tightly wound. But he couldn't let this one just go. He knew he should apologize, but he couldn't pull the words up into his throat. Instead, he got angry. The blood rushed into his face. His words were getting louder and louder, but Bone kept walking. Whitey reached out again for Bone's shoulder and spun him around. "What, did you fuckin' rape her? Is that why you won't talk about it?" But as soon as the words left his mouth, he regretted them.

Bone's face drained of expression. With it went anything resembling friendship for Whitey. An image of his father in his cell flashed through his mind. Bone nodded, his voice taut and low. "Watch your ass, motherfucker."

Whitey swallowed hard. He thought of the spare bike lock that could be in Bone's bag and took a step back. "I didn't mean that," he began, but it was too late.

Bone was backing up toward his bike. He spit on the ground. "Don't let me catch you out there." He was still nodding. "Ain't gonna be no warning." Then he turned, unlocked his bike, and rode off without looking back.

Whitey stood there for a moment, mouth hanging open. How had he gone from the one who was hurt to the one who was being threatened? He felt a lightness in his head. The insides of his stomach began to liquify. He turned around and paused for a moment. The messengers who were outside the office had stopped talking. All of them sat there, staring at Whitey.

As he climbed the stairs, Voodoo grabbed his arm. "Keep your eyes open," he said.

Whitey nodded and sprinted up the remaining stairs to the office bathroom. He closed his eyes and tried to keep a picture of Yurika smiling in his mind, but he kept seeing Bone's face. He got angry. He ground his jaw. Who the fuck was Bone? The Prince of Puerto Rican Punk Ass Motherfuckers? What was he going to do, attack him in the middle of Sixth Avenue? Sic his convict pop on him?

Looking down, he noticed the dead waterbug was still lying there. Sliding his foot over, he slowly raised his toe over it. "Kiss my royal white ass," he whispered. He lowered his shoe, crunching down on the lifeless bug until his sole was absolutely flat on the dirty linoleum.

. . .

Yurika lay on the beach at Coney Island wearing a stars-and-stripes bikini. She had found it at a Russian sportswear store near the subway exit on Brighton Beach Avenue. Pleased with the purchase, she wondered if Riya could draw her wearing that instead of her posing nude. She had also purchased an orange-and-white striped beach towel, some coconut suntan lotion, and a cheap pair of oversized, square black sunglasses she called Big Square.

The sun beat down on her and droplets of sweat ran from her face and filled her belly button to overflow. Sleep mingled with the soft ocean sounds. Half a bottle of warm beer sat on the sand by her side. Whitey would like this, she thought. Maybe they could ride Big Red double whammy here some time. She hoped he wasn't too angry at her or hurt. He looked so sad as he left Bone's apartment. Should she have told him at first about Hector? But how could she know Hector was Bone? Whitey was the one who invited her up there. Before last night, the thought of Hector was a secret pleasure she held out for herself to relish, even though it was more like some exquisite torture. She grinned. Now it was the same, really, only she had real memories. Then she felt a knot in her stomach. All her memories ended with her in an empty bed. Not even her boyfriends had done that.

She sat up and leaned back on her elbows, pushing her sunglasses back up her slippery nose. Some young, brown boys were body surfing and splashing in the waves. Their wet, caramel skin reminded her of the curves of Bone's back. She felt the knot again and had to look away. A pale young Russian couple a few feet from her lay beneath a beach umbrella listening to music on a transistor radio. They occasionally spoke Russian to each other and sounded to Yurika like they were having a quiet argument.

She thought of her aunt and uncle. Who knew what kind of a state they were in by this time? Yurika felt bad about not having called them, but she couldn't seem to do it. What would her aunt and uncle do? Send her back to Japan? She would run away before going back when *they* wanted her to. She could find another job. Maybe Whitey would let her stay at his place. She began to doze in the heat, trying to imagine what it would be like to be lying in sand that was part of her new home country.

"It Miss America," sang a thickly accented voice from behind her. She swung around and for a second thought it was Whitey. A pasty man in a large sun hat and a checkered bathing suit hovered above her, squinting down. "Dat svim suit," he said, "very patriotic." He spoke with a slur in his speech. The accent sounded Russian, like some of the store owners she heard talking around Lucky Market.

"I sit?" he asked as he plopped himself down on the sand beside her, falling onto his back and knocking over her beer. He was drunk, she realized, but she didn't know quite what to say. He pulled out a small bottle of beer from a bag he was carrying and tried to give it to her, but she just pulled her bag closer and lay back down. Her mind was reeling for some English. How do you get someone to leave you alone? What would Suzie say? Suzie would use bad language and the man would be off to bother someone else. Yurika decided to ignore him. He kept trying to talk to her, find out where she was from. He was loud, persistent. Giving him a sidelong glance, she could see his large lips gleaming in the sun. His skin was blindingly white, with tufts of hair here and there. He was from Russia, he was saying, a suburb outside of Moscow. No beaches.

Yurika thought about gathering her things and just leaving, but she heard Suzie telling her to practice English every chance she had. She managed a smile. "I'm from Spain."

He didn't believe her. She repeated herself, then fell silent and pretended he was not there. But she could hear him moving the sand around with his feet, digging some kind of hole. She could also feel him glaring at her from behind his sunglasses. He opened another bottle of beer and offered it to her. She said nothing. The proximity of his voice, though, gave her goose bumps, and she moved over. His breathing bothered her. It was labored and through his nose. She could hear the pasty sounds of his mouth opening and closing. Occasionally he would say some words in English or Russian as if he were carrying on a conversation with himself, half in his mind and half aloud.

"You Chinese?" he asked.

"Korean," Yurika replied, hoping her answer would shut him up. It didn't. He was trying to figure out why she was Korean from Spain and began venturing guesses, most of which she didn't understand because he either didn't finish sentences or he spoke in Russian. She closed her eyes again, and for a while he remained so quiet that she actually began to fall asleep in the hot sun. She awoke with a start to the sound of the man's voice close to her face.

"I give up. Tell me."

She jerked away and asked why he didn't go to another part of the beach.

He stared at her bikini. "I like American flag so much," he said, shaking his head. "And you, Miss America."

Yurika was annoyed but did not want to move from her spot. She imagined Suzie telling her to just make something up, just lie.

Yurika began. "My family has circus—"

The man sprayed beer over his bathing suit and the sand. It was true, Yurika told him. They were based in Spain but traveled to places like Thailand and Marrakech, she explained, thinking of the places Whitey had traveled. She said she was a clown named Whitey. "Do you know clowns?" she asked.

"Of course." The man grinned. "My grandfather vas clown in Bolshoi Circus. He suck his own penis."

Yurika wasn't sure about what he said, but she knew the word "penis" and grew nervous at the sound of it coming from his mouth. She spoke quicker. "My clown name is Whitey." She waved a hand over her face. "Everything white paint."

The man grinned and nodded, showing a mouth full of oversized teeth. He stretched out his legs, and Yurika was disturbed to see a very noticeable bulge in his swimming suit. He leered at her. "And who vas lucky painter of everything vhite?"

"My mother," Yurika said, suddenly missing her. She imagined her at that moment probably fast asleep on her futon dreaming of making endless cups of coffee, phones ringing, her jaw grinding with each ring.

The man flopped onto his side. "So, I call you Vhitey?"

Yurika wished Whitey were there. This man would never have sat down then, and she wouldn't be having this conversation with a drunken Russian instead of sleeping on the sand. She thought of Whitey telling her his other names, his real names. She felt the man's eyes on her, so she reached for her T-shirt and put it on.

He slapped a hand to the sand. "Ah, don't cover great American flag." He said something in Russian. Like the couple nearby, he sounded annoyed. He had managed to move closer to her again and turned jerkily onto his side. His eyes darted over her breasts, her legs.

"Vhitey," he said, putting down his bottle and extending a hand. "I'm Valery. Call me V."

Yurika hesitated, then reached for his hand. He grabbed it and pulled it toward him, throwing his body on top of her arm. She gasped. He pressed against her body and his other hand held her shoulder down. She lost her breath and felt her body go stiff. His right leg was holding her legs down as he mumbled in Russian, covering her face and neck with wet kisses and licks that smelled of beer and stale tobacco. Her hands seemed the only part of her that could move as she clawed at the sand. Grabbing a handful of it, she closed her mouth and eyes tightly and flung some at his face. He jerked away with a loud curse, throwing away his sunglasses. She flung another handful of sand at his head and reached for her things. He was on his knees now, cursing loudly in Russian and English, making people around them turn to look—though without much alarm—as Yurika fled the beach.

. . .

It was midafternoon when she slipped the key into the door of Whitey's apartment. Stepping inside the dark studio from the street, her eyes took a moment to adjust. She closed her eyes. Sweat poured down her forehead. Somewhere around Fourth Avenue on the F train, she had stopped shaking. But, afraid to doze off, she had dug her nails into the skin of her fingers and bit her bottom lip until she had left the train. She decided against going back to the store or calling because now she was in no state to see anyone—except maybe Whitey, so she had decided to go to his place.

The tattered shades were drawn on the two open windows. She could see the silhouettes of the security bars behind them. Yurika listened to their rustling in the slight breeze. Enough light filtered through their curling edges and through silver dollar–sized holes so that she could see the posters on the walls, the bike racers, and the piles of books around the bed, which was unmade, the covers strewn on the floor. An open pack of cigarettes and a lighter lay on one stack of books. Yurika had smoked for a while in Kawasaki but stopped when she noticed the nicotine stains on her teeth and parts of her fingers. She lit one now and sat on the mattress, her back against the Beatles poster.

People walked by outside. They sounded so close; she was surprised that she had never noticed this before. A man was shouting in Spanish to someone on an upper floor of the building. Some teenagers bounced a basketball as they passed. A shopping cart rolled across the uneven sidewalk. How did Whitey sleep? She closed her eyes and took a long drag of the cigarette, comforted by the sound of the tobacco burning in soft crackles.

Her eyes grew heavy. She let them close, opening them sometimes to tap her cigarette ashes into the ashtray that sat beside the mattress. Finally, she nodded off in her sitting position. She dreamed that Whitey was there, the two sharing a cigarette as they sat on the bed. Whitey blew spectacular smoke rings of bike wheels complete with hubs and spokes. He was telling her that when you're messengering, everything became some kind of sign about your safety. Clouds meant caution. Hearing a car screech meant keep to the sides of the street. Hearing strange sounds coming from your bike meant it would be a hard day. Seeing a beautiful woman meant your day would be a good one or would improve instantly. "By the way," he said, his voice clear as if he were speaking into her ear, "you got fire."

Yurika's eyes sprung open. Something was burning. Smoke rose up from a hole in the sheet. Glowing cigarette ashes slowly burned their way through the mattress. Yurika gasped and slapped the spot over and over, but this only caused a small flame to shoot up and begin to burn more steadily. She leapt up, knocking over a pile of books. At the kitchen sink, she got a mug full of water and, with a lunge, threw it at the bed where the flames were already dancing a few inches high. She grabbed a pot from the stove and filled it with water, watching as the flames began to burn the Beatles poster. John took on a new, singed leer. Swinging the pot of water against the poster and onto the burning bed, a great hiss and burst of smoke rose up from the mattress. She dropped the pot and stamped on the charred bed and a few glowing embers still on the floor.

An irregular diamond shape of char spread from the wall to the bed and floor. Smoke filled the room. She squinted and coughed as she covered her mouth with the bottom edge of her T-shirt and lifted all the shades. There was a loud banging on the front door.

"Everything okay?" said a round face that appeared in the window.

"Jesus!" said another voice. More banging at the door.

Yurika opened it. A billow of smoke rose out above her head. Two young men stood before her, a chubby one and another who was tall and skinny with stringy hair. Staring at this woman before them, the two didn't know what to say. They were scouting locations for a student movie and suddenly this person with hair like flames rising from an angry face emerged from a smoking Alphabet City portal to hell. She also had pale squares around her eyes that might have been tan lines, but given the whole scene, they weren't sure. She could have been on the set of a low-budget science fiction movie. They wondered how this could be used for their film.

Yurika blinked at them. They looked like idiots standing there staring. "What the fuck?" she exclaimed, bulging her eyes at them.

"You . . . you okay?" ventured the round-faced guy.

Yurika snarled, "Don't look at me!" She coughed.

"You wanna go to a hospital?" asked the taller one, his voice almost a whisper.

Yurika shook her head with another cough and went back inside, closing the door.

The two mumbled to each other. The taller one appeared in the left window. "Cool . . ."

Yurika didn't understand a word of what he said, but she wanted them to leave. Now. She was sick of men. They did whatever they wanted and exhausted all the women around them with their selfish ways. That foul Russian at the beach. Bone gone without a word. Her uncle probably exhausted Riya as well. She walked to the window. Before pulling down the shade, she made a neat mix out of Suzie's vocabulary and Whitey's slang. "Beat it, dickhead."

"Jesus Christ," she could hear the tall one say to the short one, who appeared in the other window. "You're a bitch."

Yurika pulled down the other shade.

They kept talking outside her door. ". . . fucking crazy Chinese bitch," one of them yelled.

A rage rose up in her that she had never felt before, one that passed any understanding and turned her hands into fists. The young filmmakers heard loud gutteral noises from within the apartment. The door flew open and the woman with flaming hair began swinging at them with a large aluminum pot.

"Okay, okay!" They backed away, arms in the air.

Throwing the pot at them, she shouted, "I'm Japanese!" then

turned away. "Or Korean," she mumbled before going back inside with a slam of the door.

Bone slowly rolled past Lucky Market, glancing through the open door. He had resisted coming to the store all morning, but he was haunted by images of Yurika from the night before: her arms reaching up behind her, fingers tangled in his hair, his hands moving over her breasts, down her belly, between her thighs. He wanted that again. He wanted to know her name once and for all. She wasn't around, though. He rolled past again from the opposite direction, and this time, Sang Jun saw him.

"Bike boy," he shouted to Daniel, who came jogging out from the back. They had worked out a system. Daniel or José would talk to any bike boy in or around the store if he was Spanish-speaking and ask if he had seen the girl. Sang Jun pointed to Bone, who rode by again. He watched as Daniel flagged him down and the two spoke, though it seemed to be in English. The bike boy was shaking his head. He took a long glance at his watch. Then he stared down First Avenue and so did Daniel, who began speaking again and gave the bike boy a card from the store. The bike boy nodded, then rode off.

"What he say?" Sang Jun asked.

Daniel shrugged. "He no see her."

Sang Jun grunted and paced back and forth behind the counter. The girl had left the store yesterday afternoon. Where could she be? Hyun Jeong saw the bike boy with the bad skin early that morning, and he hadn't seen her either. His mind flashed to his brother and sister-in-law on the other end of a phone call. "She's missing?" they would say. This is unthinkable, Sang Jun thought. Someone doesn't just disappear. He and Hyun Jeong should have made clear guidelines with her when she first arrived. No going out except if they knew exactly where she was going, how she could be reached, and when she was coming back. Why hadn't they learned with Suzie? He recalled his daughter coming home that morning, the slam of her door. Strumming his fingers against the counter, he grit his teeth then sucked his lips in. What would he tell his brother—she's only been missing for twenty-four hours? It was ridiculous.

He grabbed the phone and called Riya. He didn't want to involve her in all this, but he wanted the comfort of her voice. Since he had met her three years earlier in the store, everything in his life had become easier to take—not being in Korea, missing Jong Eun, the endless store hours, Hyun Jeong's never-ending list of grievances, Suzie's disdain. Riya was the secret gift he gave to himself for the price of exile on this overwrought island city. The phone rang and rang, and then a man's voice answered. Sang Jun hung up. He dialed again, more carefully. Again a man's voice. He sounded American. Sang Jun slowly returned the phone to the receiver. His heart dropped to his stomach. Who was that? Maybe there was a student or a model at her apartment; she sometimes had them come to her place. His mind raced. Riya could have stepped out. She might have been in the bathroom. Visions of her with a young American boy flashed through his head. He felt his face flush, nervously checked his watch.

"Daniel!" he shouted. "Take register! I come back soon." Sang Jun didn't even wait for Daniel's reply before he was practically running out the door for Riya's place.

Hyun Jeong had left the store as soon as Sang Jun arrived. At dawn, Sang Jun had been sitting in the kitchen sipping his black coffee with six sugars when he heard the downstairs door open and Suzie enter coughing.

"Is Yurika with you?" he asked in Korean.

More coughing and then the closing of her and Yurika's bedroom door.

Hyun Jeong found Suzie still fast asleep at eleven o'clock that Friday morning. She was curled up on her right side beneath her pink sheet, her long hair pouring back over her pillow.

"Where's Jae Hee?" Hyun Jeong demanded, opening the curtains.

Suzie did not stir except to lick her dry lips. Hyun Jeong threw back the sheet and gasped at Suzie's naked body. Suzie's hand reached to her thigh for the sheet and pulled it back up over her shoulder.

"Where's your cousin?" Hyun Jeong asked in English.

"I don't know," Suzie whispered, licking her lips again.

"What?"

"Ja geh heh," Suzie said, getting irritated.

"No sleep." Hyun Jeong shook Suzie by the shoulder, and it was like an electric current shocked the girl as she twisted her head toward Hyun Jeong. *"Man jee jee ma,"* she hissed. The older woman reeled backward until she was sitting on Yurika's bed, stunned that the girl would tell her not to touch her. Suzie dropped her head back to the pillow, pulling the sheet over herself completely.

"How come no work today?"

"Day off. Get out."

"Get out, get out, I know—"

"Yeah. Now."

Hyun Jeong rubbed her hands together in her lap. She wanted to ask why and when the two of them had started to hate each other, but it seemed that it had begun a long time ago and for too many reasons besides the fact that Suzie was not told about Jong Eun being her real mother. Even before Hyun Jeong had started finding the tiny, half-filled bottles of Kahlúa in the drawers, the girl seemed to harbor so many secrets—stolen dollar bills along with lipstick, combs, even a kitchen knife once. Hyun Jeong glanced around the room. There were strange, twenty-year-old remnants of Suzie's childhood like the poster of the kitten hanging from a branch and the Raggedy Ann desk lamp. She missed the girl who still thought Hyun Jeong was her real mother. The easy smiles and laughter. Trying to pull off each other's noses. Catching pouring water when they took baths together. They enjoyed each other. But after Suzie found out the truth, it was like this down-stairs room became a separate universe from the kitchen and living room and bedroom upstairs. What kinds of dark deals and promises had that twelve-year-old girl made to herself here? Hyun Jeong wondered. She was not sure she wanted to know.

Suzie was familiar with the brooding silence and the sound of Hyun Jeong's hands rubbing together. She was feeling sorry for herself, Suzie thought. Same old Korean freak show. She imagined Hyun Jeong outside a circus tent in a tattered tuxedo, barking for customers, her greasy Tiger Balmed hands waving through the air. Suzie rolled over, her eyes still closed.

"Ol guh ya," Suzie told her. "She'll turn up."

Whitey had no cleaning products at all except for a shrunken, stiff little sponge beneath the kitchen sink and a can of some abrasive cleaner so old the powder had turned into one large chunk. His place was a disaster. Water formed large and small puddles everywhere. Bits of soot clung to the wall, the ceiling, and parts of the wooden floor. Yurika would have to buy Whitey a new mattress and sheets, too. She would have to replace the books that lay soaked and slightly charred on the floor. Maybe she could even find a new Beatles poster, she thought as she threw out the burnt remains of the old one.

She left for Lucky Market to get some cleaning products and finally to tell her aunt and uncle where she was. Thinking of Bone, the drunken Russian, the fire, the stupid guys, she no longer cared what her aunt and uncle had to say. Plus, the afternoon had grown stifling hot, and she just couldn't be bothered with anything except cleaning up Whitey's place before he got home.

Everyone on the streets seemed to be moving in slow motion. People sat on the stoops of their buildings fanning themselves with newspapers and pressing cold soda or beer cans to their necks. Passers-by seemed to shuffle past, sleepy-eyed, though she noticed that she kept getting stared at. She reached into her pocket for a hair band but, finding her sunglasses instead, she put on Big Square.

Turning onto Tenth Street from Avenue A, Yurika froze. Sang Jun was leaving a building. He turned away from her, stopped to light a cigarette, then kept walking. Yurika recalled the address of Riya's place and realized that that must be it. There was so much she needed to do, she told herself—clean Whitey's apartment, tell her aunt and uncle she was alive. Now was not the time to pay a visit to Riya. But she was not quite ready to return to the rest of her life.

The pillow smelled of his hair tonic. Musk, sweat, a little cigarette smoke. She could trace him onto the sheets and onto her arms, her shoulders. Their sweat still mingled on her neck and chest. Closing her eyes, she could still feel his weight on her, pressing down. She already missed stroking the back of his neck, the line where his hair and skin met. He had come over so hungry for her, and she went right for his neck, though he was full of questions. Who was it? he wanted to know. Was he American? Was it a model? A private student? She just said yes to everything while she undressed him. In fact, it was a model who traded posing time for private drawing lessons, but he was obsessed with his own body, and this was a bore to Riya. Even though he made a beautiful subject, she was glad to see him leave. Sang Jun, on the other hand, was obsessed with *her* body, and she liked that. And not with the parts that had begun to show signs of age like breasts and bottom, though he showed a healthy interest in those. He always returned to her hair, her neck, her hipbones, her feet, her collarbone, where he had begun his lovemaking that afternoon, earnest like a boy. He slowed down only once he was inside of her. Then he became a man again and took his time. He left her smiling, eyes slowly blinking.

When the bell rang, she thought it was him again and did not use the intercom to ask who it was. There had been times when he had returned after only minutes. She swung open the door still naked except for a pillow in front of her.

Yurika gasped and Riya jumped back as the heavy metal door swung shut.

"Just a minute!"

Yurika could not hold back a giggle. This was what it meant to have a lover: you could answer the door wearing only a pillow.

"You are a week early," said Riya.

She sat on a large batik pillow, wearing a dressing gown that was a sheer, pale blue. Her hair was piled on her head, and tendrils of it—some gray—hung down the sides of her face. Yurika thought she was even more attractive up close than she was in the store. There was not a wrinkle on her face. She moved gracefully as she prepared two tall glasses of iced coffee, Thai style, sweetened with condensed milk. Yurika stirred in the milk, watching the creamy swirls. They reminded her of what her day had been like, a whirlwind of movement through the city from one borough to another. She tried to form a good explanation in her mind as to why she had decided to come to Riya's but was unsure where to begin.

Instead, they made small talk. Riya asked if Yurika missed Japan, but Yurika didn't, except for *tonkatsu don,* fried pork on a good bowl of rice. They talked about food and cooking. Riya gave her a few of her favorite recipes. Yurika was trying to figure out how to bring the conversation around to why she had come over. She found an opportunity after Riya mentioned that Sang Jun loved *som tam,* a Thai salad made with papaya and chili.

"I think," she began but was unsure of her words. There were so many vying for her attention—about Bone and Whitey, questions about her uncle and aunt. She glanced away at one of the photos of an elephant on the wall. Riya's eyes were large and watchful like a bird's. There was a wildness to this woman and her home that made Yurika shy. She went on anyway. "You know many thing." Riya smiled faintly. Yurika pointed to a large drawing pad lying on the floor beside the bed. "After you show me picture of my uncle, so, I imagination . . . why she show me the drawings?"

Riya laughed.

"Is big question to me."

"Any answer?" asked Riya.

Yurika nodded and paused to collect her words. "Maybe you can tell to me something"—she cocked her head—"to me? about me?" She shook her head. "You understand?"

Riya resisted the urge to grab her drawing pad. Instead, she asked about the bike messengers. The girl seemed surprised that she knew of them but went on about one bike boy named Whitey, whose real name was Jim, then another, whom everyone called Bone but whose real name was Hector.

Riya watched Yurika. Her face was so animated, even though she was clearly tired. She was an intriguing mix of softness in the cheeks, the chin, the full lips, and a sharpness around the eyes. Of course, the bike boys were all crazy about her. With her looks and her English, she was adorable, especially with the square sunglass tan lines. Riya wanted to draw her face in ink, and again she tried to fight the desire but gave in and reached over for her small journal and a pen. She opened to a page and began drawing the girl's face.

"I'm listening," she said, "but I also draw."

Yurika was surprised to hear a bit of Riya's Thai accent. It was easy to forget about because her English was so correct. Even as she told the story of her and Whitey and her and Hector, she wondered how long Riya had been in the States, if she had a green card, how she had learned English, if Sang Jun taught her any Korean and if he was learning any Thai. With a timid smile, Yurika admitted she had decided to visit Riya after seeing her uncle leaving the building.

"Did you speak to him?" asked Riya, staring at the line of Yurika's right cheek.

Yurika shook her head.

"He is not your father, you know," said Riya, picking up a spoonful of iced coffee. "You can talk to him."

Yurika was surprised to hear mention of her father. "Why you say about my father?"

"As you said"—Riya smiled—"I know many things."

Several minutes of silence passed between them. Yurika wasn't sure how much time passed. She listened to the scratching of Riya's pen against the paper and wondered what her face was looking like in the drawing. Sitting there, surrounded by the elephant photos and Thai weavings that hung from the walls, Yurika felt like she could be sitting somewhere in the hills of Thailand. She wondered if Whitey had been to Riya's province. Suddenly, Riya asked if Yurika knew how her parents had met.

Yurika thought for a moment. From Thailand to Japan. Her parents. They would be asleep on their futon, maybe happy in their sleep that they didn't have to worry about their daughter. Then she imagined her mother awake in their living room reading one of the historical romance novels she loved so much. Maybe, thought Yurika, she was able to do her *O.L.* job for so long because she spent all day dreaming about the characters in romance novels. Yurika had always assumed her parents had met in Japan, and she told Riya that. Her father had been working there. In fact, her parents had been at the same company then as they were now, twenty-something years later.

Riya looked up from the drawing. Yurika and her family were in fragments, no one talking to anyone. She knew this pained Sang Jun. They were lovers, and he came and went as he liked, but she knew he would always return. For this, she would always want to help him. The girl was a wake-up call to her family and didn't even know it. Riya smiled. "That's nice story, but truth is always more interesting." And with that she turned the drawing around.

Yurika's jaw dropped open. It looked exactly like her. She was surprised, though, at how young she looked, like a high school girl with the pigtails and eager face. "So young," Yurika mumbled as Riya handed her the book with the drawing.

"We can do more when you come again." Riya stood. "I have to get ready to go now."

"Ah, me, too," Yurika said, thinking of Whitey's apartment.

"Find out how your parents met," Riya said as she walked Yurika to the door. "Talk to your uncle, maybe your cousin, too."

"You know Suzie?"

"I know about Suzie," Riya replied. "Maybe we can meet one day."

At the door, Riya touched her fingers to Yurika's shoulder. "Would you like some advice about your bike boys?"

Yurika looked at her face. It was very open and clear, untroubled, yet she was full of surprises. Yurika nodded.

Riya waved a finger at her. "You must talk to Whitey and make sure he knows you are still his friend."

Yurika nodded again and thought of his apartment full of smoke and ash.

"With Hector, if you stay where you are, he will come to you."

A warmth rushed into Yurika's face at the thought of seeing him again, and she could not help but smile.

"But be careful."

"I know," Yurika said, stepping into the hall, "he's kind of not good guy."

A smile crept across Riya's face, and then there was a moment of awkwardness as the two looked at each other. Yurika was sorry to go, and Riya was sorry to see her leave but resisted the urge to call her *Nangsao,* Little Sister. "See you in a week," she said, closing the door.

"Bye-bye," Yurika waved, but then after the door closed she regretted doing that because it made her feel young like the Yurika in Riya's picture. "Truth is more interesting," Riya had said. As Yurika left the building, she wondered if this were really true.

FIVE

Spoke

A week later, on a Thursday, Bone was weaving through traffic but thinking about the small of Yurika's back. She had returned to his place that past Monday and had spent the night again. He liked sliding a finger in a line from the groove of her spine on down. The thought of this spot, of pressing her against him with his hand splayed there, made him speedy. To a pair of cops parked on a corner, Bone looked like a traffic violation waiting to happen. To a small group of tourists near Rockefeller Center, he became the instant New York story of the lunatic biker in wraparound sunglasses. To a college boy cautiously pedaling his ten-speed alongside parked cars, Bone looked like a centaur with wheels instead of horse legs, doing a jig between lanes of traffic. He watched as Bone came to a perfect track stand at a light, balancing on his two wheels, his body frozen.

Regular sex was good for Bone's disposition. On that Thursday, he was feeling satisfied about his place in the world. It was one of those days when Manhattan Island seemed to belong to bike messengers. They owned the streets. Everywhere, he saw them—on the avenues and cross streets, on the sidewalks locking up their bikes to parking meters, garbage cans, bus signs, stair railings; they came in and out of office buildings. All the while he kept an eye out for Whitey or his bike.

The messengers all nodded when they saw each other and shared words about the heat or a warning about cops on Third Avenue. Business in this city would be nothing without them, Bone thought. Fax machines were starting to become popular in business, but it wasn't the same; you couldn't fax a package yet. The bikers were the way. He thought of what Whitey liked to say about how the only faster way to move things was by helicopter.

Slipping through crowds of people crossing the street, Bone was always amazed that people had no idea how close they had come to being nailed by a fast-moving biker. But then, a second of time to a pedestrian was much shorter than a second to a biker. A pedestrian moved a step and a half or two in that time. A second to a messenger could be two full turns of the crank, shooting across several yards of pavement, seeing an opening in a crowd and speeding through before anyone realized it. It was the sight of a beautiful woman followed by a sagging-faced hot dog vendor half a block away. He thought of Freddie and how a second meant the difference between being alive and the end of everything. The same for Angel. The same for Hugo. El Gato used to tell him that a bicycle was like a time machine because if you rode enough, everyone you had ever known and every moment you had ever experienced would pass through your mind over the miles, and sometimes you would even start seeing things. He was so right, Bone thought, as he entered a Park Avenue office building where icy air-conditioning wrapped around him; the guard at the front desk looked a bit like Whitey, tall and pale, bad skin.

Bone's anger at Whitey and his mouth had festered during the course of the week since they had last seen each other. So the man lost the girl, Bone thought, that's how it goes; Whitey should've been a man about it and sucked that up instead of bitching to everyone, plus that line about rape. Bone shook his head. He imagined his hand slipping into her panties, and her gasp. Nothing like rape going on with that girl.

At least, he thought, Whitey was smart enough not to show his face around the office in the mornings. Over the course of the week, Bone had dreamed up ways to fuck Whitey up. He imagined ripping the new wheel off his bike and putting Whitey's head through the spokes. The thought pleased him. El Gato would not have approved, of course. Wheels and tires had been El Gato's specialty. He was the one who taught Bone how to lace up wheels, how to true them, how to sew up holes in racing tires. Once, Bone had asked if his father had worked with bicycles. "No," was El Gato's answer, then a long pause followed by a rare response. "Your father didn't believe in work." Bone had pressed him for details about what his father actually did, but El Gato just told him that the less he knew, the better.

As Bone rode the elevator to the eighteenth floor, he could hear El Gato asking him, *"¿Qué pasa?"* The old man crouched next to little boy Bone, cradling his broken pinkie, crying as he sat on the sidewalk beside his first two-wheeler. El Gato waved a hand as if to slap him, looking serious. "No *pinche* tears, Hector. Don't be no girl." Bone grinned to himself. That was El Gato. Always threatening and only sometimes slapping him across the back of the head.

The elevator opened to a floor of legal offices as he lifted his sunglasses to the top of his head. Reaching into his bag for a manila envelope, he brushed his fingers against the edges.

"If it ain't Tarzan," said one assistant, rising to her feet as Bone entered the office.

She had emerald green eyes, long, straight brown hair, and she tanned really dark, all of which had caused Bone to notice her when she had first started working there a few months earlier. She was even more tanned now, and her pale pinstriped skirt curved tightly around her full hips.

"How's my Jane?" he said in a low voice, following her over to a file cabinet in the corner behind her desk. Other assistants looked up and whispered to each other. Phones rang on the other side of the office.

"You don't even remember my name," she said, feeling the heat rise off his body behind hers.

"You remember mine?"

She closed the file cabinet and moved back to her desk. "You never told me your real name, and I ain't callin' you Tooth or Nail, or whatever." Bone stood above her, waiting for those green eyes to look up. "Besides"—she lowered her voice—"you never called again."

Bone glanced around her desk cluttered with paper and office supplies. An open envelope addressed to her lay beside a Puerto Rican flag paperweight, and then he remembered. Bending down, he whispered close to her. "Samantha. But you like Sammy." She didn't look up, but a smile was starting to make its way across her glossy lips. He softened his voice into a version of hers. "Say my name, baby, say my name."

Her face flushed as she grinned and pushed him away. "Are you making a delivery or just harassing me?"

He dropped the envelope to her desk. "Trying for both." He grinned and turned toward the door. "But you don't like neither." He glanced back. "Check you later."

Her eyes were soft and sad to see him go. "Bye, Tarzan," she said, holding up a hand.

Putting on his sunglasses, he swung open the office door and was gone. Sammy the Howler, he nodded. How could he forget? She had clawed the walls of his apartment until there was paint beneath her manicure. For days afterward, his neighbors couldn't look at him without grinning. Yurika made noises, too, but Bone liked hers better because he could tell that she couldn't help herself. Sammy had been putting on a show. Yurika just couldn't stop.

Back in the lobby, he glanced around for the security guard who reminded him of Whitey, but a different guy was there, who didn't look like anybody he knew. An Asian woman entered the building as he was leaving. He squinted at her and for a second she looked like Yurika wearing a business suit. Bone was glad he finally had her name down. On the second night they had spent together, he was sly and asked her how to spell her name, which she did with a finger on his chest, him guessing the letters.

He liked that she wasn't a talker. Mostly, she seemed eager to say what she needed by pressing her sweaty parts to his. He liked that her hands, eyes, or lips started and ended every sentence. She enjoyed parts of him that no woman had before—the long bunches of muscles in his forearms, his ribs, the dimples in the sides of his behind. He couldn't tell, though, if she was an inventive lover or if she was still just inexperienced and trying out every possible new thing. He didn't really care. She was willing and didn't need to open her beautiful mouth every time they changed positions. Some women did it like they were drowning or about to lose their minds. Yurika did it like she was satisfying a long-neglected thirst.

She was supposed to meet him at his place that evening. As he rode crosstown, he thought that the only real problem with her coming over weekdays was that he lost money since he left work early to go home and rest. But that past Monday, instead of taking a nap or lying down, he found himself restless with energy as he waited for her to arrive. He scrubbed the bike grease from under his nails, showered, picked out a clean pair of shorts to put on, fixed the bed, checked to see if there was cold beer in the refrigerator. He smiled, recalling how she had shared a tall neck with him after their first time, then pressed her cold lips to his chest and stomach and cheeks.

Yurika spent much of her waking time daydreaming about Bone's body. She was amazed, too, that Riya had been right; he had come to her. The Monday morning after their first night together, she caught sight of him riding up First Avenue as she had done so many times before. There were some customers in the store but not at the counter yet. Her heart pounded. This time Bone didn't just pass the store. He steered across two lanes of traffic, then hopped off his bike before it touched the curb. He smiled at her. Her limbs went weak as a surge of energy swirled in her stomach. For a moment, she forgot all about waking up alone in his bed. The muscles in his arms and legs rippled as he leaned over to lock up his bike to a parking meter. Yurika lifted her nose slightly to sniff him in the air but the fans in the store were blowing too strongly from behind her.

They couldn't help grinning at each other. Yurika glanced nervously around for her aunt and uncle. Bone stood to the side while she rang up one customer's coffee and cigarettes and some fruit for another. Yurika was tanned, and he liked how her skin contrasted with the yellow Campagnolo tank top she was wearing.

The customers left the store and Bone stepped closer to the counter. He looked her in the eyes. "I went for a bike ride that morning. Where were you?"

He had answered the question Yurika had been spending three days trying to figure out how to ask, but she could only hear herself using bad language to ask it. Her eyes moved over his face and body. He looked like a superhero with his **V**-shaped torso and the sleeveless bike jersey with a Puerto Rican flag on the front and back.

"I don't know reason you left."

He lowered his voice. "That's what I'm telling you." He repeated himself. Yurika had understood the first time and wondered why he was saying it again. But she was so pleased to see him she could barely remember what she had just said. He was telling her that he hadn't wanted to wake her up, that he went for a bike ride every morning. Yurika thought of the bike stuff she had stolen from his workshop and felt bad. She imagined him coming back from his ride, his body covered in a sheen of sweat like it was now, slipping her hands into his moist shorts. She looked toward the back of the store, then at him, trying not to stare at his legs.

Leaning forward on the counter, she managed a smile but found it hard to look into his eyes. Instead, she glanced down at the bubble gum. "I finish five o'clock."

Bone lowered his voice and spoke quickly. "You remember how to get to my place?"

Yurika looked up. She heard the last word but not the rest and was embarrassed. "Place?"

Bone had a surprised look on his face. "You don't wanna?" he asked.

Yurika sensed that their English had somehow gotten off sync. Suzie had explained this to her. When it happened at the store, sometimes the conversation ended with "never mind," with the customer getting frustrated and sometimes leaving. One miscommunication followed another. Whitey called this a "snowball effect," and it was bad.

Yurika waved a hand to start over. "I said, 'I finish five,' then what you say?"

Bone raised his eyebrows. He spoke a bit too slowly this time, and she felt a little stupid. But she understood that he was inviting her up to his apartment for that evening and that he would meet her there. She wished he would smile at her. He looked so serious, blinking at her and asking if she needed directions. She didn't. Why, she wondered, wasn't he going to pick her up at the store? Whitey had done that. Maybe he rode his bicycle back home. He smiled before he left the store, but Yurika was afraid to say anything else; no Hector snowballs, she told herself, none.

They had less conversation in bed than in the store. On that Thursday when she arrived at his apartment, they did not speak at all. With a kiss but no hello, he had again undressed her in the workshop. They wasted no time. The sound of her quickening breath excited him. He slowly turned her around and pressed himself to her, his hands slowly exploring the front of her body. She wanted to bury herself in his smell. His fingers seemed everywhere—running along her collarbone, caressing a hipbone, brushing against her inner thigh, urging her to bend forward.

They did it standing. He didn't speak at all this time. She clung to the wheel-trueing stand mounted on the end of a table as she pressed back against him. Her own arousal left her speechless. Images of Suzie and her standing man flashed through her mind. Reaching between her legs to touch his thighs, his *tres huevos,* she let out a cry when she felt how warm they were. A groan made its way from her insides out to her lips. Their first sounds to each other were wordless and loud. When she opened her eyes, the sight of the bike parts seemed to swim by them. By the time they made it to bed, they were both exhausted. Their speech had become one-word thoughts—"yo" from a satisfied Bone, "yeah" from a grinning Yurika, then another "yo" from him.

The faint laughter of some kids playing rose up from the sidewalk. In the dimming evening light, they lay on their sides, legs intertwined, staring into each other's eyes. There was a darkness in and around his that she could not penetrate. She touched and caressed the skin of his forehead, his eyelids. She wanted to disperse the web of shadows there, soften them, but they remained.

"What do you think about now?" she whispered.

He rolled onto his back and moved her head on his chest. "Nothing," he replied. His mind was a crowd of images from his day: a good sprint he had up Park Avenue, a tall blonde woman he had seen walking across Thirteenth Street wearing nothing but a slip and how he had slowed just to watch her walk, a homeless guy down on King Street shitting into a sewer while he held a steaming cup of coffee in one hand. Bone never shared these details with anyone, even other messengers. The city took so much from him in sweat and time and sore muscles; these passing images he kept for himself because he had earned them. Closing his eyes, he could still feel the streets rising up through his tired feet and hands.

Yurika had a sense of this as she listened to his heartbeat. She liked to end her evenings with him in this way. They would make their wordless love on the floor of the workshop where she preferred it, and they would eventually end up in bed, her head on his chest. A sadness filled her then. She wanted to remain there listening. In the beat of his heart, she heard many things that he could not or would not say. She heard the steady cadence of his long workdays, the countless miles pedaled, the cranking of tools in his strong hands. Always alone. He was the most solitary person she had ever met. In their mutual silence, she began to understand that she, too, kept to herself much of the time. In Japan, when she was with her friends and speaking a lot, she still wasn't saying anything, really, not what she wanted to say, about how boring and stupid their time was spent walking along the streets, drinking, playing *pachinko,* going to *robu-ho*. She had been quiet with her parents as well. With them, she didn't know where to begin. Their lives seemed frozen in the same routine for decades. They woke up. Her mother cooked miso soup, rice, some vegetables, maybe an egg. Her father ate and read the morning paper. They left for work together. They came home. Her mother cooked dinner. Her father ate and read the late edition. They watched television. They went to sleep. They barely spoke.

In New York, though, Yurika could speak to Whitey, to Suzie, and now to Riya. She felt like a new person around these people. Why was she so different with them? Why couldn't she be more like that with Bone?

Whitey did not get it. How could it be so easy for Yurika and Bone to hook up? He asked himself this over and over as he smoked and wrote his way through his sleepless nights.

His apartment still smelled from the fire, but he was growing used to it. He had put duct tape over the burnt part of the mattress and flipped over the whole thing. A part of him felt that he must have deserved what had happened with Yurika and Bone, with the fire; literally and figuratively, he was burned because he had been stupid enough to bring Yurika up to the Bronx.

He just wanted to be with her, but he knew he was being stupid. Hadn't he learned that when you want something so badly, in a needy way, you never get it? The char on the wall of his apartment and the empty wall space where his beloved Beatles poster once hung served as reminders: nothing lasts. The day after he had left her at Bone's, Yurika had left a note explaining why the fire had happened and filled a page with apologies, but Whitey knew that cosmically, the fire had happened to remind him not to be foolish and needy when it came to love.

Yurika and Bone together gnawed at him. The answer was almost too simple, too primal for him really to get his mind around, so he kept returning to it in his journal writing: *Yurika lusts for that fuck,* he wrote. *It was sex, pure and simple. Sex with a bad boy. Appalling.*

The only moments of relief Whitey experienced were on his bike. It was the only place that he could, for short stretches of time, forget his problems. He couldn't help but smile sometimes as he snaked through the obstacle course of traffic or sprinted up an avenue. There were even moments of elation after a few hours of work when his endorphins kicked in and he would feel high as he bounced from one drop to another, the Mighty Whitey of days past. Tall, lean, fast.

Then he had lunch or got tired, and his life caught up to him. His body sagged. He felt small. Yurika appeared in every doorway, crossing every street. He felt her absence in his gut. Yet she called and left messages.

I know you so angly, maybe, so, how can I say? To you. My feeling so bad.

It wasn't enough. He wanted to see her face in *his* doorway. She had a key. She could use it sometime when he was there. Didn't she miss him? There was no way Bone was picking her up at work and taking her out on dates. He didn't seem like the dating kind. Naturally, the man never talked about his private life, but he didn't have to—there didn't seem to be any. He was a man of no attachments except to his bike parts and whatever went on inside his head. Whitey recalled that it was months before Bone had even said a word to him, and then it was to tell him that his bike seat was too low. Whitey used to watch him breeze into the office in the morning. He always wore his wraparound sunglasses, a bike cap backward, clean jersey, shorts or tights without holes, gloves without tears or rips. He went straight to the dispatchers. They seemed to save the best runs for him—he was always getting the rush deliveries, the ones that paid double rates. He was a big earner, Chain told him once. On a great week, he had moved close to fifteen hundred dollars in runs. That means he could go home with almost half that. That was fast. "You need a van to do better," Chain had said. At Quick Service, Bone set the standard. Everyone wanted to messenger like him.

Fuck that noise, Whitey wrote in his journal. He didn't want Yurika to become another thing Bone could do or have that Whitey couldn't.

Where is she? he scribbled.

She was at Riya's. She had left Bone's that morning, gone to work, then to pose. They drank Thai iced coffee. The air-conditioning was on and the room was cool.

"If my models sweat," Riya explained, "it tickles and then they have to move."

Yurika liked to watch this woman move around the apartment as she set things up for their sitting. A chair, a small trunk, sheets over them. Riya moved with clear purpose. She had things to do in her life.

Colors to produce and wear, like the red tank top she wore now and a sarong intricately embroidered in swirls of white and gold. The whole apartment, in fact, was full of color everywhere Yurika looked. She felt so immature around her, as if she knew nothing compared to Riya's life experiences.

"How do you feel about posing nude?" Riya asked after everything was set up.

Yurika could feel herself blush. This was one reason she was different around Riya and Whitey and Suzie. They said things that embarrassed her, and this made her feel bare, raw, alive. She thought of Hector, how he was the only person in New York to have seen her naked. Now Riya would be the second. New York was a good place to be naked. Riya offered her a robe and said she could change in the bathroom, but Yurika shook her head and began taking off her clothes, though she avoided looking at Riya.

"Well," said Riya with a slight smile, "I guess we can get to business."

Yurika felt her whole body turn red. She felt a new boldness and shyness mixing inside of her. Thankfully, Riya gave her very specific directions about how to position her body parts for poses.

Riya liked that Yurika's body had a pleasing balance of strong and soft lines, not unlike her personality. The face was round but the neck and shoulders were thin, the breasts slight but hips nicely curved, legs strong. Riya could easily imagine her as a mother one day, breasts slightly engorged, baby resting on one hip. The girl had a way to go yet, but one day.

They began with short poses. First Riya told Yurika to stand facing her with her hands raised and her palms pressing against an imaginary glass wall. Then she asked her to crouch sideways, lower her head, and wrap her arms around herself. Listening to Riya's charcoal moving quickly against the drawing pad, Yurika imagined her drawing pages and pages of bowling pins. But Riya distracted her, giving her continuous directions. When they got to a long pose, Yurika began asking Riya about her life—when she came from Thailand, how she survived in New York.

At first Riya answered with short phrases, drawing in between speaking. She had lived in New York for ten years. She had lived in almost a dozen apartments.

"That's when I began feel like real New Yorker." Riya laughed. "I was lucky. My husband very helpful."

Yurika was straddling a chair, staring out the window with her chin resting on her arms, but she suddenly spun around at this information.

"Turn back," said Riya as she continued. "It's green card marriage. Beside, he's a gay. We good friends."

Amazing, thought Yurika. Whitey had mentioned something to her once about a Haitian man he knew who was in a green card marriage. This kind of thing was impossible in Japan. She never heard of anyone marrying for immigration purposes. The only immigrants who seemed to show up there were Chinese laborers and the Iranian guys selling phone cards and pot.

Riya explained that for two years, wherever she lived, she kept pictures of her and her gay friend all over the walls and tabletops. The closet and bureau were full of his clothes. The bathroom had two toothbrushes, two razors, two deodorants. When immigration came to visit one day by surprise, all was the picture of domestic bliss. Then, after two years, they went for their interview. They took them into separate rooms and asked them details about each other's personal habits. Riya explained that they had a lawyer coach them on the questions, so that by the time of their interview, they were bickering like an old married couple about who should buy toilet paper.

"People make their own arrangements," Riya said.

Yurika was confused by this sentence and asked Riya to explain. Riya took a long sip of iced coffee. In New York, she explained, it was possible to become a new person. Not actually a new person, but maybe a different person. The person you really wanted to become. There were ways. "Everyone," she concluded, "can decide for themselves."

They finished the sitting in silence. Yurika forgot she had a body. Her mind was full of questions. What kind of person did she want to be here? Would it be possible to stay here? Would Whitey want a green card marriage with her? Would he ever talk to her again? She couldn't see Bone having a marriage with anyone. She didn't know how much time had passed, but by the time she noticed, Riya was finished drawing. She turned over the pad. Yurika was surprised at how grown up her body looked, even sexy, especially the slope of her back into her bottom. Her eyes looked off to the side of the paper as if staring at something very interesting; they seemed so sharp and clear. Thinking of Bone, she wondered if she should tell Riya about him but then didn't. She felt quite exposed enough for one visit.

Did Suzie know about Riya? Yurika wondered. During their morning lessons, she wanted to ask her so much that she almost forgot all the good information about Hector she had to share. Over rice and lemongrass soup that Yurika had made based on one of Riya's recipes, they talked. This time it was Yurika who was shoveling bowls of rice into her mouth. Suzie was impressed with the variety of her and Bone's activities and liked to think she was a good influence that way. She asked lots of questions about size and shape and color, speed, angles, smells, textures, and she made sure Yurika had all the right vocabulary to do "proper dish," as Suzie called it. They would sometimes spend the whole hour just going into the minute details of one or two positions. Suzie made Yurika practice the *r* in "hard on" and the *f* in "stiff."

Their lessons had taken on new meaning for Suzie. In total secrecy, she had sent off the application to the English teacher–training course. The school seemed to be able to work around the fact that Suzie hadn't gone to college. They mostly wanted to know why she wanted to teach and how she would pay the two-thousand-dollar tuition to be in the one-month intensive course. Suzie planned to ask Sang Jun for the money. Since she hadn't gone to college, he might feel lucky that he was getting off paying only that much for more education. He had paid for her manicurist certification but had called that a high school graduation present. Now, if she got in, and he could pay, the classes would begin in August, and she could be teaching by September. A wild thought. Pronunciation instead of polish. Phrasal verbs instead of foot scrubbings. The Latin men and their beautiful mouths. The Italian men and their eyes. She refocused on her lesson with her cousin and said how glad she was that Yurika was finally having good sex.

It was more than just good sex for Yurika. She had never enjoyed a man's body and her own so completely. The variations and sources of pleasure seemed endless. Talking about it with Suzie gave her the opportunity to relive those moments of intoxicating pleasure. When Suzie asked what Bone was like afterward, Yurika described them looking into each other's eyes. Suzie smiled. Yurika described listening to his heartbeat. Suzie nodded.

"But," Yurika added, "he don't talk."

Suzie made a face. "Good for sex. Bad for a relationship. Which do you want?"

It was a good question. Yurika had already begun to think about it. She realized that she liked to talk—if there was something to say and something to listen to. Hector didn't seem like much of a talker, though. She would try to talk to him next time, she resolved. Why not?

This was more difficult than she had imagined. The next time they got together, a Friday two weeks after they had first spent the night together, he seemed particularly exhausted and sleepy. He lay on top of her, still inside of her, his hands behind her pressing the small of her back, his breath deep, steady.

"Hector," Yurika whispered.

"Hm?"

"You sleeping?"

He rolled over onto his back. "Nope," he said as he stretched, then reached over to put her head on his chest.

Yurika whispered his name again, but this time there was no answer. He was out. She said his name louder.

He was drowsy but not asleep. In fact, he was in a foul mood and was trying to cloak this in silence. He was hoping to feel better after they had done it a couple of times, but that was not the case. Normally, on a Friday, before he left work he would have arranged for a number of messengers to drop off bike parts on the weekend and have work done on their bikes. This had not happened. Only a small handful of messengers were coming over. From them, Bone found out that Whitey had been talking to the other messengers, convincing them to quit stripping bikes. He had noticed that a lot of the messengers were acting differently toward him but didn't give it much thought. Usually, they gave him small parts at the end of days and asked about what they needed to strip in order to have a chain replaced or a derailleur adjusted. During the last two weeks, there had been less and less of that. Bone kept looking around for Whitey but had not spotted him once.

As he lay there that evening beside Yurika, he tried to think like Whitey. He would have to come by the office sometime to turn in any CODs—that wasn't the kind of thing you asked other messengers to do for you. Whitey would need more tickets to write down his runs. He would need to show his face. But when? Where would he lock up his bike? Bone was having a hard time thinking because Yurika kept talking to him. At first he could make sounds as though he were interested, but then she started asking him questions, trying to stir him by tickling his stomach. He wasn't ticklish.

"What's with the questions?" he finally mumbled, eyes still closed.

She propped herself up on her arm. "You can ask me some question also."

"What time is it?" he asked with a weak smile.

Yurika couldn't tell if he was joking or not, but she pretended he was and gave his belly a slap. "You know my meaning."

"What do you mean?" He yawned. "Tell me."

She wasn't sure how. How could she say that she liked sex with him so much but wanted him to be someone she also liked to talk to. Why hadn't she practiced saying something with Suzie? Yurika began telling him how she used to see him riding up First Avenue in the mornings. How her heart used to beat faster. He looked so free. When he came into the store, he never really saw her until that time he had the accident and she said something about his bicycle.

"Do you remember?" she asked.

He was sound asleep. She knew he was tired from work, but was it okay if he fell asleep while she was talking? Yurika felt like she had a large, hollow pit lodged in her stomach. She used to fall asleep from boredom in school. She thought of her parents and their nontalk. When her father read the paper, he grunted periodically in response to her mother's telling him about her day.

She shook Bone's shoulder. He didn't stir, so she shook him harder and said his name.

He awoke for a second to throw an arm around her. "I need sleep."

"You hear me?"

"I'm so tired, baby," he whispered as he pulled the sheet up to his waist. "Shut that beautiful mouth, baby. Sleep."

He said "shut up," thought Yurika. Almost kindly. Like it was okay. She tried to imagine how tired he was. Whitey had told her how exhausted he could get some days, that he could just fall asleep while he was reading on his bed and not even notice until he woke up in the morning. Once he had even fallen asleep on a date, right at dinner. The only time Yurika had ever been so tired was when she stayed up all night in Japan and had to wait for the trains to run again so she could get home.

She decided not to wake Bone again. They could talk another time. There was no reason sex needed conversation just at that moment. She sat up cross-legged next to his body. The light of a street lamp filtered into the room, giving it a yellowish glow. Slowly, she pulled the sheet down from his body. It was golden brown and beautiful. All hers. She moved her hands so they levitated just above his body, one down his thighs and one over his stomach and chest. Then they met again over his privates. She closed her eyes and inhaled deeply. His smell was everywhere. She wanted to take in the whole sight of him at once but couldn't, so she swung a leg over his thighs and lowered her body onto his, her head on his chest. He gave out a long exhale, his arms wrapping around her.

She couldn't sleep. After a while, her thoughts drifted to Whitey. She imagined asking him if he would marry her for her green card. Then she felt guilty. He had not come into the store since the Thursday they had come up to Bone's place. She tried to call him. Still, he hadn't stopped by. She had even gone by his place again and left another note, asking him to come by the store or call, but he had not. The thought of Whitey not speaking to her made her feel sick. She could still see him in the hallway outside the apartment, giving her subway directions. He looked so serious at the time, but Yurika understood now that he must have been angry and couldn't or wouldn't show it. Then Hector had closed the door on him. She fell asleep dreaming that Whitey was asking her over and over how she could do this to him, how could she?

Whitey was, in fact, busy having the worst week of his life. Worse than his first week of messengering in the winter. Worse than the week he dropped out of college and had to face his father. But he was asking these and other questions in his myriad imagined conversations with Yurika. The rest of the time, Bone's threat weighed on his already heavy heart. He did everything in his power not to be seen by Bone, arriving at work when they opened at 7 A.M. and not returning until the next morning. In his inner ear, he could hear Bone hiss, "Ain't gonna be no warning." Almost as bad was that he wasn't sleeping. Mostly he took catnaps but could not remember falling asleep. He couldn't stop thinking of Yurika. The yearning for her kept him awake. He didn't even have his Beatles poster to console him. It had survived his teen years at prep school, nearly a full year of college, and several moves afterward only to be lost now—and by Yurika's hand, no less.

Everywhere he went, he thought he saw either her, Bone, or the two of them together—having ice cream on a bench in Washington Square Park, walking past the Empire State Building along Thirty-fourth Street. When he remembered standing outside Bone's apartment while she called out that she would phone him later, he felt his limbs go weak. Taking her up there was what he now referred to as "his foolishness."

In more lucid moments—usually when Whitey was riding—he understood that there was no way he could have known that she already knew him and had something going on for him. She had written this in her note and apologized for not telling him. She had apologized for not being a good friend, but this was a moot point to Whitey because to him she was already more than a good friend. He was hopelessly losing himself in the belief that he and Yurika had been very close to having a real relationship. He tortured himself by imagining Yurika and Bone doing it on the floor beside moist piles of inner tubes and handlebar tape.

His sleeplessness took its toll. He would suddenly find himself exiting a building in Hell's Kitchen or Turtle Bay and not remember which dispatcher had given him the run or how he had gotten there. His bag would be empty, but he could not remember how many runs he had completed. On several occasions he had to think hard about where he had locked up his bike. Time sped up then slowed to a surreal crawl. It would suddenly be three o'clock, but then the next half hour would stretch on and on for the rest of the afternoon. The city offered up scene after scene of a never-ending waking dream. An attractive blind woman emerging from the shadows of a stretch limousine and led by the driver into a tall black box of a building. A bus driver sticking a pudgy hand out his window to give Whitey the finger. A man in a sweat suit on his knees praying on a carpet facing east. A cab driver stopped at a light leafing through a porn magazine. A wooden cross covered in gold glitter emerged from the sun roof of a van. A Chinese man standing between two cars relieving himself as a cigarette dangled from his mouth, the smoke crawling up the side of his face. A pair of white men in business suits walking down a street in the sweltering afternoon heat without a single bead of sweat on either of them.

All of Whitey's conversations with messengers seemed the same. He talked about Yurika. He worried about Bone. He hadn't intended to convince any messengers to stop doing parts for labor exchanges with Bone. It just seemed to happen, beginning with Voodoo. They had run into each other outside of 666 Fifth Avenue. Voodoo was worried about Whitey.

"Take that shit with Bone seriously, bro," Voodoo said, shifting uneasily on his bike seat. "He don't give a shit 'bout no one."

Whitey nodded, then explained how and why his days of stripping were over. "That's the only good thing about all this."

This gave Voodoo pause to think. He had always felt the stripping was wrong, but he loved getting free labor on his bike. But he didn't like having to deal with Bone. He talked down to all the messengers and was not generous with his barter. There was little choice, though, given the amount of riding they all did—forty or fifty miles a day, probably more. The bikes were in constant need of attention, and Bone was a pro. Like Whitey and his ever-problematic brakes, Voodoo was in constant fear of having his bike stolen as some cosmic retaliation for all the stripping that he had done over the years. He locked his bike up with two **U**-shaped locks and a thick bike chain but hated having to carry all three of these around all day, every day, in addition to all the packages. The idea of no longer stripping unsuspecting bike owners of their derailleurs and their hubs seemed very appealing.

A similar train of thought went through other messengers' minds after talking to Whitey. In one way or another, all were unhappy with the trade with Bone because of the added burden they felt from guilt and worry that something bad would happen to either themselves or their bikes. They were already a superstitious lot on the whole. Not unlike the dream Yurika had before the fire at Whitey's, many messengers counted on signs to lead them through a day, though they rarely spoke of this. If they felt unsafe, they wouldn't go out or they'd play paddleball for a few hours. Hearing a car screech was a bad omen. So were mechanical problems with their bikes, which was why Bone's work was so valued.

Still, many had wanted to stop their stripping at various times. Problem was, it was almost second nature; when they saw a nice pair of handlebars or pedals, they just took them. Seeing Whitey's transformation into a humorless sleepwalker got them talking and fueled their change of minds. They watched as the circles under Whitey's eyes got darker and deeper. They talked about how Whitey stopped smiling and cracking jokes, how he no longer had the energy to rock back and forth and clap his hands together when he talked. In the mornings before work, they sat on the stoop of the messenger office and shared stories of their own heartbreak and shook their heads that a guy as nice as Whitey should have to go through such misery. In their talks, Yurika became Whitey's girlfriend and Bone became a woman stealer. Out of their already existing feelings of intimidation around Bone, they turned him into an ogre who never gave them fair trade for their parts. Formerly secondhand stories like the one of his breaking another messenger's nose suddenly had eyewitnesses. They stewed in their dislike of Bone until they felt justified in their actions. When Bone came up to them as he often did to see if they had any parts, they just shrugged or told him they had nothing for him.

On the first Monday of August, after more than two weeks of poor sleep, Whitey arrived at work again at 7 A.M. He convinced himself that Bone wouldn't arrive until at least eight-thirty, so he locked his bike to a parking meter just down the street from the office. His caution about where he had been locking it up had been excessive; even in his state of walking insomnia, he could see that clearly now. So he entered the office and went in to take care of business, use the bathroom, and down his first dose of caffeine pills for the day.

Across the street, Bone sat in a window seat of the diner where messengers often got coffee and breakfast. Sipping a black coffee with no sugar, he was watching for Whitey to arrive but thinking of his father. Bone had a recurring daydream that he would get busted by the cops one day for some crime he hadn't committed. In prison, he would meet his father. In one scenario, they got into a fistfight first and nearly killed each other. In another scenario, they were cell mates. They traded stories of betrayal on the outside—how they had gotten revenge or how they planned to get revenge when they got back on the outside.

Whitey came into view. He coasted up to a parking meter, locked up his bike, then went inside the office. Bone left the diner and got on his bike. His plan was to wait for Whitey across the street, then follow him for a block before knocking the shit out of him with his bike lock. A few other messengers had arrived with coffees and sat on the stoop outside the office, smoking. As Bone stood staring at the front door of the office, his eyes drifted to Whitey's bike, to the wheel he had built. A new plan formed in his mind. Coasting across the Sixth Avenue, he caught Lefty's eye but looked away. As he approached Whitey's bike, he dismounted and stood his bike up using the pedal as a kickstand against the curb. Crouching, he removed wire cutters from his messenger bag. In eight quick cuts, he removed four spokes—one from the top, one from the bottom, and one from each side of the wheel he had built. By midday, the wheel would look like an accordion. The next day, Bone planned to strip something else. Then again. And again. He grinned. Cutting the spokes took no more than a few seconds, and Bone thought that to the messengers on the stoop he would look like he was making an adjustment on his own bike. Stuffing the spokes into his bag, he hopped on his bike and pedaled up the avenue.

Whitey emerged from the bathroom feeling dizzy. He had nodded off on the toilet and awoke not knowing how long he had been out. The phones were ringing. Ian was taking runs; so was Chain. Jim had arrived and was in the back wearing one of his beige linen suits as always, standing by his desk, speaking his swearless English to someone on the speakerphone.

Making his way outside, Whitey took two caffeine pills with a sip of Lefty's second cup of coffee of the day.

"Mira, yo," Lefty said. "Bone was just by your bike."

"Whatever," Whitey mumbled as he kept walking. He inhaled deeply and felt a chill even though the day had already grown warm. The sky was blue. Sparrows could be heard somewhere above him. He unlocked his bike and swung a leg over the frame. He wanted to go by Lucky Market to see Yurika, to have a laugh with her, to see her dimples again. As he rode up the middle of Sixth Avenue, he was trying to recall the feeling of Yurika's kiss but was having a hard time because his front wheel was making funny ticking sounds, as though it were under strain. He coasted and leaned toward his front wheel to listen for the problem. As he drifted into the intersection of Grand Street and Sixth, there was barely enough time for him to jerk his head up at the sound of the horn and the screech of the speeding car's breaks.

Time slowed. Whitey felt the pressure of the car against his shoulder and leg. He was embarrassed that this could make him lose his balance. He was more embarrassed still that this contact could separate him from his bike. In fact, he seemed to be hanging in midair and even had time to think, I'm flying, and how that was a good idiom to teach Yurika when she wanted to say she was feeling good. He saw his bike disappear beneath the wheels of the white Buick, the terrible swerve of the car up the avenue.

There was time to remember being six years old, in the back of his father's new Continental, the smell of the new leather, the low vibration of the engine, playing with the electric windows, that fine electric hum. The hum turned into the reprise of music in the Beatles' song "Helter Skelter," and he suddenly missed sitting in Lillian's Pizzeria with his buddy Phil at the age of twelve, listening to that song that would forever change everything.

His memory of time sped up and his past longings welled inside him. He recalled the blue eyes of Cassie Windsor and how he kept a picture of her taped to the headboard of his bed. Hers was the first face he saw in the morning and the last he looked at before he went to sleep. He longed for the time he spent traveling—the smells of the night market in Bangkok, the air full of mint in the *souk* of Marrakech, the sardines in Barcelona that melted in his mouth.

His skull made a loud crack against the pavement. As his memories drained out of him, time sped up again. He could see himself moving into his new apartment, doing his first run as a messenger, seeing Yurika's heart-shaped mouth for the first time, riding tandem with her around Central Park. Then he saw his own death, crumpled against a parked car on Grand Street, a pool of blood spreading around him. He saw his burial in the Virginia cemetery where his ancestors were and where the rest of his family would one day join him. This disappointed him because he had hoped to be cremated and scattered to the winds in the high Atlas Mountains of Morocco.

Time moved far beyond the present. He saw people moving, traveling, migrating, filling the land around where his body lay. The streets cracked then turned to gray dust. He saw the masses of people crossing the borders, changing borders. New York and America became distant myths like Atlantis and the Hanging Gardens. He understood for the first time that history accomplished one thing: it faded memory over unspeakable amounts of time so that there could be more room for life, more death, and endless opportunities for humans to relearn exactly the same things over and over, from the fact that fire burns to the fact that death means you do not always get to say good-bye to the people you love.

SIX

Through Night

The news of Whitey's death spread through the ranks of the messengers. Those like Lefty, who witnessed the accident from the stoop of the office, told others they met during the day, and those messengers broke the news to others, even if they weren't from Quick Service. By midday, more than a few found it difficult to keep their minds on work and the road. They wound up taking long breaks every few drops. They lay on grass in Central Park. They sat on benches or even the sidewalk staring at passing traffic. They didn't believe Whitey was gone and couldn't help but wonder who was next.

It was a high-volume day at Quick Service. The dispatchers were instructed not to tell any messenger the news or even talk about it until the day was over. This was even the case when Bone called in. He had heard about Whitey shortly after noon. A messenger named D.S. from another company told him. D.S. stood for Deep South, and usually Bone tried to avoid even being seen with him because he wore jeans when he worked along with a T-shirt and an Afro pick sticking out of his hair. Rubber bands around the cuffs of his pants kept the material from getting caught in the chain ring. Yet he always acted as if he were the coolest thing on two wheels. He rode around on a department store bike that he treated like a top-of-the-line model. Heading the wrong way across West Thirty-sixth Street looking for an address, D.S. saw Bone and practically crashed into him.

"Yo, Bone, I got some news." He began picking his hair and excitedly licking his lips. Bone had never seen him so animated. "Um . . . there was a accident . . . yo . . . Whitey got kill."

At first Bone thought D.S. had finally lost his mind. He kept blinking at Bone as though he would stop only when there was some acknowledgment of what he had said. But what he said made no sense to Bone, especially with him looking so excited.

"Whitey dead, yo."

It was a trick, Bone thought. Whitey was pulling some kind of stunt and somehow managed to involve this idiot. Bone knew better than to believe any word passed on the street, especially from D.S., who always seemed and, in fact, often was, lost. He usually asked Bone obvious bike questions about how to clean his chain or how much grease to apply to cables. But now he was saying something very different, and it seemed crazy. The whole city seemed to get thrown out of whack—noises louder, the traffic moving faster, too many people crowding the sidewalks.

"Whitey's dead," D.S. repeated.

"I heard you," said Bone as he rolled away toward a phone. D.S. followed him.

"The fuck are you doing?" asked Bone.

"I gotta call, too," said D.S., swinging around his empty bag.

Bone waved up the block. "Find another phone."

D.S. dismounted his bike and glanced up and down the block. "All right." He nodded. "I check you later."

Bone quickly called the office. Chain picked up. "Quick Service. Hold."

It couldn't be true, Bone thought. No way. Absently, he reached a hand into his bag for the spokes from Whitey's wheel. They were warm.

He took one out and tapped it against the phone as he glanced up and down the block. The city was dense and hot. Traffic became thick on Thirty-sixth Street with delivery trucks unloading and loading racks of clothing.

Chain came back on. "Where are you?" Phones were ringing in the background.

"It's Bone."

"You empty?"

"What happened to Whitey?"

"Can't talk now. You empty?"

Bone grit his teeth and grabbed his packet of tickets. "Come on, Chain."

"Ready?"

"The fuck, Chain?"

"Are you ready?"

Bone shook his head. "Go."

Chain read off a series of pickup locations and drops that Bone wrote on each ticket.

"Call when you're empty," Chain said, and he hung up.

It wasn't long before Bone ran into other messengers who confirmed what D.S. had said. He heard two stories. In one version, Whitey had a bike problem that caused an accident. In another version the accident just happened. Bone still found both stories hard to believe. He had had the same feeling when Freddie got killed. An unreality shrouded everything. Time should have stopped, but it didn't. He kept thinking of the spokes in his bag. He told himself that those couldn't have caused an accident. It was impossible. The bike would have been fine for miles. Then it would have gotten a warped wheel. He tried to put it out of his mind and raced toward his first pickup. Today could be a two-hundred-dollar day if he kept his head together and emptied fast. He thought of Yurika at the store. Did she know?

He was curious but decided she wasn't his problem. El Gato would say, "She's a fine pussy but don't get sucked in."

He wasn't going to be the one to tell her. For the rest of the day, if he was downtown, he swung up Third Avenue, away from Lucky Market, took Twelfth Street or St. Mark's Place if he needed to go east. Mostly, he managed to stay out of the neighborhood altogether.

Yurika kept an eye out for Bone. He was late for his morning ride-by. In fact, she was surprised that she hadn't seen any messenger all morning. She was sure that this would be the day Whitey would return to Lucky Market. Each time she envisioned him coming through the door, a smile growing across his face, she was distracted by a new customer.

It was a busy day at the store. There were deliveries that her aunt and uncle were taking care of in the basement. Daniel and José were restocking the outside. As the day grew hotter, more and more people came in to buy cold drinks. Her right fingers were starting to hurt from all the cash register activity. Many regulars came in and Yurika had lots of opportunities to speak English aside from saying prices, offering matches, or asking, "Bag?" Mrs. Manton came in and the two of them complained about the heat. From her, Yurika learned the expression, "It's killin' me." Riya stopped by as well to buy some juice and ask if Yurika would still be here in September.

Yurika glanced around the store. "I hope."

Riya told her that if she were, she could be a paid model for her drawing classes. Yurika understood that this meant nude modeling, and she blushed.

"You'll have more chances to practice before then," Riya said as she handed Yurika a five for a large bottled water. It was then Yurika learned the expression, "You're a natural," which Riya told her.

Yurika never thought of herself as anything natural. Could someone become one? Maybe she was with bicycles. She saw herself at Whitey's apartment working on his bike. A dull ache began in her stomach: she missed him. How could he still be so angry? she wondered. She decided to go to his place after work and wait for him to return.

Toward the end of the day, business slowed. Hyun Jeong went home early, complaining of a headache. Sang Jun was in the back on the phone. Daniel and José were outside. Yurika was replacing the Camel hard packs when Voodoo came in the store. He had that glazed look in his eyes and that slow walk that told Yurika it had been a busy day for him, too. As he stood before the counter, he could see by Yurika's bright smile that she had no idea about Whitey and that it had fallen to him to give her the news. He, too, had avoided the store all day, hoping that someone else would be the one to do this. But now here he was. He felt heavy.

"Gotta tell you what happened," he said, glancing outside.

Yurika laughed. "Something happen your bike?"

Voodoo shook his head and this time looked right at her. He swallowed hard and spoke slowly and clearly, not wanting to repeat himself. "Whitey was in a bad accident. He got killed." He paused, unsure if she knew what those words meant. "He's dead."

She heard what he said but it took a few seconds to register. Voodoo was nodding, answering the question in her eyes. Then Yurika's face seemed to melt around the mouth and eyes. Her hands, as though in slow motion, rose up to her mouth. The dull pain that had been in her stomach seemed to well up now into her chest as she let out a cry and ran from the register. She locked herself in the back bathroom.

Hearing the commotion, Sang Jun came into the store. With a bike boy standing there in front of an empty counter, he immediately grew suspicious.

"What happen?" he barked at Voodoo.

Voodoo told him about Whitey. Sang Jun recognized from Voodoo's description who it was, and he pressed his lips together and shook his head. As far as he knew, no one had ever died in Yurika's life except her maternal grandmother when Yurika was probably too small to remember. And now her boyfriend—since that was who he decided Whitey was, especially with her often not coming back at night these last two weeks. Her sobbing could be heard all over the store.

"Tell her I'm sorry," said Voodoo, turning to go.

Sang Jun nodded and watched him leave. He got Daniel to take the register, then went and stood outside the bathroom door. It was so long ago now that he had sat on the side of a bed in Korea, crying after Jong Eun died. He gently knocked on the door. Yurika didn't answer, so he walked away and told Daniel what happened. They stood behind the counter together. Both were lost in thought—Sang Jun about Jong Eun and Daniel about two friends who had died trying to cross into the States; they got lost in the Yucatán and were found weeks later shriveled like dried fruit.

Yurika saw Whitey standing outside of Bone's apartment calling out train directions. She saw him rocking back and forth in the store, clapping his hands together. He sat on the floor beside her while she worked on his brakes. Each memory made her cry harder, her face buried in handfuls of toilet paper. She wanted to think in Japanese, say Japanese words, hear Japanese come from her lips, but none came out. It was like that part of her brain was clogged or shut down. Instead, she found only English: Whitey's dead; Whitey was dead.

Customers who came into the store glanced at the muffled wailing coming from the back. Sang Jun paced back and forth outside the bathroom waiting for Yurika to emerge. He lit a cigarette. The bike boys knew what they were getting themselves into, he thought. It was a crazy job, and he was surprised that there wasn't some kind of death or terrible accident every week. Well, he considered, maybe there was. It was not the kind of news they said on TV. When there was a lull in Yurika's sobbing, he knocked on the door again, and to his surprise, the doorknob turned and she emerged. Her eyes were swollen and red, tears still falling down her face with each blink.

It was the first time all summer that Yurika wished Sang Jun were her father and that her mother would be close by. He was looking at her with great concern but did not seem to know what to say. She didn't have any English or Japanese to describe the feelings inside of her, so she remained mute, her breath broken and quick.

"We go outside," he finally said, stubbing out his cigarette in an ashtray. He led her through the store. She could feel the eyes of customers on her. She saw Daniel looking at her and thought he said, "Sorry," but she wasn't sure because her crying was still echoing in her ears.

They crossed First Avenue and walked down Tenth Street. Sang Jun stopped at Riya's stoop, where he sat down and invited Yurika to join him. She wanted to say that she knew whose apartment house this was, but she couldn't muster the energy to speak. She drew her knees up and rested her arms on them. Staring across the street at a tree that was growing at an angle and cracking the sidewalk beneath it, she could hear Whitey's voice. It was warm and punctuated with laughs. She didn't catch his words, but somehow she understood that whatever he was saying was hopeful, maybe about a trip or a plan for his bicycle. She thought of Bone and the nights she had spent with him, the two of them never mentioning Whitey, never mentioning anything, never talking.

"You know . . ." Sang Jun felt awkward in his English because he'd never had to use it in quite this way. "I have first wife she died."

Yurika turned to him. Her parents had sometimes mentioned a woman in connection with Sang Jun, a young woman who had died. Yurika had always assumed it was some Korean relative or some old girlfriend, but now she understood that she just hadn't really cared enough to pay attention or to find out. Sang Jun stared across the street, but he seemed to be looking beyond the buildings. He described for

Yurika the first day he had met Jong Eun, how she would not make eye contact with him except for the brief moment when they were introduced outside of an economics class. He knew he would marry her then.

"Her eyes told me everything," he said, shaking his head. As he described the spark he saw in those eyes, her long shiny hair, Suzie came to Yurika's mind. A clear space opened in her thoughts. In it, Suzie walked up to this woman and gave her a long embrace. As a daughter gives a mother. The way Suzie never touched Hyun Jeong.

"Suzie," Yurika began, and her voice trailed off, no energy to speak.

Sang Jun lit a cigarette and nodded at her. "She needed mother. Hyun Jeong is aunt." As if he read the question forming in Yurika's mind, Sang Jun explained how Suzie found out when she was twelve, going through some pictures in his closet. "She so angry then." He shook his head. "She feel something about Hyun Jeong not her mother." He took a long drag and flicked his ashes. "Maybe, not so angry now."

Especially, Sang Jun thought, since he gave her two thousand dollars for school. It was all top secret still. Suzie told him that she was taking a month off from the salon, then would see if she would go back or not. Sang Jun wasn't sure what to think and was hoping she wouldn't take the money and run off to Florida or the Caribbean. Still, he was glad she thought of something for her life besides nails. He couldn't stand the smell of all that nail polish or the thought of his daughter touching so many strangers.

They sat in silence. A young couple walked past arm in arm, staring into each other's eyes. Sang Jun turned to his niece. "So, I know your feeling about your boyfriend."

Yurika thought of Bone, then realized that Sang Jun was talking about Whitey. She didn't correct him. Her head dropped to her arms as sobs welled up again. She felt hopeless. Whitey was not her boyfriend, but her heart was breaking, and from it, sadness poured out.

Sang Jun put a hand on her back, and Yurika felt herself go weak in the limbs as she cried, occasionally opening her eyes to see the wet spots on the stair beneath her. Sang Jun's hand moved to her shoulder, and he pulled her closer. Yurika cried into his chest, covering her hands with her face. People who walked by glanced up at the two of them. Reaching into his back pocket, Sang Jun pulled out a handkerchief and gave it to Yurika. She wiped her eyes and nose as her cries subsided again.

Sang Jun glanced at his niece and thought for the first time how she looked like his brother. "Your father," he began, "think I make mistake to marry Hyun Jeong. Because he love your mother, he think only that way for marriage."

This was news to Yurika. The idea of her father loving her mother seemed like a novelty item people won at one of the *pachinko* parlors she had worked at. Her mother was more her father's servant than wife—cleaning, making his meals, speaking about mindless shopping excursions and other *O.L.* adventures that never caused her father to look up from his endless supply of newspapers and magazines that she brought him to read during meals.

Yurika shook her head. She could hear Riya telling her to talk to Sang Jun, to ask about how her parents met. But she didn't want to hear or think more. She needed to go to Whitey's apartment and just be there. She wanted to be alone in his space. But she didn't know how to begin to tell her uncle any of this.

Sang Jun kept talking. He was explaining about Jong Eun's illness. Riya was the only person in America who had heard this story. Now he was telling his niece. He hadn't expected to, but here he was, sitting on a stoop just talking. In English, no less. In her way, he thought, she was already more a New Yorker and an American before she arrived than he could have ever hoped to be. That was why she could get along with the bike boys. Have a boyfriend. Have other places to go besides the shop and their home. Maybe it was her age. Maybe she was just so open. He was surprised, then, when she sprang up from the stoop and walked away, turning only to say that she would call them later.

He did not go after her. She would be okay. Remaining on the stoop, he lit a cigarette. He thought of how Riya liked to draw him after they made love. Then he imagined a young, naked American boy in her bed. He shook his head. It was silly to be jealous. He was lucky she shared anything with an aging businessman like him. Of course she had her own life. His niece was like her in that way. Strong head, strong heart. Glancing behind him, he imagined the door would swing open at any moment and Riya would exit with her young lover. The image faded when he thought of the dead bike boy, of Jong Eun and her illness. Sadness settled on his shoulders. Youth, he considered, didn't spare anyone from an early death. He shook his head and looked away, stood up, and began a slow walk back to the store to call Hyun Jeong.

Death, illness, true crime. Daytime TV was much better than prime time, and Hyun Jeong was thrilled to be home on a weekday without having to clean. A little headache went a long way. There were the talk shows and the court shows and the soap operas; she couldn't decide on one program, so she unplugged all the phones and settled herself in Sang Jun's armchair and surrounded herself with rice crackers, two kinds of pound cake, some Cheez Doodles, and even a beer, picked up the remote control, and watched about a minute of every program on every channel—except the news, which had grown boring since the hostages of Flight 86 had been released and the trial of the man who had poisoned his wife ended with that man walking free.

For years she had tried to get Sang Jun to buy a small TV for the store, but he insisted that it was not good for customer service. Radio was okay; television was not. To Hyun Jeong, though, the Korean radio station was boring. Who cared that Seoul was having the worst traffic problems in its history or that a new movie was banned in Korea because there was too much sex in it? They were in America, and none of that mattered to them, really. It was a big country with enough of its own problems, and Americans were free to have their own special troubles. Daughters, husbands, nieces—all trouble.

She wondered if Yurika was becoming a slut like her cousin. All those bike boys and staying out all hours. She was going to get herself pregnant. Or worse. If she and Sang Jun had to give the girl's parents some bad news, it would serve them right. Once, an American woman had told her, "You get what you pay for," and Hyun Jeong had never forgotten it because it was so true. The girl's parents hadn't even offered to pay for rent or food, even just some kind of courtesy money. The presents they sent along were cheap, too: a box of rice crackers and a tin of green tea—not even the finest kinds but the sort that she had seen in Korean and Japanese airports for decades. In fact, the girl was probably instructed by her parents to buy it at Narita airport just before she boarded the plane. So, Hyun Jeong concluded, they paid for nothing so they should get nothing.

It was bad enough to be so tired of working all the time without ever hearing a thank-you or having a complete day off from everything. Hyun Jeong was sick of having to do her hair in the mornings, put on makeup for the thankless customers in the store. Why was she the only one who did laundry, the dishes, who cleaned the house? Why should any woman have to do that maid's work alone? The girl was too much. Hyun Jeong thought of the girl's action figures and of how much money she would take out the next day. She washed down a mouthful of pound cake with beer and thought, anything she did for the girl was above and beyond what anyone should expect.

She changed the channels. On one of the court shows, the judge was deciding to make a man pay a woman back for using her car for too long a period. Hyun Jeong smiled as she brought the bag of Cheez Doodles to her lap. She imagined the girl and her parents on the show, looking guilty as a judge demanded they pay Hyun Jeong a few thousand dollars for taking her goodwill and hospitality for granted. You thought you could get something for nothing, the judge would say, but you know what? You should pay for what you got. Cut to a commercial.

Hyun Jeong could hear the bathroom door close again downstairs and the air going on. Suzie hadn't gone to work that day. She seemed to be spending the day moving from her bed to the bathroom and back again. She stopped crunching on the Cheez Doodles and turned down the volume, listening carefully. Suzie was vomiting. Maybe it was dry heaves. Unfortunately, it was a familiar sound with that girl. Too much drinking again, Hyun Jeong thought, shaking her head and turning the volume back up. You would think that after all her years of drinking, that girl would finally know how to do it. Some people never learned, Hyun Jeong considered, reaching for her beer. That was the cause of most problems, she thought as she landed on a Christian station—people just didn't think. They could pray all they wanted, and it would do no good without a little common sense.

Yurika knelt on the floor of Whitey's studio. Clearing away some books, she prayed, trying to remember how she was taught to when she was a girl at the local Buddhist temple. When people died, the priests told her, their souls needed prayers to help them become aware that they had died. Prayers helped them become spirits. Without prayers, the dead were often lost. But Yurika knew no words of prayer in English and couldn't remember the ones in Japanese. So, with her eyes closed, palms pressed together, she tried to keep Whitey's image in her mind. Occasionally, when it felt appropriate, she bowed to the ground as she had seen people do at temples.

The problem was that her mind could not be still. Her mind's picture of Whitey became memories of Whitey, moving pictures of Whitey, talking Whitey, rocking Whitey. Then she remembered herself as she was in Japan, always worrying about not having enough money to go shopping with her friends, having arguments about whether Ultra Man could defeat Godzilla in a fight, struggling over whether she should wear her imitation Gucci jean jacket or her knockoff Versace sweatshirt. It was all so pointless and stupid, she thought as she squeezed her eyes tighter to hold on to the picture of Whitey. Her life in Japan was the same as everyone else's, as all her unemployable, half-educated, designer-fixated friends. In twenty years of living, she had nothing to show for herself. The thought made her bow low to the floor and whisper, *"Sumi-ma-sen,"* sorry, to whoever might be listening. She was sorry for wasting so much precious time listening to *pachinko* machines instead of teachers, trying to pronounce Ralph Lauren instead of practical English words, being part of *mindu conturoru* instead of having a mind of her own.

"I'm sorry, Whitey," she whispered.

She prayed to and for Whitey as other Japanese people prayed to their ancestors. She apologized for her ignorance, for not knowing what a Nazi was and why Japan was involved in World War II. She apologized for being a bad friend to him, for abandoning him for a beautiful man who didn't care half as much for her as he did. It was just like Suzie had said: Bone was good for sex, no good for a relationship—and it was a relationship, she realized, that she had always been secretly hoping for. With Whitey, she got the relationship. With Bone, the sex. For this, she bowed down again and apologized.

Hearing the key turn in the door, she sat up. For a second, she thought it would be Whitey, and she smiled. This vanished quickly. She gasped when she saw Bone standing in the open doorway. He wore his messenger clothes, his long arms and legs shiny with sweat in the early evening light. At first she thought he had come to find her, to tell her about Whitey, and she felt relief. Then his smell reached her, and she had to close her eyes again. She grew confused. How would he know where she was? What was he doing there?

Bone had expected an empty apartment. She was the last person he wanted to see. His afternoon had taken a strange turn. Mid-afternoon, when he called the office empty, Ian mumbled a confirmation that Whitey was dead. He also suggested that Bone stay away from the office. Some of the messengers had the idea that Bone had tampered with Whitey's bike and caused the accident. "They're pretty pissed off," he said. So Bone hadn't returned to the office. Instead, he thought he would use the key Whitey had given him to take back the bike stand Whitey had gotten in exchange for parts.

Yurika had been on his mind on and off as well. She would want comfort from him, soothing words, things that he had no desire to get into with anyone. At the thought of it, a fear tightened his insides, but he took it to be revulsion. Good sex was one thing. Getting involved was another, and it was for someone else. Nevertheless, when he saw Yurika kneeling on the floor of Whitey's apartment, he felt a spasm of jealousy. A picture quickly formed for him: Yurika and Whitey had actually been involved, and she had betrayed both Whitey and him by being with both of them. That was why she came uptown with Whitey when he picked up his wheel. That's why she had the key to his place. And, his story went, she was easy. Whitey was weak, and she betrayed him. Bone wanted pussy and there she was. She came back to Whitey after all because she realized no one could have him—Bone—no one could own him. And here she was, waiting for a dead man. For a second, he was glad Whitey had been killed.

Then he noticed she had been crying and understood that she knew Whitey was gone. He moved past her and picked up Whitey's bike stand.

"What do you do?" she exclaimed, grabbing the repair stand.

"It's mine," Bone said.

He knew Whitey was dead, thought Yurika, and he still couldn't say anything to her. He was there to take something from Whitey, and this filled her with rage. Holding on to the repair stand with her left hand, she began slapping wildly at him with her right. "Whitey died!" she screamed. "It's not yours!"

Bone yanked the repair stand away and shoved her hard so she fell into the middle of the room. She scrambled to her feet.

Lifting the repair stand like a baseball bat, Bone growled, "Get the fuck back."

Yurika froze. This was not the man she saw riding up First Avenue in the mornings. His eyes were wild like a trapped animal's. She had no doubt that he would hit her with that stand. Her animal man, she realized in a flash of clarity, was just an animal.

His hands tightened around the stand. "I'm taking it."

Yurika stood motionless and watched as Bone turned and left, leaving the door open. She could hear him unlocking his bike and the clank of the repair stand as it hit his frame. Then he was gone.

Standing for a moment as the sound of his tires on the pavement faded, Yurika felt a wave of anguish surge through her. Again she saw Whitey standing outside Bone's apartment and the door closing. How could she? English curses burst into her mind. Fucked once by Hector. Now fucked twice. Self-loathing collided with grief. She grabbed fistfuls of her hair and sank back to her knees. Tears began to stream down her face again. She gritted her teeth, trying to hold back a terrible groan that burst from her anyway, leaving her sobbing, her forehead against one of Whitey's books from his true crime pile.

She sat on the floor of Whitey's apartment until the light was gone from the room. In a stunned silence, she stared at the front door as a Monday night emerged outside the window—a game of dominoes being played a few doors down, the sad horns of a ballad in Spanish blaring from a car stereo.

Then she heard a key in the door. Again she sat up. They began to arrive—messengers Whitey had given keys to over the years. Lefty, who had seen the accident, told others, who contacted yet others. It was a small messenger world; word traveled fast. Some brought friends along. They came in and piled their bikes against the wall behind the door. Some Yurika knew, but some were from other messenger companies; some had gone back to school or moved into other lines of work like cooking or construction. They were all black or brown and most spoke a smooth mix of Spanish and English. They were sad and polite. Some recognized Yurika from the grocery store. They called her the Lucky Market girl, then after a while, just Lucky.

With each new arrival it became clearer to her that Whitey was really gone. Grief brimmed inside her. She could barely say more than a few words before tears ran down her cheek. Some messengers she met for the first time asked if she had been Whitey's girlfriend. They had been just friends, she told them, but they didn't seem to believe her. One husky, brown man with piercing blue eyes came up to her and put a thick hand on her back. His voice was like a rough stone.

"Yo, my nigga Whitey found a good woman."

His name was Samson, and he was the landlord's son. He assured her she could go on staying in the apartment, and as she began telling him that she didn't live there he cut her off. "Is cool." He said his father was right outside playing dominoes with the super, then someone called to him from across the room. "I'll take care of it," he said, and he walked away.

For an instant, she was confused. Could she really stay in New York? Could she pay rent? But the apartment began to fill, and she became distracted. The pile of bikes got thicker. There was beer, some harder drinks, cigarettes, and a few messengers passed a ceramic pot pipe painted to look like a bike wheel. They talked about Whitey and traded stories about his messengering and the times they rode with him. They picked up his books and passed them around. Yurika explained to Lefty and Righty, who had been among the first to arrive, that in Japan on the night before a funeral, the family of the dead held an *otsuya,* which translated into "through night." The family would cook and serve drinks to guests all night long while everyone remembered the person who had died. The slightly drunken brothers couldn't pronounce the Japanese word for this, but they could say "through night," and they staggered around clinking their bottles of beer with other people's bottles and cigarettes, shouting in drunken melancholy, "Whitey's through the night! Through the night for Whitey!"

Yurika felt the alcohol immediately, and her head began to get lighter. She had the feeling of her body moving automatically as she collected the empty beer bottles and emptied ashtrays. She was surprised that she was speaking to everyone who came, and even more surprised that she was introducing herself as Lucky. The pattern of conversation was easy to follow with introductions, then talk about Whitey. She didn't have to think very hard. In fact, her English seemed to improve dramatically the more she drank and smoked whatever was being passed around. Her sadness mixed with the comfort of easy conversation. She found out a great many things that Whitey had never told her and many idioms he had never gotten around to teaching her. She was "set straight" that even though Whitey was called Whitey, he was "one hundred percent" nigger, according to Lefty. On warm summer evenings, Whitey liked to "drop acid" with other messengers and "bug out" through Central Park.

"One fast motherfucker," said Tank. "Even trippin', man, he dropped my ass!"

Whitey loved speed, they all said. Some of the messengers had even encouraged Whitey to get into bike racing and maybe even get a sponsor, but Whitey would have none of it. When Yurika asked why, the answer was always the same. "He liked things his own way."

Voodoo told her about Whitey's family. According to him, they had made a small fortune doing some kind of business with the government. Whitey was the only person in his family who hadn't finished college. His sister lived in Washington, D.C., and was married to a military man who was bald and collected handguns. Yurika was surprised at how much he knew. He explained that he and Whitey used to loan each other books and talk a lot whenever they saw each other. Yurika watched Voodoo as he spoke and thought that in another setting he could be a teacher. He wore round, gold-rimmed glasses that contrasted nicely against his brown skin. His face was sturdy, square in shape. His voice was soft and intelligent, his smile easy. Plus, just like a teacher, he used his hands when he spoke, his long fingers pointing and splaying as he moved from one story to another. From him, Yurika also learned the idiom "black sheep," and she realized that she and Whitey had had that in common, for she was certainly the black sheep of her family. The thought made her cry again, and Voodoo gave her a roll of toilet paper that was being passed around.

"Whitey dug you," he said, trying to cheer her up. "He was always talking about you." This made her sob harder. She began telling Voodoo about how Whitey taught her to fix bicycles. Almost everyone was sitting on the floor, and many listened now as Yurika, in between sobs and the occasional laugh, talked about how she and Whitey had met at Lucky Market and how it took her a long while to understand Whitey's fast English.

"Yo," shouted Tank, " 'member dat time in the Rambles he had us all crackin' up?"

There were several raucous imitations of Whitey around the room. Righty stood up and began speaking so fast that spit flew from his mouth. Voodoo launched into a Whitey-style story about how his brakes weren't working and isn't that what happened to Che Guevara when he was motorcycling through Chile a couple of years before the revolution in Cuba, which was a big influence on the Beatles song probably because what song about revolution couldn't have Fidel in mind? He pointed at one person, then another, stretching his head this way and that, then acted out a revolution, turning his hands into pistols and shooting wildly around the room and finally shooting himself and falling back to the floor.

"Whitey!" everyone shouted, raising their drinks and smokes again.

More beer was bought, and cloud after cloud of smoke appeared and dissipated in the studio. Someone had brought in a boom box and put on a mix of hip-hop and Latin music. People began to dance. Yurika sat on the bed talking to Lefty and Righty. Lefty told Yurika about the accident and how Whitey had never seen the car coming.

"He flew like a motherfuckin' bird," said Lefty, moving his hand through the air, "and when he hit the ground, that was it. I think his neck broke."

They were silent for a moment, and Lefty shook his head. "I know why tha' shit happen, too."

"Word up, yo," said his brother, his eyes widening.

"You know Bone?"

Yurika nodded, surprised to hear his name. She kept getting flashes of his naked torso and his pubic hair, of all things, but was trying to keep these images from her mind.

"Mira," said Righty, pointing around the room, "that nigga ain't here, right?"

Yurika didn't understand and thought she was missing something. "They were friends," she said.

Righty and Lefty began talking at once. The two of them told her about Whitey coming into the messenger office a couple of weeks back, telling everyone that Bone and her were together the night before. Bone was so angry, Lefty said, and just that morning, had done something to Whitey's bike that caused the accident.

Yurika sat back, drew up her knees, and buried her face in her hands. Could Bone have killed Whitey? What had she done? She saw Whitey in the hallway outside Bone's apartment shouting train directions. She pretended that it would be okay. She wanted to believe it would all be okay just so she could be with Bone's skin, his smell. She could still feel her hands moving over his chest. If she had only known who Bone was, she could have just left with Whitey. Instead, she stayed. She woke up alone. She was attacked by a Russian. She almost burned down Whitey's apartment. The Japanese expression *jigo-ji-toku* came to mind—what goes around comes around, as Whitey sometimes said, and she realized that she had been a bad friend, plain and simple.

She reached into her pocket for the good luck pouch Daniel had given her. It was gone. Maybe it had fallen out at Bone's place or at the beach. It was just as well, Yurika thought. The paper just had "Hector" written on it, and the flower petals were falling apart. Anyway, the pouch lasted weeks longer than their time together.

A weight seemed to fall upon her as she collapsed into Lefty's shoulder, a fresh round of tears wetting his sleeve. To him and the others, this was further evidence of her love for Whitey, and they mumbled to each other, wishing they had a woman who would cry for them. Those who had heard about her being with Bone no longer believed it. They decided that Whitey must have gotten this wrong because he was jealous.

"See?" Wolf told Lefty. "Love mess up his mind."

Lefty lit a cigarette. "Yo, how could he know that shit?"

They all agreed that if Whitey hadn't caught Lucky and Bone together, he couldn't really have known. No one pressed Yurika for further details. They didn't ask if she had been with Bone or not, and no one mentioned Bone's ways with women. The fact was that they all had grown fond of her. They wanted to give her every benefit of the doubt the way they would for a messenger on the road the first day. Any mistakes were excused; it was just good to still be alive.

Yurika did not know what to say. She wiped her eyes and asked Righty for a cigarette.

"There you go, girl," he said, lighting it for her.

She took a long drag. She didn't want to tell them she had been with Bone. Still, maybe it was wrong to lie during an *otsuya.* Was it a lie if she didn't tell them something that she had done? She wasn't lying about Whitey, after all. When she thought of Bone now, she felt a dark cloud gather around her. What had he done to Whitey's bike? How could someone so beautiful be such trouble? The idea of him killing Whitey filled her with bitterness.

She pointed her cigarette at the front door. "Bone came to here before."

"What?" those around her exclaimed. "That fuck was here?"

Yurika told them about how Bone had arrived when it was still light out, how he had his own key. "He take Whitey's bike stand," she said, narrowing her eyes.

The messengers all began talking at once. They knew that bike stand because many had used it and remembered when Whitey got it from Bone. They argued for a moment about how many and which bike parts Whitey had given to Bone for the stand, but Yurika didn't understand what they meant. What she understood was that everyone knew it was Whitey's.

Yurika then learned about how all of them stole bike parts for Bone, that Whitey had been a part of this, too. She learned phases like "rip someone off" and "nab something."

Jesus laughed. "Whitey was fast strippin' that shit."

"Yo," said Righty, glancing sideways at him, "you know anyone who ain't?"

"Not like Whitey, man, no way." Jesus jerked his hands back and forth until they were a blur.

Everyone laughed. Yurika couldn't see Whitey doing this. They told her sometimes the messengers stripped in pairs. One watched out for police or bike owners while the other did the job. They had all stripped with Whitey because he was so fast that he would give them some parts to trade with Bone as well. In exchange, they greeted Whitey with coffee or a bagel in the morning. In stores, they treated him to his favorite apple juice and plums. Yurika nodded. Now she understood why they always seemed so generous to him. They were actually just paying him back for being a faster thief than they were.

Her eyes grew heavy; each time she blinked, her eyes seemed to stay shut for a longer pause. She watched the faces of the messengers around her. In the store, she had never really looked closely at them. Now as they sat next to her, they looked so different, not like tough messengers at all, but people who could be anything. Wolf, in fact, who still had his sunglasses on, looked much more wolflike. His jet-black, wavy hair swept up away from his narrow face, and he was darker than she had imagined, his nose smaller, his teeth longer and pointier. He could be a famous painter, she decided. A painter who might howl at the moon at any moment. She laughed.

"Check her out." Righty grinned. "She noddin' off, laughin', I like that."

She noticed, too, that Righty had much larger eyes than she had thought. He opened them unnaturally wide when he spoke so you could see large amounts of the whites of his eyes. Between his eyes and unshaven face, he looked a bit like one of those toy monkeys that played cymbals. This made her laugh, too, which made those around her laugh. She turned to Lefty, who was laughing the loudest. He looked much more devilish than she had noticed earlier, his features much smaller, sharper, his eyes darting back and forth as if constantly checking on what others were doing. He reminded her of the Iranian guys in Tokyo who sold pot and phone cards to her friends.

At some point everyone who had a key to the apartment took it out and told why Whitey gave it to him, then tossed it into the center of the floor.

"Fucked-up family," said Wolf, letting his fall to the floor.

Others dropped their keys right on top of his and everyone laughed.

Voodoo had gotten his key in case he ever wanted to have a new book to read. Tank had his so he could use the shower sometimes.

Lefty and Righty had a key so they could use the bathroom and keep a stash of cold beer in his fridge.

"Whitey good *pinchi* brother," said a short, round Mexican named José, who was now working in a nearby restaurant. He hesitated with his English but others encouraged him to talk on. "Four years ago, messenger." He pointed to himself. He held up his key. "For put bike here at night." He pointed to the corner with the stack of bikes. "Then I back to Bronx." Some applauded for the Bronx. José continued. "Then *no mas* messenger"—a chorus of cheers rose up—"now I cooking"—he laughed—*"mas* safety *para* me. Whitey say keep key." He shook his head, staring at the pile of keys. *"Buena persona."* He trailed off and dropped his key. People around him slapped him on the back and everyone raised whatever drink or object he was holding in his hand to toast Whitey.

When it was Yurika's turn, she roused herself and, in slightly slurred English, told them about Whitey giving her his phone number. The messengers liked that and high-fived one another. She explained that Whitey gave her the key at first because of family problems but later so she could learn about bikes. She also told them Whitey was a patient English teacher.

"Yo, what you learn?" Jesus wanted to know as he packed another pipe with ripe Guatemalan buds.

She told them some of the slang Whitey had taught her. In her tipsy state, though, she knew she was saying them wrong. "Bu-row my ten pound dan-gu-ring su-ram bacon, mazafaka!" A burst of laughter rose up from the messengers. Holding his side, in between gasps for air, Voodoo told her Whitey had taught her things that would make a messenger blush. Yurika searched for that phrase, the one that she realized she had used incorrectly once before, and tried to get it right this time. "Up yours!" she shouted, and the room erupted.

• • •

The noise in the room seemed to be coming from far away, from some muffled source. Occasionally, a word or two came across clearly. She sensed movement around her, but it was all too quick. Moving slowly, as if in a dream state, she believed she was wearing Whitey's messenger outfit—bike shorts and one of his T-shirts that read 100% PURE.

Whitey was suddenly sitting before her. The room was empty except for him. The bikes were gone. Empty beer bottles lay in a messy pile in the sink and stood on the floor next to the garbage. He wore a clean white T-shirt and bleached cutoff jeans, his skin smooth, totally free of pimples or scars and giving off a healthy glow.

He smiled. "Good soap and no white lawyers."

He asked if she was going to live there now. Yurika pointed to where she thought Samson had been standing. "He said okay for me." She looked at him. "Is it okay?"

He nodded.

She tried to concentrate, to fight her overwhelming desire to sleep because there were things she needed to tell Whitey, but it was so difficult to focus. The names of bike parts flew through her mind: axle, ball bearings, crank. She remembered the chain remover, the male and female parts of the chain.

Whitey put a hand on her shoulder. "Next time I'll have better skin." He laughed. "The teeth . . ." He shrugged.

Then he stood up. The room was filled with the faint light of early morning. Reaching into his pocket, he pulled out a gold key and dropped it onto the pile in the middle of the floor.

SEVEN

Kick Stand

Only one thing on that Saturday morning could have satisfied a hunger bordering on homicidal: banana pancakes. Marching down the street to the corner store, Suzie bought some pancake mix, two bananas, and syrup, then returned home. As she cooked, she ate some pitted black olives and small chunks of Parmesan cheese she had bought a couple of days before at an Italian deli on Main Street.

The warm, sweet smells made her salivate. She was glad Yurika was not yet there. No one could teach how to say the same thing five different ways on an hour's sleep and a hunger the size of South Korea. Plus, these days she was preoccupied with thinking about everything from the first two weeks of her teacher training. There were all these new people who had suddenly entered her life who didn't need manicures. The first day of class that she had missed seemed like a long time ago. Her nerves had seized up. The thought of being in front of a class made her completely nauseous and gave her a slight fever. All day long it was bed, bathroom, but never beyond. She called the school to tell them, and they were very understanding. The next day Suzie mustered the energy to get herself dressed, fed, then to class. There were fourteen other students, ages ranging from a few years younger than her to one retired woman moving into a second career. Suzie was the only Asian, the only nonwhite person. People seemed surprised when she opened her mouth.

"You speak such good English," the guy who sat next to her said during a break, as if he'd never met an Asian American before. Each time she talked to a different classmate she had to explain how she had come to the States at the age of five. Yes, she was bilingual in English and Korean. No, she didn't have any serious language troubles when she began school. Yes, she had been back to Korea for visits. And yes, she loved kimchi.

In two more weeks, when the class finished, one student was on his way to Rotterdam to teach junior high school students. Another student was going to a university in Istanbul and another to a government-sponsored program in Tokyo. Suzie was one of the few who did not have plans to teach overseas. She was intimidated by the other students' worldiness and their academic degrees—B.A.s, B.B.A.s, M.A.s, M.F.A.s—it was another world from Number Thirty-two red nail polish and almond-honey scrubs. When she told people she was a manicurist, it tended to kill conversation. "Oh," was all they said, their voice rising as if suddenly recognizing her from their neighborhood nail salon.

In class, she lost her self-consciousness. She became completely absorbed in the material. In the mornings, the class went over different approaches and exercises for teaching grammar, speaking, listening, reading, and writing to each level of English-language learner. She studied her two teachers' moves, copied down their jokes. In the afternoons, the class broke into small groups and each member taught twenty minutes of a lesson to either beginning, intermediate, or advanced students. It was terrifying and thrilling, and Suzie threw up only occasionally in the mornings. In the last hour of the day, the trainers would give them feedback on their teaching. Both teacher trainers said that Suzie had a great advantage by being Korean because students, especially Asian ones, identified with her. They also assured her that she moved through her lessons smoothly. But, they said, she had to try to relax, speak louder, move around more, and make more eye contact.

It was strange to make eye contact with her students, though, because she was looking at a fifty-year-old Polish man, an eighteen-year-old Russian girl, a middle-aged Colombian woman, a bookish Chinese woman, and a handsome young Croatian guy with huge blue eyes, among others. These were people Suzie had seen before in a kind of abstract way around the city—working as cab drivers, in delis, on the subway—but she had never really *looked* at them. They were immigrants as her father and Hyun Jeong had been twenty years earlier. Like Yurika was becoming. Perhaps because of this, there was something that felt like home the first time she walked into a room full of people with accents. It was familiar and gave her a measure of confidence.

She thought of her cousin. The girl was taking Whitey's death hard. She had all but stopped smiling. Tears welled up in her eyes constantly. She didn't eat much. She spent a lot of time alone at Whitey's place and visiting with some Thai woman she had made friends with from the store. Suzie and Yurika usually met at an East Village café after school ended. While she would babble on about the students in her classes, Yurika would stare out the window or down at the table, her eyes brimming with tears, then say something like, "I miss him." She had gotten rid of the pigtails and dyed her hair black, letting it hang wherever it landed, so her eyes were often obscured, which gave her kind of a mod look. Any day, she was supposed to move into Whitey's place, but that had not happened yet. Some evenings, Suzie helped Yurika pack up Whitey's things, which was slow going. Whenever they found pictures, they sat on the floor and looked through them. There was one rubber-banded thick pile of old photographs from Whitey's childhood and teen years. It was amazing to see him before his skin had gone bad. He was a cute little boy with bangs and a slightly surprised look on his face. Most of the pictures were from Whitey's trips—a beach in Thailand, a sunset in Morocco, a flamenco dancer in Spain—and mostly he wasn't in them except when he'd gotten someone to take a picture of him in front of a monument or with a new friend.

Yurika spent nights at Whitey's place. She was trying to get in touch with Whitey's parents but without success. She had left three messages, and they still had not called back. Quick Service had notified them about Whitey and had told them that Yurika was going to pack up his belongings, but they had not called yet and didn't seem to be home when Yurika phoned.

In light of Whitey and what Yurika had to do, Suzie felt guilty for feeling so excited about her class. She couldn't help herself. It *was* exciting. When the course was finished, she could teach anywhere and imagined herself in far-flung places where the temperature never dropped below cozy and a beach was always nearby. There were a lot of good beaches in the world. South Pacific Islanders probably needed English. People on Bali no doubt needed it for tourists. What was the native language of Tahiti? Did the men wear sarongs?

Reaching into her dressing gown pocket, she pulled out a small bottle of Kahlúa. It had an old, familiar taste. Lately she'd been craving it again—maybe it was being back in school; the smell and taste of the stuff always reminded Suzie of high school. How many of those little darlings had she gone through then? A nip before geometry, another before social studies. It made wasting all that time bearable. Plus, then she could suck on mint candies during classes. The teachers thought she was so cute with her little candies. Share with the class, they would say, and she would—Kahlúa at lunch and mint candies afterward.

My God, thought Suzie, that was seven years ago. She poured a little Kahlúa on her pancakes before adding the syrup. Then she brought them to the table and dug right in. It was heaven. Sweet and squishy in the middle, a bit more well done around the edges, the bananas just chewy enough. You could smell their warm sweetness before each bite. She sighed. For a moment, she imagined what it would be like to live in that house by herself—or even if it were just her and her father. He acted less pussy whipped when Hyun Jeong wasn't around. Good word to share with Yurika, she thought, returning to the counter for a pen and piece of paper. "Pussy whipped," she wrote, and then, "don't be such a pussy" and "no pussyfooting." She imagined teaching that set of vocabulary and gave a laugh. Drawing a little doodle of pubic hair around the word "pussy," she wondered if her standing man liked oral sex. The thought had occurred to her before. She would have to find out. Her insides tingled at the possibility. She could see herself standing with one foot on the toilet seat and one foot on the toilet paper dispenser.

She dripped a bit more Kahlúa on her pancakes and wondered if her cousin just needed a bit more proper sex—but from someone other than Bone. Yurika had told her about seeing him at Whitey's place. Too bad he turned out to be so psycho. In general, Suzie thought, sex with him did wonders for the Japanese in her. It helped her relax. Her Korean side could use a bit more, too, because that half seemed full of bad temper and strong opinions. A kind of schizophrenia, really, the Korean side saying whatever popped into her head, arguing with people, talking back, and the meek and polite Japanese side always thinking of what others might be feeling, what she should or shouldn't say. No wonder her parents sent her away. How was anyone like that supposed to get along in Japan?

She stopped chewing. Her skin tingled. She froze, her hands flat on the table. It was a Saturday; this wasn't supposed to happen when she wasn't teaching. She leapt up. In the bathroom, she fell to her knees before the toilet as she lost it all—pancakes, cheese, olives, bananas, even Kahlúa.

. . .

Yurika found her cousin lying on the couch in the living room looking miserable as she filed her thumbnail. Pancakes remained unfinished. She had deep lines and dark circles beneath her eyes. A little bottle of Kahlúa sat on the table, and Yurika could also faintly smell the stuff in the air. Her cousin's hair was up, but it looked like an abandoned nest with small strands sticking out here and there. The ashtray on the coffee table beside her was full of cigarette butts, one still smoking.

"There you are," said Suzie with a weak smile as she tossed the emory board on the table.

"What's happen to you?" asked Yurika as she lowered herself into the armchair. "You look so bad." Yurika reached for one of Suzie's cigarettes and the lighter.

"Smoking?" Suzie asked, surprised.

"So stress," said Yurika, lighting up. She said she had found cigarettes at Whitey's place and sometimes had one as she went through his things. She thought of how she also liked to smoke at Riya's apartment, but she didn't mention this.

They sat silently for a moment, each dragging on a cigarette. Suzie lay back down and blew smoke rings into the air. Yurika looked down at the Kahlúa and ashtray again and wondered what was going on with her cousin. Standing man? This all seemed too much to be just about him. There was an expression she had learned from Whitey that was good to use now, and she tried to recall it. She waved a hand around the table and toward Suzie.

"How come you so beat?"

Suzie smiled at her cousin's English, then exhaled loudly. She looked hard at Yurika for a moment. "I think I'm pregnant."

Yurika blinked at her cousin, unsure she understood.

"You know 'pregnant,' right?"

Yurika nodded, but she couldn't believe it.

"Well, that may be me."

Questions flew through Yurika's mind, but they were an impossible mix of Japanese and English, and she wasn't sure they were all questions. She could hear Whitey saying over and over, "Holy shit!" and she wanted to scold her cousin for her standing man and her Indian man and her Rastafarian who liked to do it from behind. Instead, she asked Suzie if she was sure. Suzie shrugged.

"There's no way I'm staying like this." She pulled another bottle of Kahlúa from her dressing gown pocket, unscrewed the top, and held it in the air in a toast. *"Campai,"* she toasted in Japanese as she took a swig.

Yurika wiped the sweat from her forehead. The day was growing uncomfortably hot. She sat back in the armchair, looking at Suzie and exhaling loudly. The conversation she had had with her uncle weeks earlier came to mind. Yurika was unsure how to bring up the subject of Suzie's real mother, so they hadn't spoken about it yet. She looked at Suzie and tried to imagine her with a baby on her hip, a cigarette hanging from the corner of her mouth. She considered an even scarier possibility: Hyun Jeong raising the child. And then she had a scary flash of herself pregnant with Bone's baby, and she was filled with horror.

"Don't look at me like that," Suzie said.

"Just I'm thinking."

Suzie shook her head. "That I should keep the kid, stop smoking, quit drinking—"

"No, no." Yurika thought of Suzie's real mother and then her own mother, who was probably getting ready for bed just then, placing her slippers neatly in the corner of the *tatami.* Japan seemed so far away. If she stayed in New York, would her parents visit? Would they call? Would she ever tell them about Whitey? Would she ever find out how the two of them met? Riya had seemed to know but wanted her to find out from someone else. She turned to Suzie. "Do you know how my parents met?"

Suzie was getting used to her cousin being preoccupied and the non sequiturs that she came up with since Whitey's death. "Yeah," she replied with a smirk. "Your dad dumped my real mother for *your* mother."

Dump. The word was familiar. She saw a truck emptying tons of black dirt on an open hole in the ground in front of her parents' apartment building in Japan. Whitey had talked about office workers and store owners dumping on messengers. It was negative. Her father did something negative to Suzie's mother because of her own mother. Hurt. Break up. Her father and Suzie's real mother? A clearer idea began to form as her eyes widened in surprise.

"I know all about my mother," Suzie went on. She explained that one rainy Saturday when she was twelve years old, she had been going through Sang Jun and Hyun Jeong's things. Grabbing Yurika by the hand, she pulled her cousin into her parents' room and threw open the door to the walk-in closet, crawling to the back. In another moment she pulled out a dusty dark blue cardboard box. Yurika lowered herself to her knees as Suzie removed the top, shuffled through some papers, then produced her real mother's passport, Suzie's own birth certificate, a color photo of Suzie as a baby with Jon Eun in a hospital, and a death certificate, which Suzie translated for her cousin. Even sick, her mother was a beauty, thought Yurika. Suzie had her eyes, chin, and lips. Hyun Jeong, Yurika thought, barely looked at all like her sister.

She put everything away except for the picture. They returned to the living room as Suzie finished the story, often glancing at the picture. Jong Eun and Yurika's father had been dating seriously at their university. Then Yurika's mother came on the scene as an exchange student.

"They lost their shit for each other," Suzie went on, enjoying the look of surprise on her cousin's face.

"Love?" Yurika asked.

Suzie nodded. "He followed her back to Japan."

Yurika was amazed. Was Suzie making up the whole thing? How could that passionate young couple be her parents?

Suzie lit another cigarette. "My poor mother." She sipped some Kahlúa. "She was heartbroken."

Sang Jun, as it turned out, had been in love with her from the moment they met outside of economics class. But she was with his brother.

"No brother," Suzie went on, "no problem." A shadow passed over Suzie's face as she stared at the picture of her mother. "No one knew that she was already sick."

Yurika wondered what her parents did when they found out about Jong Eun's illness. Did the brothers talk? she asked Suzie, but Suzie only shrugged. What she knew was as much as she could get out of her father over the years. Since she found out about Jong Eun, though, she had stopped calling Hyun Jeong *Umma* or Mom and stopped listening to anything she had to say.

"I can't stand her."

Yurika sat back in her armchair. That was when they stopped being a family, she thought. Thirteen years ago. Same house, same food, same water. Nothing else. Thirteen years. That's why the house felt so heavy sometimes and so empty at others. It was maybe why Sang Jun and Hyun Jeong practically lived at the store at times. She watched Suzie light another cigarette and stare out the front window. Her will was too strong, Yurika thought. And now, at twenty-five, she was still living there. She thought of all the things she had learned about Whitey at the *otsuya,* and now seeing Suzie differently, like it was the first time she was really seeing her, a kind of motherless daughter who could be a mother herself. Yurika shook her head. There was more going on inside a person than could ever be noticed or even understood from the outside.

"Why are you still live here?" she asked.

Suzie tapped her cigarette over the ashtray. Her answer was disturbingly simple but very New York. "Free rent."

Sang Jun was in one of his quiet moods as he thought about Jong Eun. He smoked, and he watched Riya drawing, her dressing gown hanging nearly open. She liked drawing him when he got this way because his face took on a Clint Eastwood kind of look—jaw tight, eyes narrowed, lips straight with a touch of menace.

"You look like real tough guy sometimes," she told him, pressing a finger to his lips. "Maybe I put your picture in a post office." She showed him the red pastel drawing.

Sang Jun thought he looked like an old man, his cheeks hollow, his eyes sagging. Would Jong Eun think he looked old these days? What would she look like? Riya, it seemed, was the only thing in his life keeping him young. For a moment, he wondered again if she had a young, American lover but quickly put the thought out of his mind. He was making things up, he told himself, when there were other problems, real problems to face. His niece. His daughter. His wife. He dreaded having to be at the store on a Saturday, but he knew Suzie liked to have the house to herself. Of course, she never told him that, but she seemed a little friendlier when he saw her on a Sunday or a Monday, and he liked to imagine her upstairs in the house, planted in his armchair drinking or smoking or whatever she liked to do, the TV on, no parents around.

Riya came over to him and scratched lightly at his scalp. "What's inside your brain today?" She pulled gentle fistfuls of hair. "More quiet than usual."

He put his cigarette in an ashtray and put his arms around her, lowering his head to her shoulder, exhaling loudly. She was surprised by this but only rocked him gently, scratching the back of his head.

He was like a big, wordless boy sometimes, she thought, who liked to smell her neck and fill the area of her collarbone with small kisses. She closed her eyes, nuzzling closer to him, sliding a hand down the back of his T-shirt.

They didn't usually see each other on Saturdays because Riya often had a class somewhere, but Sang Jun had called earlier. He sounded tired, almost troubled. She scratched his back lightly, and he let out a gentle groan. It was not a sound of pleasure. It was like he had a clogged chest, like there was something hiding in there or was stuck, so she decided to perhaps look for that something. Naked people spoke more truthfully than clothed ones. Slowly, she pulled off his T-shirt and looked him in the eyes. They looked angry, confused, though still wordless. She sat back and slid her robe from her shoulders. For a brief moment, he sat looking at her, breathing hard, his nostrils flared, his eyes glancing over her body, her face. She stood up and dropped her robe to the floor, raising the corners of her lips as she turned away, but he grabbed her arm and pulled her down to him.

Riya liked when Sang Jun felt so strong inside of her. She gripped his shoulders as she raised and lowered herself on top of him. Maybe it was all the garlic in his diet or the *soju* he drank, but he could keep it going longer than most any man she had been with.

She didn't know how he could stand his wife. Whenever Riya saw her at Lucky Market, she smiled, but the woman was cold, cold, cold. How could he have possibly married the sister of his true love and bear to see an uglier version of her face every time he looked at Hyun Jeong? She stopped moving, opened her eyes, and grabbed his face in her hands.

"Look at me," she commanded. His eyes remained closed as he pulled her closer. She gave him a shake. "Open your eyes." He did. "Keep them open," she said as she moved on top of him again.

Sang Jun lowered her to her back, all the while staring into her eyes. They were beautiful eyes, large and clear, and they reminded him of Jong Eun. Riya, of course, was wilder, but her body was long and languid like Jong Eun's. Her eyes smoldered; she was having a hard time keeping them open. Gasping, she opened her eyes wide as she thrust her hands into his hair. He moved slower in her now. She narrowed her eyes and slid her hands to his bottom. Her lips parted, a faint smile on them. Sang Jun wondered why he didn't keep his eyes open more of the time. Her face at such moments became the kind of image that would keep him warm during winter nights at the store or the next time he came into his bedroom late at night and heard Hyun Jeong's snoring.

A bud of a thought suddenly flowered in him: a life without Hyun Jeong. Suzie was old enough. He could give Hyun Jeong money and send her back to Korea with some job to do, say it was temporary, that he would have to watch the store, and of course she would never come back, and he would just have to keep sending money. He felt the adrenaline rush into his body. It was time, he thought, as he felt his insides erupt. It was time, he wanted to cry out as he opened his eyes wider. It was time, he almost shouted out as he pressed down, letting out a groan that shook the bed and made Riya tremble beneath him.

Yurika glanced around the room in panic. Where were her Ultra Man figures? Where were all her magazines? The bike pictures on the wall? She went through her drawers, looked under the beds. Anything that had been outside the drawers was gone. Yurika glanced at her cousin. Suzie covered her face with her hand and shook her head.

"It was her." Suzie sighed, explaining that earlier in the week Hyun Jeong must have gone on one of her cleaning sprees. "She cleaned *out,* not up."

Yurika pulled her hair back from her face and grit her teeth. "My money."

She ran upstairs as Suzie followed, back into her aunt and uncle's bedroom. Images of Hyun Jeong cluttered her mind. Her going through Suzie's cosmetics. Her pestering questions. She must have found the money. That's why there had been some missing weeks back. Opening drawers, she rifled through her aunt and uncle's underwear and socks, shirts, and pants.

"What are you doing?" Suzie asked, amused, as her cousin ransacked her parents' room.

Yurika explained about the money in the action figures as she went through drawer after drawer.

"That's what those were," Suzie mumbled, joining in the search. They went through everything in the room, under the mattresses, and even inside the framed wedding picture and the one of Suzie at the age of six dressed like a princess for Halloween. When they were finished with that room, they checked the bathroom—shaking the half-filled jars of Tiger Balm, looking behind and inside and beneath the lime colored septic tank, in the medicine cabinet filled with bottle after bottle of generic aspirin Hyun Jeong bought on sale. In the kitchen, they pushed aside bags of Cheez Doodles and half-finished pound cakes, looking through the refrigerator and even the garbage. Finally, they returned to the living room to check every corner of the brown wall-to-wall carpeting for hiding places, beneath furniture, inside cushions.

The Ultra Men were gone. The money was gone. Suzie fell back to the couch, exhausted. Yurika paced the living room, trying to think of where that woman would be keeping her money. She imagined her aunt standing behind the counter, smiling her phony smile at customers, being very pleased with herself and already planning how she would spend the cash. She wondered what Riya would do in such a situation, then headed for the stairs.

Suzie sat up and asked where she was going, but Yurika was already reaching for the door when she called back, "The store."

Daniel couldn't bear the smell of Tiger Balm. He avoided Hyun Jeong as much as possible and tried to get José to do the shelf stocking near the register. But José was on to him and went outside to cut flowers. The smell was bad for business, José told him and Daniel agreed. That woman—*La Loca* they called her when she went overboard with the Tiger Balm—she was bad for business, too. They had noticed that over the summer she began taking less and less care of her looks, her ponytail a bit sloppier, her face pale.

La Loca seemed so agitated. She kept mumbling to herself in Korean between customers and patting her pant pockets like she was keeping some strange rhythm to herself. The energy around her was like a television stuck in between stations. The customers didn't seem to want to stay very long in the store when *La Loca* was behind the register. Today was particularly bad. Occasionally, a short line would form and, more than once, a customer was watching *La Loca* one moment, then decided to get off the line and put things back.

To the customers in the store that afternoon, the cashier seemed particularly ornery. She answered their questions with choppy one- or two-word answers. She handled the merchandise roughly. A few regular customers smiled and said thank you, trying to get some warmth out of the woman, but there was nothing except a slight scowl and English that sounded forced and irritated. They much preferred the girl, but she usually didn't work on Saturdays. The cashier seemed only to get more sour when someone asked where the girl was. When another customer seemed to leave because of her, Daniel took a deep breath and went up to the register.

"I can take register?"

"No, no," Hyun Jeong began, "oh, *sí, sí,* come, I look for Mr. Song."

She walked out on to the sidewalk. It was a sleepy Saturday afternoon. First Avenue was empty. She glanced up and down, looking for her husband. He said he was going to visit some of the other Korean markets in the neighborhood. They all did that a few times a month. With him, though, one cigarette always led to another, and he was always late coming back. Lazy man, she thought.

The rolls of bills felt full in Hyun Jeong's hands. She had one in each pocket. In the left were yen, and in the right were dollars. They were right at home there. It's where they were supposed to be from the start. When customers entered the store, she resented it because she had to stop touching her money.

The girl's stuff was gone, and Hyun Jeong was glad to be rid of it. If she was not going to come home at night, her toys and magazines shouldn't be taking up valuable space in the house. If she wanted to act like a stranger, she would be treated like one. Strangers didn't keep their things in that house, Hyun Jeong thought. She didn't care what her husband or brother-in-law might say.

She wanted to go shopping on Fourteenth Street to price a tiny transistor radio she could listen to with an earpiece, a new cordless phone, a palm-sized automatic camera with a zoom lens. She had enough to buy or put a down payment on any number of things, and the thought made her feel strong.

Sang Jun was glad his wife had left before he arrived back at the store. He stood outside the store smoking, a slight grin on his face. She had gone shopping, Daniel said. That was fine. Sang Jun needed time to work out the details of his plan. Why would he need his wife to go to Korea? Why wouldn't he go himself and leave her to watch the store? In the past, they had gone back together only to visit family, and he took care of any business things himself. He could tell her he slowly wanted to make the store more Korean and needed her to do some investigating. That might appeal to her. She loved the police shows on TV and always tried to figure out the endings before they were over. She could investigate the shops in Seoul for things that their usual Korean importers didn't carry. She would have to look hard, he would tell her, and it might take some time. Of course, she would do nothing. Once she was there a month with his money and no work, there was no way she would come back. Sang Jun was sure of this.

The heat was getting worse. He leaned against a parking meter. A truck was unloading produce for a restaurant across the street. Maybe he could tell her he was thinking of opening a restaurant. He imagined himself in a dark green suit, greeting guests, and he was completely immersed in this fantasy when Suzie and Yurika walked up to him. He turned around, startled. Suzie never came to the store, so he immediately knew something was wrong. And why was she there with her cousin?

Yurika had been practicing what to say on the subway ride. Suzie had helped her choose words that were clear and direct. But the more Yurika thought about her money, the angrier she got. She needed that money now to pay rent. Her words mixed with bits of slang she had learned from Whitey and other messengers.

"Bitch rip me off," she yelled.

Suzie explained it to her father in fast Korean. He couldn't believe it. It was true he didn't trust Hyun Jeong to do the books for the store, but he couldn't tell the two girls that. She was his wife, and without real evidence he would have to stand by her. Their conversation got more heated, and Suzie and Yurika pressed him. Yurika told him about catching her aunt going through Suzie's makeup. Suzie reminded him of past times they had both caught her listening in on phone conversations or when she had steamed letters open or was caught in some ridiculous lie about what had gone on in the store. The more of these things she could recall, the angrier she got, and the louder she got, until she was yelling at her father, and he had to insist that they go inside the store to talk. This only made Suzie more angry. Sang Jun grabbed her by the arm and walked down the street as Yurika followed. He tried to appease her in a soft voice and in Korean, saying that it was true a lot of wrongs had been committed, but she was not a thief.

Suzie pulled away and stopped walking. "She's worse!" she shouted in English. Several passers-by turned around.

Sang Jun suddenly felt weak and wanted to crumple onto the sidewalk. Backing away until he was leaning against a car, he let his head fall into his hands. Suzie was speaking Korean now, her voice sharp and bitter. It was amazing, she was saying, that that imbecile and thief could even be her aunt. From the rear pocket of her cutoff jeans, she pulled out the picture of her and Jong Eun, waving it at her father, asking if *she* would have wanted Hyun Jeong to be her mother. He couldn't look at the picture. He couldn't look at Suzie either. She had asked him the same question so many years ago when she had first found out, and he hadn't given her an answer then. Now it seemed that all he could do was feel the blood draining from his limbs.

It was then Yurika spotted Hyun Jeong coming down the street. She moved toward her. Suzie and Sang Jun glanced over at Hyun Jeong walking toward them carrying a bag from a nearby electronics store, her eyes narrowing at them as she approached.

"Where my money?" Yurika asked. "My stuff?"

Hyun Jeong's face flushed as she pushed passed her. "I don't know your thing."

Sang Jun and Suzie followed the two of them into the store. Hyun Jeong motioned for Daniel to move from behind the counter, and she stepped up and stuffed her bag beneath the register. Yurika kept asking where her money was. Suzie and Sang Jun were talking to Hyun Jeong in Korean, their voices loud and agitated. He was asking what was going on, and Suzie was accusing her of stealing money.

"You talk to your mother that way!"

"You're not my mother," Suzie shot back in angry Korean.

Hyun Jeong grew hysterical at this. "Who fed you and dressed you? Ungrateful wretch!" She grew increasingly shrill as she asked why they were all attacking her when all she ever did was cook and clean and take care of all of their needs.

Customers who were in the store looked up from their shopping. They had never heard an outburst coming from Asians, not even in Chinatown. They were all talking at the same time, one in English, the rest in Korean. The woman behind the counter was clearly being accused of something and she was getting very worked up over it, raising her voice and pointing at the young woman speaking English.

"Jae Hee takes advantage of all of us," Hyun Jeong yelled.

"You look through Suzie stuff also," Yurika said, following her own line of attack.

Sang Jun moved closer to the counter. "Where are the girl's things?"

"How can you accuse me?" Hyun Jeong was red in the face now, her lips twitching as she spoke. "What do you want from me?" she cried. "Do you want my money? My things?" She reached underneath the counter and pulled out her purse, opened it and emptied the contents onto the counter. Coins and credit cards and bills fell out, half spilling to the floor. She threw the wallet at Yurika's face.

"Fuck!" Yurika shouted as she lunged at her aunt. Suzie grabbed her and shouted, *"Do la suh yo!"*

Hearing Suzie call her crazy was more than Hyun Jeong could bear. She reached from under the counter and pulled out her bag from the electronics store. "Crazy!" she shouted in English. "Sure crazy!" Ripping open the bag and the boxes, she hurled a transistor radio then a new phone to the floor, where they shattered. Then she began breaking up the Styrofoam they came in and throwing that to the floor.

The customers who were in the store had left. Sang Jun, Suzie, and

Yurika stood in a stunned silence as Hyun Jeong came from behind the counter and kicked debris at them. She raged on in Korean. None of them cared about what she had to do in a day, she cried. They were all selfish. "It never ends!" Her face was completely red now. "Enough!" She covered her face as her whole body shook with uncontrollable sobs.

Sang Jun put a hand on Hyun Jeong's back and slowly moved her toward the back of the store. He nodded to Daniel to take the register. Suzie and Yurika stood in the center of the store for a moment, staring at Sang Jun and Hyun Jeong's back. Suzie stopped Daniel just before he went behind the counter.

"Hang on," she said, moving to the register and pressing the sale key. "It's okay," she told Daniel. The cash drawer opened and Suzie lifted up the edge of it. She removed a hundred-dollar bill and from the bill slots she took another hundred in twenties.

"That should do it," she said. Then she tore off part of a receipt and, grabbing a pen from the counter, wrote, "$200.00 stolen by Hyun Jeong." She put the piece of paper into the cash drawer and closed the register.

"Here," she said, handing Yurika the cash. "Keep it in your wallet."

"Is it okay?" Yurika asked, wide-eyed, glancing at Daniel, who only shrugged.

"I've always wanted to do that," Suzie said, moving her cousin toward the door. "Let's split."

Daniel watched the two leave. He sighed and shook his head. José was already sweeping up the mess on the floor. Daniel got a garbage bag and began throwing out the radio and phone shards scattered across the floor.

Bone felt a bit broken. The day before he had ridden a hard thirty miles before breakfast, then had gone to work. On this Saturday, he skipped breakfast because Righty and Lefty stopped by for some bike business. They said they had needed to take a break because of Whitey. Others, they said, were coming over later as well. Sunlight streamed through the open windows, reflecting off the bike parts scattered around the room. The three of them stood for a moment in an awkward silence, each thinking of Whitey. Righty fingered the strap on his messenger bag. Lefty rubbed the back of his neck and readjusted his bag. Bone tapped an Allen key against his palm.

"He's gone," Righty finally said. "Can't believe it."

When these two came with parts to trade for repairs it was always on a Saturday and always together, even if only one of them needed something. This time it was Righty who wanted to take off his rear wheel and derailleurs and finally use a fixed-gear wheel. It was cleaner for work, Righty said—no freewheel cog, no gears, no brakes—he was sick of cleaning all that. Plus, he went on, track bikes looked cooler even if it was harder on the legs.

"Esta, bro," he said, slapping his brother's arm. "The wheel turning, my legs turning. Is beautiful."

It was beautiful, Bone thought, until it rained or you had to stop suddenly. He had been riding a fixed gear until Freddie got killed on one. Righty knew all about that, though, so Bone didn't say anything. Righty would be another cool-looking messenger getting fucked up as the cartilage in his knees turned to dust after a season of work. After all, Righty was getting old for this business, too, maybe almost thirty. That's about when Chain moved behind the desk with his neck arthritis and his knee with metal pins.

Righty was hoping to trade Bone his own rear hub for a fixed gear. As Bone dug around in a box of hubs for one, Righty said it was impossible to strip a fixed gear from a bike unless you wanted to take it from the wheel of a messenger's track bike. He shrugged. "They're the only ones riding that."

Bone nodded, but he remembered the time Whitey took ten seconds to cut one right out of a wheel, not caring whose it was.

"Yo, I'm a get a fix gear one day," said Lefty.

Righty slapped him on the back. "You gotta learn to ride first, bro." He turned to Bone with a laugh. "Check him out, this *culo* on a fixed gear?"

Bone smirked and shook his head. Lefty could barely ride a straight line when he had the choice of twelve speeds. It was amazing he had lasted as long as he had on the street.

"But Bone, man," said Lefty, "maybe a straight block, then."

Bone couldn't help but laugh. He was talking a racing freewheel now with a narrow range of gears meant for one thing only: speed. In his prime, Chain had ridden a straight block. Bone used a straight block now. Whitey had done a subfifteen-minute lap around Central Park with one. He shook his head. *"Mira,* you ain't got legs for that shit, yo."

"Listen to the man," Righty added, "you gonna make yourself old soon." He turned to Bone. "Just lace me up a fine wheel like you did for Whitey."

Bone glared at him. Whitey must have told all of them about the wheel he was getting. Him and his fucking mouth. Righty was examining a brake pad on the worktable. Lefty was checking out the prices of used frames hanging from the ceiling. It was like business as usual, but Bone wanted them to leave. All night and morning, he felt restless, like there was an itch moving around under his skin that he could never quite get at. He didn't want to see any messengers, but he was relieved to have some semblance of normal business again. He didn't want to think about Whitey or the wheel, but the two stayed paired in his mind.

Once three years earlier, he had been riding north on 9W, just past the New York State line. He was doing thirty or so as he began a descent with a turn in it, the road a blur beneath him. For a split second he imagined crashing, then something twitched or shifted on him—a shoulder or a knee, he couldn't remember—and less than a heartbeat later he became an avalanche of flesh and bike.

Why was he thinking of this now? He was feeling out of control and didn't like it. So he tried to keep his mouth shut and his focus on the work. There were just too many damn distractions.

Wolf took a long drink from his bike bottle, which was full of malt liquor. He wanted new brake cabling. Voodoo needed a new chain. Bone glanced at their bikes against the wall, then at the two of them. They looked ragged. Both were still in their messenger clothes, still wearing their bags. They said they had stayed out riding and drinking all night then took a nap in East River Park.

Their talk returned to Whitey. Lefty began describing the accident again, and everyone but Bone listened closely as if it were the first time. Bone didn't want to hear it—he didn't need to—and he started lacing up Righty's hub with spokes while the four went on behind him. He had been imagining the whole scene just as he always imagined Freddie's death. Whitey was dead, and all their talk wasn't going to change that. Lefty was saying how Whitey didn't even see it coming because he was leaning forward down the left side of his bike. He slapped his hands together, then sailed one through the air to show how Whitey flew in an almost perfect arc. The other messengers shook their heads.

"Damn," Voodoo whispered beneath his breath.

"Driver's probably back home just chillin'," said Wolf.

"Word," Righty high-fived him. "Another fuckin' biker down."

They traded stories of drivers who had done them wrong—the Indian cabbie making a turn from the middle of Sixth Avenue, the delivery truck that stopped short on Eleventh Avenue, the Jersey driver not staying in one lane down Second Avenue. They laughed about the way Whitey used to speed by drivers who had cut him off and whack the trunk or hood of their cars with his bike lock.

Bone had taught Whitey that move, but he remained silent. He had also taught Whitey the fine art of shattering sideview mirrors with a U-shaped lock, riding by and using a good underswing. A thousand uses, he used to tell Whitey about these locks. Bone hated repeating stories or the same catchphrases over, but that one about the locks was a good one. With these guys, it was the same stories over and over. He had heard about Lefty's Jersey driver for weeks now, and each time the driver got a little wilder and Lefty a little bolder. With Righty, too, every story was a new opportunity to wag his tongue a bit more and bulge his eyes a little wilder. He even laughed hard at his same old jokes.

"You talk a lot of shit," Bone mumbled at them without looking up or turning around, "lotta *mierda."*

The conversation stopped and everyone turned to look at Bone. He was adding nipples to the ends of spokes. Righty looked at the others, then at Bone, who still hadn't turned around.

"Why you gotta talk like that, yo?"

Bone turned the spoke wrench, making a creaking sound. "I talk whatever I motherfuckin' want in my place." He could feel the blood rush to his face.

"But why you gettin' all up like that?" asked Righty. "Everybody pissed about Whitey—"

"Mira." Bone swung around and pointed to the door. "Take it outside so you can talk all the shit you want."

Righty put his sunglasses on but didn't move for the door. The four messengers fell silent and glanced at each other. Wolf slipped his hand into his bag and put it around the rounded part of his bike lock, feeling its cool steel against his sweaty hand.

It was like a damn open house, Bone thought. Tank and Jesus had also arrived for tune-ups, but they had to leave their bikes outside the apartment. The two of them had brought some very new parts they had stripped just that morning—a pair of touring pedals from Tank and a set of Campagnolo shifters from Jesus. The two of them looked like hell also and still wore messenger bags.

Bone's only comfort was that he was starting to get into the rhythm of that morning's work. His hands began waking up when he got to the trueing stage of Righty's wheel. There was no need to think then because his hands knew what to do—how many clockwise turns of the spoke wrench for the wheel to bend one way and how many counter-clockwise turns to bend it the other way. His restlessness slowly lifted as he felt the strength in his fingers, which began to be covered with black spots of new grease.

The six messengers were talking and occasionally looking over at Bone working. Without any of them ever saying it, this was one of the reasons they didn't ever just drop off their bikes and pick them up when they were fixed: they liked watching him work—the precise, knowing motion of his hands, his eyes focused like a hawk's. His hands seemed to know each bicycle the way some know a lover's body—every curve and hidden place, how much tension to apply in one place, every sound that rose up from each part.

Wolf watched Bone and thought about Whitey, how Bone had given Whitey that new wheel, then stole his girl, just like that. Moved right in. He sipped from his bike bottle. Bone was taller than him, and he had those long arms that always reminded Wolf of thick brown snakes. What kind of woman would say no to a taste of that? Compared to Whitey especially, with those teeth like unshuffled playing cards and skin like half-eaten pizza. Wolf shook his head and turned back to the others.

"Yo, 'member dat time Whitey tried using some kinda skin lotion, and he come in smellin' like hippie shit?"

They remembered. It was early spring and Whitey was telling everyone that he was on a mission to improve his skin. Chain kept telling him to quit smoking and drink two quarts of water a day, but Whitey liked cigarettes too much and didn't want to be peeing at every drop he made during the week. So he tried some homeopathic remedies that dried his skin until it was pink and itchy. For a week, he walked around looking like one of those freak hairless animals, his skin raw, angry, and exposed. Then he found some patchouli moisturizer that he applied liberally, not realizing how strong the smell would be. The messengers and dispatchers in the office were sick with the smell of him all day.

Bone listened now as he was finishing up Righty's wheel. The motions of his hands reminded him of Whitey's wheel, and again he thought of the spokes that were still in his messenger bag. Nobody dies from missing some spokes. He pictured Whitey leaning forward on the left side of his bike to listen for a problem, the car smashing into him, and his body flying through the air.

The voices of the other messengers began to irritate him again. They sounded loud and stupid, a bad combination. He spun around and threw a spare spoke at them. "Yo, I told you, if you talkin' shit, take it outside." He nodded to the door.

Tank was trying to spin his bike lock around his wrist, and he stopped and shrugged. "We just talkin' 'bout Whitey."

Bone pointed at him. "You want a tune-up?" Tank nodded. "Then shut your fuckin' *culo,* man."

A silence fell in the room as Bone returned to his work. The messengers looked at each other, at the floor, out the window. Then, slowly, Lefty slipped his messenger bag from his shoulder. With the strap in his hand, he held it midair. It swayed slightly. He glanced at the others. They turned to him and each let a hand slip into his own bag. Lefty turned to Bone and let his bag fall to the floor.

Wolf swung first. His bike lock hit Bone on the side of the head, knocking him down. The others were upon him instantly with their own locks, just as they had planned during the early morning hours of that day. Bones that had been broken from past bike accidents were broken again—ribs, a collarbone, an elbow—and new ones were shattered on Bone's face, his pelvis. Blood began to smear the wooden floor where the messengers' feet stamped and kicked at him.

No one said a word. Their minds were speeding. They beat him for whatever he did to Whitey's bike that got him killed right in front of the office. They beat him for sleeping with Whitey's girl and stealing Whitey's bike repair stand. They beat him for the times he had talked down to Whitey and each one of them. They beat him for the times he dropped Whitey or one of them when they wanted to ride next to him. They beat him for not being unconscious yet, for still trying to put up a fight. They beat him for all the bike parts Whitey and they had stripped for him, for the terrible need they had to use him just as he used them, to have another day to ride, to deliver envelopes and packages to people who wouldn't even look at them or give a nod or a smile in an elevator. They beat Bone because they wanted to and because they could. Mostly, they beat him because he was alive and Whitey was dead. Then they stopped almost as suddenly as they began, out of breath, sweaty. They gathered up their bags and bikes, took Whitey's bike stand, and left Bone on the floor, a mangled, whimpering mess.

EIGHT

Lucky Song

It was on a misty Tuesday evening that Yurika finally finished packing up Whitey's things. She lay on the floor, still occasionally crying, imagining an iceberg melting inside of her. Whitey's belongings were in boxes around her, each labeled accordingly: books, clothes, personal things. There were actually only a couple of boxes of clothes and a couple for personal things; the rest were full of books that Yurika would have kept, knowing how much Whitey loved to read, but the thought of endless pages of English was more than she could bear. She thought of Voodoo, who used to share books with Whitey. Maybe he would like them. She decided to keep Whitey's T-shirts with their impossible English, and the bike tools, as she thought he would have wanted her to have them. In fact, she could hear Whitey telling her to keep everything and throw out what she didn't want, that his parents wouldn't want anything of his.

"You don't know," she whispered. "Now is different time."

"Call them and see for yourself," Whitey was telling her.

"Always I try," she said, stretching her arms into the air, "but no answer."

Actually, she dreaded ever having to use any English on the phone. You couldn't see the person's face and eyes, so half of the communication—maybe more—was lost to her. Words she might otherwise know became a bizarre new vocabulary. Riya knew about this fear of hers and sometimes called her at Whitey's so she could practice speaking English on the phone. That helped for sure, but in the past few weeks, when she needed to transfer Whitey's gas and phone billing to her own name, using the phone had been torture. Between the automated systems that could not slow down or explain vocabulary and the live operators she could sometimes reach who were mostly unhelpful, she finally gave up. She found their offices in the phone book and did her business in person. It seemed like affording the rent would be the least of her problems.

During the day, she would practice what to say to Whitey's parents. Suzie had told her that when someone died, you could usually say you were sorry even though it wasn't your fault. You could say half of the conditional phrase, "If there's anything you need," with the second part understood as being, "let me know" or "I can help." Yurika didn't know how she could help and was worried that if Whitey's parents needed something, she wouldn't understand and would make them uncomfortable by having to explain themselves.

"That's okay," Whitey was saying, "they never listen anyway."

This was little comfort to Yurika. She thought of Bone and wondered if he was also a bad listener. The more she thought about him, the more surprised she was that they had so much sex and so little talk. He never showed her anything about bicycles the way Whitey had. They never chose the parts for her bicycle that he never made for her. Her own lust for him was surprising and disappointing. It was so easy to have sex, so difficult to talk. She still tingled at the thought of his bare brown bottom cupped in her hands but forced the image from her mind.

She was beginning to lose herself in a reverie about Bone's body when the phone rang. Yurika sat up and stared at it. Her first thought was that it might be him calling to apologize. Her heart pounded in her chest.

"You gonna answer it?" Whitey asked. "Maybe it's them."

Yurika had disconnected Whitey's answering machine because she was too embarrassed about her own speaking to leave her own message and it was too creepy to have his voice tell people to leave messages. But now she wished the machine were on so she could—what had Suzie called it—"screen the call." She slowly reached for the receiver and brought it to her ear without saying anything.

"Hello?" an older man's voice said. "Hello?" He sounded a little annoyed.

"That would be my father," Whitey said. "Don't worry. He always sounds bothered."

"Ah, Mr. Pitt?"

The voice got louder. "This is Jim's father. To whom am I speaking?"

Yurika had never heard a voice like that in English. It was like something she imagined from an old movie—deep and strong, slow and so clear. She imagined an old man in a black suit sitting at a dark wooden desk, spinning a globe. Plus, he used the word "whom," which Suzie told her was not really ever used in speaking except by people who were overeducated or pretentious. Yurika had seen pictures of Whitey's father. He was tall like Whitey, with slightly bulging jaws, a small chin. To her, he looked like he could be a past president of the United States—very white skin, very straight posture, serious eyes.

"Don't let him scare you," Whitey said. "Speak up."

Her stomach tightened and her mouth went dry. "This is Whitey—ah, Jim. Friend of Jim."

"Yes, I know all about you, young lady."

She was about to say she was sorry and offer help but he cut her off.

"That's fine, Yoko," he said. Yurika didn't even have time to correct him before he went on. His voice became signals—neutral, even signals with barely a trace of feeling. He didn't sound like a man who had just lost his son. He wasn't asking her any questions because there were no pauses in his speaking, no voice rising at the end of sentences. Occasionally, she caught some words like "mother," "Mrs. Pitt," and "no need." Yurika felt sad. His tone of voice reminded Yurika of her own father—distant, practical, disappointed.

Finally, Yurika understood that there was no need to send Whitey's things to Virginia.

"Is all that clear?" asked Mr. Pitt.

Yurika nodded. "Yes." She could sense he wanted to get off the phone, but she couldn't resist asking her own questions. "Just a moment." Grabbing her electronic dictionary, she frantically looked for the translation of a word. "Where is Jim *interred* now?"

"He's in our family plot," replied Mr. Pitt.

She asked him to spell that last word, and he did so, sounding quite impatient, and as he went on, perhaps describing more, she quickly punched the letters into her dictionary and it gave her back the Japanese word for "plan," *takurami.* Yurika hit the return key. The Japanese word *suji* came up next—"story." The third one, "small piece of land," *jisho,* finally made sense.

"So that's it," he said finally, adding in an almost cheerful tone, then said good-bye and hung up.

She put down the receiver and suddenly felt very alone. Whitey was really gone. She moved her hand over the cool surface of a cardboard box labeled BOOKS. Maybe she would keep all of them after all. Whitey's silent friends. His roommates. Maybe they had secrets to share about Whitey, more stories to tell. Could she even read one of his books? Maybe she could just keep trying until she found one she could finish. Start with something that looked easy. The thought of reading made her sleepy, though. Plus, she kept hearing Mr. Pitt calling her Yoko. Would he and her father get along? She and Whitey might have had more in common than she had guessed, but now she would never know. She closed her eyes and rolled into a ball on her side.

Voices outside the apartment spoke in Spanish. They were lively and punctuated with laughter and the occasional clap of a pair of hands. She recognized the deep voice of Samson, the landlord's son. One of her new neighbors. She would have only new neighbors now. Spanish speaking. English speaking. No Japanese. No Korean. No family. Couldn't she stay rolled up in a ball? Wouldn't someone tell her when it was time to go home?

Her friends in Kawasaki would still be asleep even though it was midmorning there. She had told them she would call them, and they had said the same, but for a whole summer no one had called anyone. They were far away, and she knew she was not part of their lives anymore—their endless meanderings through Tokyo. Was that all over for her? Would she miss them?

As Yurika lay there, a distant memory emerged. She was seven years old in a little yellow school uniform with a matching hat. Her class was on a trip to see the Kamakura Buddha. A yellow puddle of schoolchildren on a train platform. One of her friends spotted a Western couple, a young man and woman. Word quickly spread through the class and soon everyone was glancing over at them and giggling. Even the teachers couldn't help themselves. The foreigners looked totally different from Japanese. Their eyes were impossibly huge, their height amazing, their hair full of waves and curls and the color of the sun, their noses huge, their skin so coarse and white. The whole class trip was transformed from that moment on. Once they got to the Buddha, everyone paid attention only to the Western tourists who were there and not the four-hundred-year-old Buddha. The *gaijin*. The foreigners. That's all anyone talked about at school. Their pale skin. Their huge noses.

Yurika had wondered what they ate in their huge homes. If they watched Ultra Man on TV. Her parents explained that they ate lots of hamburgers and hot dogs, and they ate spaghetti without the slurping noises Japanese made with noodles. It was then they told her about

Sang Jun's family living in New York, and Yurika asked if they could visit. One day, they said, one day when she was old enough, they would all go together. But they never had. The Songs had visited them in Japan once for two days, but they hadn't brought Suzie.

Yurika doubted if her parents would come visit her. She grabbed the phone and dialed their number. Hearing the Japanese-style ringing—lighter, more of a series of short beeps—she could easily imagine the off-white table her parents ate at, the pastel yellow walls, the smell of good rice. She glanced at her watch. They were at work, of course, their Wednesday morning, so she quickly hung up. In a few days, Yurika thought, she would try again.

Sitting up, she tore open one of the boxes and began reading aloud the names of Whitey's books. *"Dza Auto-bio-gu-la-hy obu Ma-ru-co-rum X, On Dza Load."* Maybe, she thought, she would be able to get through some of these after all. She had a sudden pang of excitement. It was like she was unpacking her own stuff in her own apartment.

Then she uncovered Whitey's journal. Somehow, she and Suzie had overlooked it when they were packing. It was a tattered spiral-bound notebook with silver duct tape holding the cover on. She leafed through the pages. Whitey's handwriting was nearly illegible. In one sentence, the words would slant to the right, then to the left; some of it was in script and some was printed. Many hands could have written it. She looked closely at one page. A word here and a word there she could make out. The rest might have been written in another language altogether. Some of the letters reminded her of the words she saw written on the Russian storefronts along Brighton Beach Avenue. Turning another page, she saw her name written in large black letters, slightly stylized so that the top of the *Y* became handlebars, but the rest of the bike was incomplete. She traced the lines with her fingers and thought of Whitey's kissing her on the street. Then she closed the journal, rested it on her stomach, and lay back with her eyes closed.

She thought of a story Whitey had once told her about a bike trip he had taken one summer from Seattle to the Grand Canyon. After biking twenty-five hundred miles, he sat on the rim of the canyon for days. He barely moved except to get food and water to bring back to the edge of the canyon, and then he just sat, ate, and listened to the stillness. One day his eyes were following the edge of colored rock along the canyon walls. He looked to the eastern rim, then the southern one far away at the horizon, then the western one, then along the cliff toward himself. He was so absorbed that when he was finally staring at the tips of his own toes, he didn't notice them. For an instant, the boundaries between himself and earth had dissolved. He had become just another piece of the earth.

Yurika wondered if she would ever live in New York long enough to arrive at a moment when she wouldn't recognize herself. How would her eyes change? What color would her hair be? What clothes would she be wearing? She couldn't imagine. Instead, she saw Hyun Jeong in the store cutting vegetables in the basement kitchen, mumbling to herself in Korean. She saw Sang Jun posing for Riya, a cigarette dangling from his lips. She saw Bone when he was still a nameless messenger to her, flying up First Avenue. The other messengers stood before her in the store, flirting as they lingered with their sodas and snacks they had just purchased. Suzie sat before her at the breakfast table, her eyes dreamy with the memories of men she had been with. And there was Whitey. He was pedaling on the front of the tandem the evening he and Yurika had toured Central Park. He was pointing at something and turning around, telling her to look, over there. Yurika turned and saw a young schoolgirl in a yellow uniform looking at her. A little Japanese girl. She giggled and pointed at the funny-looking *gaijin. Yes,* Yurika thought as her fingertips moved down her face, *look at big eyes and mouth so big speaking English.*

• • •

Suzie was in her favorite club thinking of her next lesson with Yurika. She had learned a great pronunciation drill based on the fact that the letters *l, d, t,* and *n* had more or less the same tongue position. Wearing her black cowboy boots and a black minidress, she stood with her back to a speaker, repeating, "la, da, ta, na, la, da, ta, na." Even though she couldn't hear herself over the music throbbing against her body, there was comfort in the pressing of her tongue behind her front teeth.

People danced around her. One guy asked her to dance, but she smiled and shook her head. This was the place Suzie had first begun her wordless encounters with standing man. They had tried to speak but couldn't hear each other and gave up quickly. He led her to a door labeled Emergency Exit, down a flight of stairs, through a corridor to a bathroom, and into the stall of her wildest dreams, where distant music pounded as she had wrapped her legs around this man's brown body, his hands and long arms pulling her toward him without a word.

Where was he? She swung her tiny purse back and forth in front of her legs. By midnight, she began to feel stupid, standing there, her thong moist from her excitement like that of a feral animal. Her head was beginning to ache from waiting. It was Saturday night. Where was he? She didn't know where he lived or what his phone number was, not that she would have called, but not knowing only added to her frustration that moment. There had been some Saturdays she had shown up and he hadn't. Why, she wondered, did this have to be the case on that particular Saturday? She wanted to lead him down the staircase of their mutual lust and down the corridor to the rest room, the Fuck Room, as she sometimes thought of it. She wanted to turn it into the Eat Me Room, the Blow You Room. Maybe he was down there already. She stepped away from the speaker and began weaving her way through the crowd, feeling eyes following her as she moved.

Glancing behind her as she made her way to the emergency exit, she noticed for the first time the warning written on it, saying an alarm would go off if the door was opened. She went through and down the staircase. The corridor seemed darker than usual, and for a moment she thought she heard voices coming from somewhere farther on. She froze and listened carefully. There was nothing. Pushing open the door of the rest room, she stepped inside. It was much dingier than she remembered, but then again, she had never looked closely. Mustard paint was chipping everywhere. One lightbulb hung down from the ceiling on a wire. The window was open. The smell of urine wafted up from the alleyway below. Suzie felt her stomach knot, and she had to take a deep breath so as not to get sick. Her boot heels clicked against the tiled floors as she walked to the sink and glanced in the tarnished mirror, making small adjustments to her hair, which was partly in a bun, except for a few choice tendrils trailing down the back of her neck. She looked good. Standing man was missing out.

It was then the first cramp doubled her over. She made her way to the bathroom stall and sat down, dropping her purse to the floor. The pain seared across her belly, causing her to gasp and bite her lips to stop from screaming. She was pregnant, and it was the baby. She was losing it. Lifting up her dress, in the dim light she could see that the moisture she had felt between her legs was actually blood. Another cramp coupled with stabbing pain, and she leaned forward, gritting her teeth. Her head felt lighter and lighter, and things began to spin as her mind grew jumbled and confused, believing one moment that she was at home, then another back in high school smoking in the girls' room as the class bell rang louder and louder until there was only ringing piercing the air and wrapping her body in a band of pain.

Yurika was the first called. She had fallen asleep trying to read *Hiroshima,* which she had chosen because it was so thin. The ringing of the phone seeped into her dream and became an alarm warning that the city was about to be bombed. Yurika sat up and for a second could not remember if she was in Kawasaki or New York.

She grabbed the phone. *"Moshi-moshi*—ah—hello?"

A nurse had found her number in Suzie's purse. Yurika had a hard time understanding what the woman was saying and had to ask her to speak more slowly. She grabbed her electronic dictionary and felt embarrassed to ask for the spelling of a word. Suzie had a miscarriage. A lot of blood was lost, but she was safe now and sleeping. After getting the address of the hospital, Yurika thanked the nurse and hung up.

She sat with her back against the wall and looked around the room. Now what? wondered Yurika. She called her aunt and uncle. They were both home. Hyun Jeong answered the phone, but she handed it directly to her husband when she heard Yurika's voice. Yurika could hear her talking in the background. Sang Jun was having a hard time understanding what Yurika was saying. He was shouting into the phone. He didn't know the word "miscarriage" either, so she kept it simple. "Suzie's in hospital."

Hyun Jeong refused to go. That sexpot of a girl had accused her of stealing money and practically disowned her as a mother. There was no way she was going to the hospital in the middle of the night for a visit.

"She's still your daughter," Sang Jun insisted.

Hyun Jeong gave a laugh. "She's not my daughter." She went into the bedroom where she grabbed the picture of Suzie in her princess costume. "This was when she was my daughter," she exclaimed, slamming the picture to the table, shattering the glass.

"You agreed to be her mother." Sang Jun swiped his arm across the table, sending the picture and glass to the floor. "That means always."

Hyun Jeong crossed her arms and shook her head. "Now it's different."

"You have to come," Sang Jun insisted.

Hyun Jeong kicked the frame across the kitchen floor. "Her mother died when my sister died." She kept talking and wouldn't stop when her husband tried to interrupt. Wake up, she was telling him. It was a good idea at first. Little girls needed mothers. But this little girl became a little devil, and all she did was torture them.

"I'm glad she's finally learning a lesson," Hyun Jeong concluded, slapping her hands together. "Let her rot. And her cousin, too." Then she began on their niece and Sang Jun's brother, his kowtowing to the Japanese his whole life, taking their name—what kind of a last name was Uda anyway?

Sang Jun stopped listening. He sat at the kitchen table and stared down at the fragments of broken glass. They looked like little, sharp pills, and he imagined force-feeding them to Hyun Jeong to stop the grating sound of her voice, to close tightly her narrow, small eyes and small ungenerous lips. He thought of Riya, the quiet and peace he felt after they had made love and she was drawing him as he smoked. Rising from the table, he walked into the bedroom, Hyun Jeong following, asking why he hadn't moved to Japan years ago when his brother had asked him to.

"Why not?" she kept asking. "And what was wrong with Korea?" She followed him into the bedroom, then out again, reminding him how he had fallen apart after her sister died, how all of Korea had become such a mausoleum to him that he had to flee across the ocean so he could try to forget Jong Eun.

Sang Jun swung around and slapped her. She let out a wail and ran into the kitchen. She threw open the cupboards and pulled all the dishes from the shelves, crashing them to the floor along with the cups, glasses, jars of pickled onions. Sang Jun watched and listened to the mayhem coming from his wife's mouth and hands. He grew calm, lucid. Slowly, methodically, he picked up his pillow, then went to the walk-in closet and removed the blue box that held the only things of Jong Eun's he had taken with him from Korea. Leaving the bedroom, he walked down the stairs as Hyun Jeong was tearing into the refrigerator, throwing everything to the floor. He walked into Suzie's bedroom, which was now half bare without Yurika's things. He dropped the pillow on the bed that had been his niece's, then placed the blue box on the nightstand. Leaving the room and closing the door, he walked down the short hallway to the door. Then he left for the hospital. Upstairs, Hyun Jeong had started on the kitchen furniture, scolding the chairs as she broke each into pieces.

Suzie spent a full day at the hospital and was released and told to rest. She was determined not to miss her last week of classes, so come Monday morning, she nearly fell asleep during a lesson on conditional clauses. Sentences like, *If you hadn't been drinking so much, you would still be pregnant,* passed through her minute-long dreams.

On Monday afternoon, the two cousins sat in their usual café. Yurika watched Suzie closely. She was surprised at her cousin, who acted as if nothing had happened. Suzie looked tired and a little depressed, but Yurika had seen her worse after one of her club nights. When Yurika asked her about the miscarriage, Suzie was very matter-of-fact.

"It was like the worst period cramps you can imagine," Suzie explained as she spooned some tiramisu into her mouth. "It was for the best."

Yurika didn't understand that expression. Suzie explained. Talking about English seemed to give her energy. She waved her spoon in the air as she spoke. Yurika was struck again at how, in English, you could use an expression that sounded so nice for something that was supposed to be so bad. Suzie came up with other expressions that were negative but could also mean something positive: the word "bad" to mean "good," for example, and "the shit," which meant the best.

Yurika remembered that one from Whitey when he talked about bikes. Columbus SL tubing was the shit. Campagnolo components were the shit. At the store, she still expected to see him walk through the door. When she looked out the window these days, it was to imagine Whitey riding by, not to look for Bone. Whenever she heard English that he had used, she thought it was his way of saying hi. As she restocked the cigarettes and aspirin, she told him about her days—her modeling at Riya's, the messengers she saw at the store.

Sang Jun caught her talking to herself on more than one occasion and worried that another woman in his life was having a breakdown. Since he and Suzie were roommates now, he asked her about her cousin one evening. Suzie was doing her homework, and he was reading the paper when he suddenly looked up. "What's happen your cousin? Now she so strange."

Suzie told him Yurika would be fine. Having her father in her room was strange. In the twenty years they had lived in that house, the times he had actually passed through the doorway were limited to when plumbing problems had arisen. There were no social visits. Now, in the evenings at least, he was a fixture. He brought home some kind of take-out food. They ate in the room, each on a bed. Then he read the paper while she did her homework.

Upstairs, Hyun Jeong was left alone. They went into the living room or the kitchen only when they knew she was asleep. Mostly, Hyun Jeong lay in bed and refused to speak to anyone. Sang Jun ended up confiding in Suzie about his wife. He had a plan to send Hyun Jeong back to Korea. Suzie politely listened but decided she would believe it when and if it actually happened. To her surprise, he actually went through with it. After Hyun Jeong had spent nearly a week in bed, Sang Jun appeared at the door of his former bedroom with a white, business-sized envelope. Hyun Jeong was sitting up in bed staring straight ahead into the mirror on the bureau. He walked over to her side and sat down. She slowly turned to look at him, her eyes smoldering with disdain.

"I brought you something," he said, handing her the envelope.

She took it in her hands but didn't open it.

"Look inside."

Hyun Jeong fingered the edges of it. She didn't need to open it because she was sure of the contents. Silently, with all the concentration she had been able to muster, she had willed Sang Jun to do just what he was doing at that moment. In fact, she had envisioned all of this, down to the size of the envelope. A smile crept across her lips. He was so weak, she thought. She could make him do anything. She could hear the TV judge say again, *You get what you pay for.* Well, she had paid with twenty years of her life—to him, to Suzie, to the store. She hadn't wanted to marry her sister's husband in the first place. It was his idea, then her parents had pushed her into it. Now, it was his turn to pay. This would be part of her pension. She turned the envelope over in her hands and felt its thickness. Unable to resist, she quickly tore it open. Inside was a one-way plane ticket to Seoul leaving the next evening and fifteen hundred dollars in crisp hundred-dollar bills.

"I'll send that much every month," Sang Jun said, rising from the bed. "Your family will be glad to see you." He waited for a reply and when there wasn't one, he moved for the door. "I'll take you to the airport."

"Don't bother," were the last words Hyun Jeong would speak to her husband.

By the time Sang Jun was ready to leave for the store the next morning, a hired town car was waiting outside the house. Suzie and her father stood in the doorway as Hyun Jeong, dressed in a navy blue pantsuit she wore on special occasions, rolled one large suitcase to the car. Sang Jun tried to help her, but Hyun Jeong just waved him off.

Suzie watched Hyun Jeong. The woman would not look up at her or her father. Suzie kept waiting to feel something herself—relief, sadness, anger, excitement—but nothing came. She called out a good-bye, but Hyun Jeong's face remained expressionless and unchanging. The woman would not look at them—not as she stood beside the car while the driver put her suitcase into the trunk, not after Sang Jun told her in Korean to have a safe trip, not when she got into the car and it slowly pulled away.

It was only when the car stopped at the light at the corner that Hyun Jeong lowered her window. Of course no one had apologized, she thought. How had she put up with so many years of their ingratitude? Never a thank-you for this delicious breakfast or lunch or dinner. Never any praise because the house remained clean day in day out. She should have left years ago, Hyun Jeong thought, after Suzie found out about Jong Eun. Carefully, she peered out because she imagined Sang Jun and Suzie might still be standing there. But, of course, they had already gone.

They were upstairs in the house. Rays of sun filtered through the living room blinds and stretched into the kitchen. Without speaking, Suzie put on some rice and tea water. Sang Jun took out a Tupperware container of Hyun Jeong's kimchee from the refrigerator and transferred it to a bowl. He handed Suzie a pair of chopsticks. They sat at the table together eating. Sang Jun asked how her teacher training was going. Suzie told him about the class, how she planned to look for teaching jobs when it was over and cut down her nail salon hours. Sang Jun nodded. They sat quietly for a few moments, eating.

Suzie looked at her father. He looked older than his fifty-three years. The skin around his eyes seemed heavier than it used to be, making it hard to see as much of his eyes as before. She took another piece of kimchee and could really taste the full flavor of garlic and chili. "Well"—Suzie smiled—"at least she made good kimchee."

Sang Jun nodded but couldn't speak because his mouth was full. In spite of this, Suzie could see the edges of his mouth slightly turned up into a smile.

• • •

After Hyun Jeong's departure, Yurika's responsibilities at the store doubled. Daniel often took the register while Sang Jun showed her how to check inventory, how to place new orders, where to file invoices, and how to make kimchi and other small, prepared foods. After a particularly grueling day of cutting vegetables, she realized why Hyun Jeong depended on her Tiger Balm. She also began to understand how much Hyun Jeong used to work between the shop and the home. Yurika returned to Whitey's place and fell into a deep sleep.

She dreamed that she and Whitey had just ridden around the park on the tandem bike. It was a beautiful evening, the sky azure, the moon full, "like a mountain bike wheel," said Whitey. They decided to go back to Flushing on the train. Exiting the subway car onto the Main Street station platform, Whitey pointed to the floor.

"See all the black spots?"

Yurika looked down. Sure enough, the ground was covered with old pieces of gum that had been stepped on by countless commuting feet. She had never noticed them before; they were everywhere—black spots the size of silver dollars.

"Watch this." Whitey grinned.

The spots began to vibrate, then spin around. Suddenly they began to dart this way and that from one side of the platform to the other in every direction. Whitey was conducting their movement, a bike pump in one hand like a baton. He laughed at the chaos swirling beneath them as he lifted both hands into air. The gum spots began to move uniformly around them then, forming a huge wheel with spokes, with Whitey and Yurika as a hub. Yurika grinned as the whole configuration of gum spots began spinning around them.

"The bicycle," Whitey intoned as he outstretched his arms, "is perfect love."

• • •

After that dream, Yurika saw bicycles parts everywhere. Traffic lights became green, yellow, and red bike reflectors; street lamps—crank arms, manhole covers—free wheels. Her vision was full of bicycles. The very thought of them made her happy for the first time since before Whitey's death. Often, she found herself thinking of all the components filling Bone's workshop—the bins full of seats, the frames and wheels on the ceiling like a hanging garden of chrome and alloy. She recalled their sex in his workshop: the smell of bike grease like some kind of mechanic's aphrodisiac, holding on to the wheel trueing stand with him moving behind her as she looked up to the frames of red, blue, and gold while her body vibrated with heat, trembling muscles and nerves.

At the store the morning after her dream, she realized what she needed: she was going to turn Whitey's apartment—her apartment—into a bike workshop. This so excited her that for a moment she forgot how to use the register. She stared blankly at the keys while her mind filled with images of the apartment with bike parts hanging from the ceiling. The first person she told her idea to was Voodoo. She hadn't seen him since the *otsuya* and was glad he was back at the store. It seemed so long ago that he had stood before her with the news of Whitey's death, but it had been only a couple of weeks. He wasn't dressed for messengering. Instead of bike shorts and a T-shirt he wore a pair of jeans and a deep green button-down Hawaiian shirt. On his feet were sandals instead of sneakers. She remembered her impression of him from the *otsuya* and thought that now he looked like a young teacher on vacation. The only problem was that he looked more tired than she had ever seen him, with dark circles under his eyes, his face unshaven.

"No bike?" she asked.

He shook his head. "I quit."

Yurika was surprised. She didn't think any of them ever quit. "Too tired?" she asked.

Voodoo shook his head and frowned. He rested his hands on the counter and stared at her for a long moment before shaking his head. There was a sadness in his eyes, Yurika thought, something heavy. He blinked and looked away. "Long story." He told her he was working with his brother, delivering mattresses. He could see Yurika was puzzling with what that meant but didn't feel like explaining. "And *you,*" he said, waving fingers toward her head. "Your hair's black again."

Yurika felt a pang of missing Whitey because he used to tousle her hair. She glanced to the back of the store, blinking, then turned back to Voodoo. "I have story, too," she began. "Actually—from dream."

She told him her idea. "I want make like Bone's place," she said.

Voodoo looked away again. She was surprised that he wasn't more excited about this. He stared outside, his eyes darting side to side as traffic passed. When he spoke, it was in a distracted monotone. "I got Whitey's bike stand for you."

Yurika looked confused and once again Voodoo leaned forward onto the counter, leaning on his hands. "Also a long story." He took a step toward the door and asked if she would be at Whitey's that evening. Yurika nodded. "Maybe I'll tell you later," he said as he turned and left.

Voodoo was determined to do something good for the girl. It was his way of making up for what he had done to Bone. Chain had told him that Bone was in the hospital and had just been moved from the critical care unit. Besides the bone breaks and fractures, he had suffered from internal bleeding and nerve damage. Even before he had found this out, though, Voodoo had barely slept. Every time he closed his eyes, he saw Bone's broken and bloody face, his twisted body on the floor of the workshop. He knew it was monstrous what they had done. He knew this even before Righty had come up with the idea and the messengers were all wishing and fantasizing about something of that sort—something swift and brutal. Still, whenever Voodoo thought of Bone, he wanted to watch him suffer. But it was done. The question for him was how to balance the scales again without having to see the man again—if that were even possible.

He and his older brother, a round man named Raphael, arrived at Yurika's in a van. First they moved Whitey's boxes to the corner of the apartment where the messengers had stacked their bikes the night of the *otsuya.* Then, much to Yurika's surprise, they replaced her mattress. Voodoo had made a mental note of the charred corner the night he was there with all the other messengers. At first Yurika protested, but they wouldn't accept this. Then she bowed to them and thanked them again and again as they carried it into the space. They then unloaded Whitey's bike stand along with a power drill and a case full of tools, a few dozen hooks and the anchors to hang them from the ceiling, wood to build a worktable, and a vise grip that they planned to install on one edge of it. They also brought a few bottles of red wine and some Cuban sandwiches Voodoo had bought at a bodega in Hunt's Point.

Yurika was amazed at how different the brothers looked and sounded. She could not understand a word of Raphael's English. He spoke quickly and under his breath, with only a vowel here and there punctuated with what sounded like a curse. When he laughed, she could see gaps between his teeth, which were yellowing. His eyes were set deeply into his brown face. He never looked her in the eye and didn't speak to her directly.

Voodoo told her to relax and start on the wine and food, so she sat on the floor, sipped from the bottle, and opened a sandwich of roast pork, ham, and cheese. She was thrilled about having a workshop. The neighborhood kids and adults could come to her with their busted chains and squeaky brakes. She wondered how she could get hold of spare parts without paying too much for them. Certainly, there would be no messengers stealing parts for her, if she could help it. Taking another drink of wine, she tried to figure out why she was also feeling so uneasy as Voodoo and Raphael worked. She looked at the bike stand. What long story of Voodoo's explained how he got it back? Was it connected to him quitting messengering? She glanced at the front of the apartment. Bone had stood in that doorway, holding up the bike stand like a baseball bat, ready to swing it. He would not just give it back because Voodoo had asked. The more wine she drank, the more she thought this made sense and the more she could see the heaviness in Voodoo's face. Even though he was working, talking, and occasionally taking a swig of wine, she started to think that something really bad must have happened between Voodoo and Bone.

"When do you see Bone?" Yurika finally asked when the brothers finished putting the hooks in the ceiling and sat down for a break. She pointed to the bike stand. "Why he give to you?"

"He didn't," Voodoo replied. "I took it." Now he was the one who didn't look her in the eye. He glanced up at the hooks in the ceiling. He looked at the floor.

Raphael mumbled something and Yurika began to wonder if he were speaking English at all. She decided to find out, so she turned to him. "Do you know about Bone?"

He nodded. "Nigga couldn't keep his shit together," he said, glancing at his brother. "That's all I know."

Yurika was surprised to understand the words but couldn't get the meaning of all of them. She looked at Voodoo.

He exhaled loudly then spoke slowly. "Had a little run-in with Bone."

Yurika imagined a gang of messengers chasing Hector through the streets. "Running?" she asked.

"Run-*in,"* Voodoo repeated, lowering his voice. "A fight."

Raphael let out a laugh and drank some wine. "Mess his motherfuckin' ass up good," he said, wiping his lips.

A smile crept across Voodoo's mouth.

"So," Yurika began, unsure if "fight" meant argument or violence, "you stop messenger work after fight?"

Voodoo took a long drink of wine, then passed the bottle back to her. He explained that he didn't feel safe anymore. For the first time since arriving, his voice rose. "Like I said, it's a long story." His eyes grew wild. "If I ride again, something bad's gonna happen." He shrugged. "That's why I'm Voodoo—I believe that shit."

Yurika could hear Whitey saying, "What goes around comes around." *Jigo-ji-toku,* she thought. Voodoo looked exhausted, his eyes sagging. She didn't want to tell him that something bad was already happening to him. Instead, she pressed him for details.

Voodoo shook his head. He didn't want to talk about it. He hadn't spoken about what happened with Bone to anyone except Raphael, and then it was just to say they had kicked the shit out of the man.

"Yeah, man," Raphael said, "details, *por favor."*

"I know Bone not such good person," Yurika said. "But"—she searched for words—"we hung out sometimes."

Voodoo nodded.

"So," Yurika continued, "I wanna know."

Voodoo was drinking more now, his eyes darting from his brother to Yurika. "There was a fight, and he lost," said Voodoo, wiping his mouth. "Nothing else to say."

Raphael, who knew some of the messengers, asked in between swigs of wine if Tank was there, if Wolf was there. Voodoo closed his eyes. He clenched his jaws. Yurika asked if Bone was still working. Then other questions from his brother. Voodoo could still feel the bike lock in his hand and the swing of his arm, the impact against Bone's face, his skull.

"You wanna know?" Voodoo's dark eyes shot open and looked wild. He laughed and blinked at the two of them, waving his hands around as though to catch some words to use. He was a little drunk. "There were six of us." His voice rose as he shook his head. "You shoulda seen his face." He told them the story from the beginning, when Righty had first suggested the plan, how Wolf volunteered to be the first to strike. Voodoo stared at the floor as he spoke, rubbing his hands, which Yurika noticed still had tan lines from his bike gloves. He paused occasionally to drink wine and glance at the two of them. Yurika watched him closely. Just then, Voodoo reminded her of Whitey the few times he had talked about his family—somber, unable to look at her; there was guilt, disappointment, failure in his face.

As Voodoo talked on, he grew more animated. Raphael began laughing and shaking his head at the details of the beating. The two brothers were getting drunk. Yurika's eyes grew heavy. The thought of Hector's face bloodied and misshapen made her stomach turn. Was it all her fault? She again saw how nervous Whitey seemed in Bone's workshop. She, too, had been so excited to see Hector. Every time. She had hurt Whitey to be with him. The messengers hurt Bone because of Whitey. But she couldn't help but feel it was *all* her fault, her at the center of a terrible, gruesome snowball effect.

Voodoo's voice was growing distant. It became sounds that she understood without needing the words, signals rising from the apartment and flying above the city, up to the Bronx, to Bone's apartment. There he was, lying on the floor of his workshop, spokes sticking from his body like he was the victim of some acupuncturist gone mad. What Voodoo was saying—what the signals meant—was that Bone was a hub—for attraction, for sex, for bicycles, for anger, for violence.

"He's broken," she could hear Whitey say.

She awoke the next morning because she knocked over an empty wine bottle with her foot. Light streamed in from the front windows. Paper bags and crumbs littered the floor where she and the brothers had had their picnic the night before. The hooks were still in the ceiling, which suddenly looked too empty. In the corner opposite her stood the crooked construction of Voodoo and Raphael's drunken labor. Each leg was a different length, and the vise grip was fixed in the center of the table, the exact place where it would be completely useless in a bike workshop.

Voodoo returned alone the following day and the day after that. He began to meet Yurika at the store and walk back with her to her new apartment. Not only did he reconstruct the worktable, but he also spray-painted her a round graffiti-style sign in red, white, and blue that read LUCKY'S BICYCLE REPAIR. They decided on the hours that Yurika wanted to include on the sign, then hung it outside.

The only problem was that Yurika had all of Whitey's tools but no parts yet. Voodoo told her not to worry. He explained that people could buy their parts at a bike store, then bring them to her, since her labor would be cheaper.

"But," Yurika wondered, "will someone come to empty bike store?"

"It won't be empty for long," said Voodoo.

He produced a sage stick and lit the edge of it on the stove, then moved around the room mumbling and wafting the smoke all around. To Yurika, he looked like some kind of young holy man in street clothes. After he was done, Voodoo explained that the burnt sage cleared a space of any bad spirits or negative energy. Yurika nodded, her eyes wide. Voodoo gave a laugh. "That's why they call me Voodoo."

"This voodoo?" Yurika asked.

He shook his head. "Native American."

Yurika was impressed. He explained to her about charms like round stones and mojo letters that had the power to protect. He pulled out a charm he wore around his neck, a round flat piece of lapis the color of the evening sky. This, he said, protected him from the evil eye.

"Ebir eye," Yurika said, trying to pronounce it. "What is that?"

Voodoo placed it back in his shirt. "When people want something bad to happen to you." He paused. "Like Bone now, I'm sure."

Yurika nodded. She remembered Whitey telling her about all the different people who didn't like messengers. Maybe, she thought, all messengers needed that kind of protection. If Whitey had worn one, it might have stopped Bone from touching his bike that morning. If Bone had one, it could have prevented Voodoo and the others from putting him in the hospital.

Yurika was about to ask Voodoo what he would suggest for good luck, but her first customer appeared. It was the member of the Puerto Rican Schwinn Bicycle Club with the bull horns on his handlebars. He was passing by in need of his brakes adjusted when he saw the sign. It took all three of them to lift the bike onto the bike stand.

While Voodoo and the man spoke a mix of Spanish and English to each other about bicycles, Yurika went to work. The adjustment took only twenty minutes, so Yurika charged him only five dollars. This man, who introduced himself as Miguel, was pleased and promised to spread the word about her work. Then he rode off with a honk of one of his horns and a mariachi tune playing on his stereo.

The contact with Voodoo and the customers who trickled into the workshop gave Yurika renewed confidence in her English. She often thought, too, of the night she spoke to Mr. Pitt and when Voodoo and Raphael were over, how she understood more of the feeling of English than the actual words. In the store, she had fewer problems and could even enjoy herself when she spoke with customers. When Mrs. Manton made a joke about her husband liking to eat meals only in his cab, Yurika laughed and suggested she get him a small TV to watch as well, so his car could be more like a living room.

It was not until Yurika finally spoke with her parents and stumbled over her Japanese that she realized how much English she had been using all summer. She called on the last day of August, only then realizing that her father's birthday had been on the thirteenth.

"Sumi-ma-sen," she said to her father, and she was sorry.

He seemed unfazed, Yurika thought. He was a man used to a lot of unpleasantries, maybe beginning with calling himself Masa, a Japanese name, instead of Tae Hyun, his Korean one. She wanted to ask him so many questions about that, his meeting her mother, Kimiyo, and other things, but she was afraid. It was too direct, too probing. There was no precedent for that in their relationship. Instead, Tae Hyun told Kimiyo to pick up the second phone, and the three of them made small talk about the family in the States. Yurika told them that Hyun Jeong went back to Korea. She wanted to tell them about how her aunt had been on her mind, about how people in New York were in your life one moment and gone the next, but there was too much to tell. When her parents asked why Hyun Jeong had returned, they were surprised at Yurika's answer.

"She's really nuts."

Her parents made grave noises of recognition. "I always thought that was a strange situation," Kimiyo said.

"How has the weather been?" Tae Hyun asked, eager to change the subject. "It's been one of our hottest summers here."

Yurika's heart sank. This was the first time she had spoken to them all summer, and her father was more interested in talking about the weather. "I'm working a lot," Yurika told them, "so I don't notice much."

Her father laughed. "I'm actually looking forward to the rainy season."

Yurika sighed. More weather. He wasn't interested in her jobs. She decided to try a more American way and be more straightforward. "I have some good news."

"How's your English?" Kimiyo asked.

"It's really funky and cool," she said as quickly as she could in English.

Her parents both oohed at the sound of it.

"That's great," her father exclaimed. "You can become a translator."

"Ano," Yurika began, "the good news is that I have an apartment, a few jobs, and I'm staying longer."

There was a moment of silence. Yurika thought of how the two of them used to stay up and wait for her to come home until she stopped coming home. Then they stopped waiting up. They didn't even ask her where she had been. What would they say now?

"Omedeto," her father finally said.

"Yes, congratulations," her mother added.

Tae Hyun laughed. "Didn't I say going to New York would be a great idea?"

Yurika wanted to remind him that the idea had been hers originally.

"You see?" her father went on. "You just needed the proper motivation. With the right motivation you can succeed."

Her father went on to talk about how difficult it was for him when he first arrived in Japan, but because he had the right motivation, he could succeed. That was a favorite word of his—"motivation." There was much for him to lecture about motivation, but Yurika decided it was time to get off the phone. They had asked her no questions about her friends, her life—nothing. She wondered how it was possible to have such little interest in one's own child—even if there was trouble. Her parents were basically having a conversation with each other, her mother talking about when she got a raise, her father talking about working overtime. Was this Japanese? Or had she just gotten used to Americans talking about everything? Yurika felt the thousands of miles between her and them, and it occurred to her that this distance had been there for years.

In junior high school she had become a *kagikko,* a kid with her own set of house keys because her parents worked. Around the same time, they all seemed to have less and less to say to each other. Or was it that she just saw them less? It was hard to recall exactly. Yurika remembered feeling sorry for herself then, having convinced herself that her parents decided their job was finished because she was no longer a child. Then as she skipped math class and chemistry, she began to feel old enough. Stay out later. Smoke. Drink beer. Hang around Shinjuku with her older friends. It seemed to her now that she had been leaving them slowly, going a little farther away each year until there was now an ocean and a continent between them. They had their lives, and now she had hers.

"I have to go," she said, interrupting her parents' conversation.

Her parents seemed in bright spirits now. Only after she got off the phone with them did Yurika realized they hadn't even asked for her new address and phone number.

Riya frowned when Yurika told her about her conversation with her parents.

"You must have been big trouble to them," Riya teased, as she motioned for Yurika to change her position.

They were doing one-minute poses. Yurika liked these. Each drawing ended up very differently. In the charcoal ones, Yurika thought she looked heavier. In the pastels, she looked taller. The pencil drawings made her look muscular. In colored ink, the Yurika in the drawings seemed most accurate. Riya explained that Yurika, like everyone, had many different looks, a different one for each pose, and she taught her the expression, "You never step into the same river twice." So Riya never saw the same Yurika twice—especially because of the hair, which had bright yellow tips now.

"Your parents," she said, "see the same river everywhere. I bet you didn't tell them about this job."

Yurika laughed and shook her head as she got ready for a longer pose.

"Maybe you should," Riya added.

Yurika could not imagine telling them. She was still surprised that she was doing this. Nude. There was no word like that in Japanese as far as she knew. Even the word "nude" sounded so exposed. Thankfully, Riya helped her with poses and explained how artists liked curves and shadows, twists that concealed and extensions that revealed. To help Yurika feel more comfortable with her body, Riya taught her some basic yoga positions to practice with funny names like "downward-facing dog" and "cow face." The poses also gave her more flexibility and strength. Riya encouraged Yurika to use her imagination as well, especially during the shorter poses that were easy to hold. You are a tree, Yurika told herself. You are a bird. You are in love. You have just killed someone. You have just had sex.

It was especially important for Yurika to concentrate on the poses since she had begun posing for Riya's classes at the art school. So many students in each class. The key was not to make eye contact with anyone except Riya—Riya yes, students no. Yurika preferred posing at the apartment because they could talk as Riya worked. Riya's English sounded almost perfect. There was an accent, but she spoke so smoothly, so differently from the Thai she sometimes talked on the phone. Yurika also liked to watch her face. One moment she would look so serious, her eyes piercing a page, and the next she would be smiling at something she had done or said or making a face at her drawing.

Riya seemed to know everything about Sang Jun's life, too, about Jong Eun and even about Suzie's English teacher–training program and her miscarriage.

"Did you ever learn how your parents met?" Riya asked Yurika one day during a thirty-minute pose.

Yurika nodded. "My father dump Jong Eun for my mom."

Riya nodded and smiled at her young friend's English. She was always surprised at how quickly Yurika incorporated new words into her everyday speaking. When Riya was learning English, she was terrible with vocabulary and couldn't remember words from one day to the next. She learned to be very proficient with the words she relied heavily on, such as "actually," "really," and "yeah," because they made her sound more natural. It was hard to believe that it had been fifteen years ago that she was taking English classes and doing grammar exercises. Her eyes followed the line of Yurika's hip up to her ribs. How many bodies had she drawn in that time? Hundreds? Thousands? How many ribs? Arms? Lips?

Sang Jun had once shown Riya a photo of his brother and sister-in-law. Yurika's mother was beautiful in a restrained, Japanese way—clear shapes of her facial parts but very little behind them. Looking at Yurika now, Riya thought the girl was prettier than her mother because of the spark in her eyes. Yurika's mother certainly would never pose nude. She probably never even looked closely at her own body. Was it any wonder that Yurika was an only child?

"You know," she began as she she added shading to Yurika's ribs, "your father was the more handsome of the brothers." She paused to change colors. "But Sang Jun was the more responsible." As she drew, she explained that Sang Jun married Hyun Jeong not only so Suzie could have a mother, but also because he felt terribly guilty about Jong Eun's death, that he couldn't save her. He lost months of sleep believing he had let her and her family down. Marrying Hyun Jeong proved his good intentions toward the family. She sighed. "It was impossible for him not to."

Riya and Yurika remained quiet for the rest of their session. When they finished, Yurika dressed and looked at the picture. She thought she looked older, her eyes sharp and curious but also a little tired. Her mouth was slightly open, as though about to say something.

"I think of you this way," Riya said, "talking, but with many more thoughts inside." She tapped Yurika's forehead with a finger and walked her to the door.

Riya smiled. "See you in class."

Yurika was always a little sad to leave Riya's place but gave a wave and headed downstairs.

The late afternoon sky was bright. A slight drizzle began, which felt refreshing against her face. She ran her hands through her hair and scratched her scalp, shaking her head, liking that she could see the yellow tips of her hair from the corners of her eyes. As she walked down Tenth Street toward Avenue D, she smiled at some of the people she was getting used to seeing in the neighborhood: the little man wearing the fedora who sold ices; Mrs. Manton, who was leaning on the windowsill of her first-floor apartment; a tall guy who wore sunglasses and smoked on his stoop in all weather. After living in the neighborhood for a few weeks and running into some of the people she knew from Lucky Market, she got up the nerve to talk to them outside of the store. She and Suzie had not started up their English lessons again, and Yurika needed more practice. Voodoo and some of the other messengers would stop by her place, and they liked to teach her new words and idioms, but talkative messengers were still not the same as lessons. Mostly, they talked about Whitey and bicycles, sometimes even Bone. When they had a bike problem, more often than not she could fix it. It was Voodoo who finally explained all the slogans on Whitey's T-shirts, which Yurika sometimes wore when they weren't decorating the walls of the apartment.

Having conversations in English was getting a little easier; it was not quite as scary either. Suzie had been right about asking people questions. People loved to talk about themselves and say what they knew. In this way, Yurika had found out that no one really called the neighborhood Alphabet City anymore. Some called it Loisaida, while others called it the Lower East Side. Still others, like some of the young Japanese people she was starting to meet, called it the East Village. Those who called it Loisaida or the Lower East Side had lived there the longest and were usually Latin or European or older Americans. Really, they said, the Lower East Side was everything south of Fourteenth Street on the east side down to Canal, but with real estate in New York, it had shrunk to just the named streets below Houston like Stanton and Rivington and Orchard. It was the young people Yurika's age who called it the East Village. That name sounded to her more punk and full of hair gel. She liked that the neighborhood had many names because she was like that, too, and if someone felt comfortable where she lived then someone could call that place home.

As she turned onto Avenue D and got closer to her apartment, she could see a tall dark woman standing outside with her son and his bicycle, a two-wheeler with training wheels. The little boy was sitting on his bicycle, pointing to the sign on the door, reading aloud. He was going over the words slowly, repeating syllables and words, and he reminded Yurika of herself when she picked up a newspaper or magazine. She also wondered if the boy looked like Hector when he was little.

"Luc-ky's bi-cy-cle re-pair," the little boy was saying, waving his finger. "Open—"

"Every day," Yurika said with a laugh as she approached the woman and child and got out her keys.

"And what's the last part?" the mother asked her son.

He read the hours and turned to his mother with a big smile.

Yurika invited them inside and asked what they needed. The little boy said he was big now and wanted to take off his training wheels. Mounting the bike on the stand, Yurika got a wrench and adjusted it to the correct width. She expected a lot of resistance from the nut but was surprised when the training wheels came off easily, as though it were time for the bike to be a real two-wheeler, like the wheel was ready to be free.

Acknowledgments

One stick cannot cook a meal or build a fence.

—HMONG PROVERB

My wife, Jaymie Adachi, has been my secret weapon throughout the writing of this book. She has a great heart for stories and the restraint of an ancient blues musician. To her I give my deepest thanks, with love.

Jane Rosenman, my editor at St. Martin's, was determined to see this novel published. She had a vision of what this story could be, then beautifully edited the work to help make that vision a reality. As I told her a number of times, she rocked my world, and I thank her for this.

Sandy Dijkstra, my agent, I thank for guidance, ongoing cheerleading, sharpshooter editorial help through numerous drafts, and for her truly great staff, especially Jill Marr, Babette Sparr, Julie Burton, and Elizabeth James.

To Mei Ng, I owe a debt of gratitude for her friendship and invaluable help in bringing this novel into the world.

St. Martin's has been wonderfully supportive for this first-time novelist. I thank everyone there, but I would especially like to acknowledge Sally Richardson, George Witte, Stephen Lee, Frances Coady, Wah-Ming Chang, Kenneth J. Silver, Susan Yang, Cynthia Merman, Dori Weintraub, Christina Harcar, Matt Baldacci, Henry Yee, Ethan Friedman, Marie Estrada, Joshua Kendall, and Emily Haile.

Over the course of the last six years, I have been fortunate enough to have a small army of readers, many of whom have also been an invaluable source of support and love. To my parents, Masazumi and Agnes Adachi; my brother, Taro Adachi, and sister-in-law, Bonnie Adachi, endless thanks. To these friends who are also ace readers, I am very grateful: Svenja Soldovieri, Claire Lev, Scott Williams, Amy Adachi, Hannah Jones, Myra Munial, Amy Heffner, Jacqueline Keren, Bernard Yee, Stefanie Smith, Nitza Wilon, Angela Vuagniaux, Glynn Lloyd, Mohan Polamarasetty, Jaya Chakravarty, Stephanie G'Schwind, and Arne G'Schwind.

Many of my students at the New School, Hunter College, Yeshiva University's Stern College for Women, and the School of Visual Arts were readers of early drafts. They gave me valuable reader feedback as well as necessary language and cultural information. To all of them I am very grateful, but especially to Maya Okamoto, Kimiyo Murakami, Maki Hota, Kayo Darlington, Yurika Ito, Hiroe Yamamoto, and Jong Eun Oh, Aliena, and Yuri Kato.

I thank my colleagues at the New School's English Language Studies department: Marjorie Vai, Victoria Kimbrough, Heather Alonzo, Nelee Sim, Nikki Westfall; and a very special thanks to Caitlin Morgan, who has been an essential reader, advisor, and the best officemate a person could have hoped for.

Many other family members and friends have continually shared their warm enthusiasm for this project, and I thank them.

I have been blessed with great teachers to whom I owe more than I can ever say: Hugo Garcia, Marcia Lippman, Ann Douglas, Deena Froomkin, and especially John Clark Pratt, a friend, mentor, and Jedi editor.

Special thanks goes to Rabbi Burt Siegal and the Congregation of the Shul of New York.

The following artists have provided an endlessly inspiring soundtrack to my writing life: Muddy Waters, the Beatles, Bob Dylan, Lou Reed, Tom Waits, Patti Smith, Bruce Springsteen, Al Green, Johnny